A Shift in Tides

Lost Legacies
Book 7

Maddox Grey

GREYMALKIN

The Lost Legacies Series

A Shift in Darkness*

A Shift in Shadows

A Shift in Fate

A Shift in Fortune

A Shift in Ashes

A Shift in Wings

A Shift in Death

A Shift in Tides

A Shift in Night

*A Shift in Darkness is available for free download at maddoxgreyauthor.com.

Published by Greymalkin Press
www.greymalkinpress.com

This is a work of fiction. Names, places, characters, and events, and incidents are the product or depiction of the author's imagination and are completely fictitious. Any resemblance to actual persons, living or dead, events or establishments is purely coincidental.

Dev/line editing by Proofs by Polly
Copy editing and proofreading by Rachels Top Edits

Cover Design by Seventhstar Art

eBook ISBN: 978-1-963368-04-8
Paperback ISBN: 978-1-963368-05-5

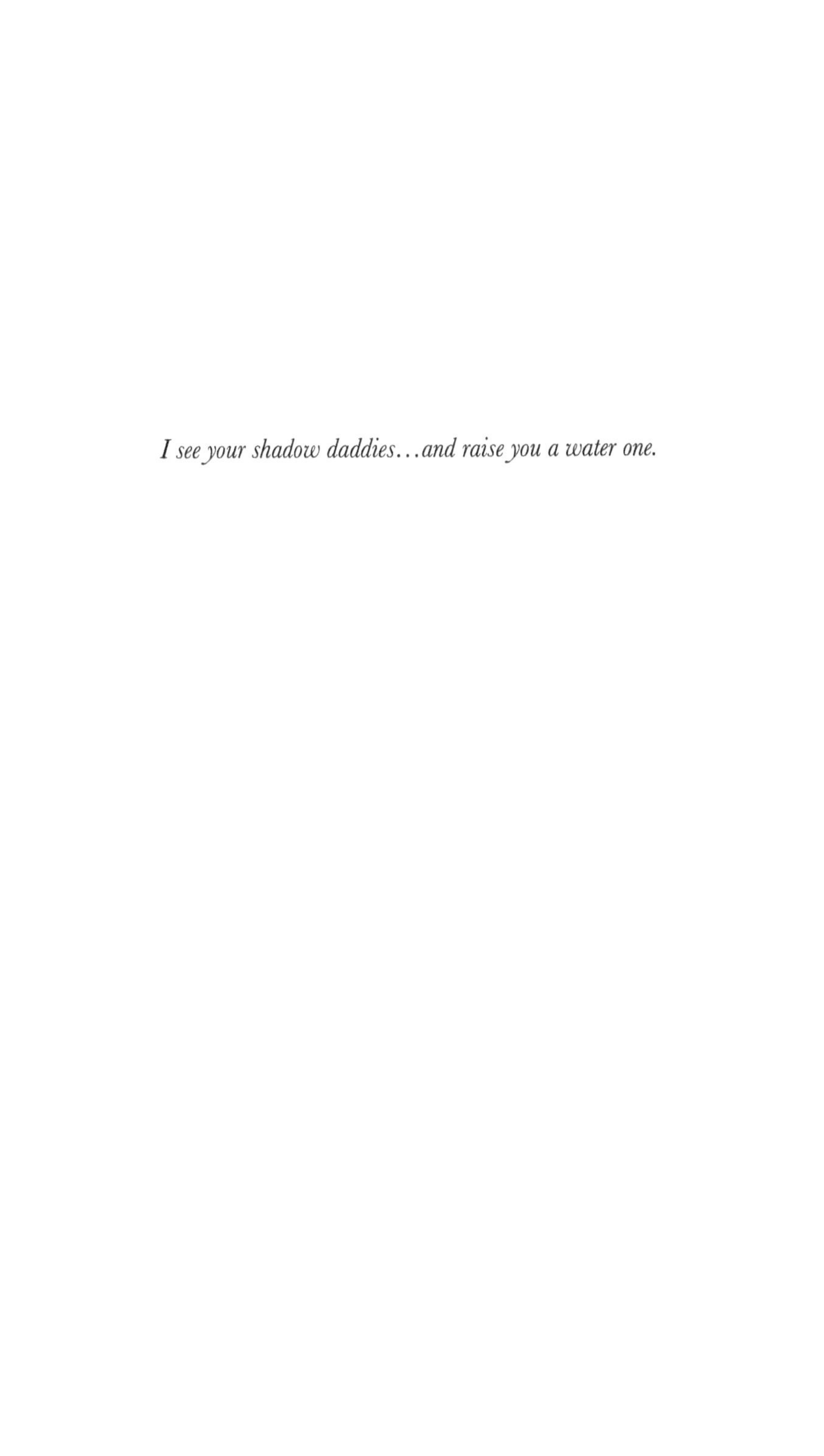

I see your shadow daddies…and raise you a water one.

Prologue

"Dragon love spat," I declared and pointed towards the group of stars directly above where I was floating in a distant sea beneath a starry night sky.

"Okay," Connor drawled from where he was floating next to me. "Assuming I'm willing to give you the dragons—which I'm not entirely convinced about, by the way, because I don't see anything that could be wings—where are you getting love spat from?"

I turned my head to the side, and he did the same. "Your lack of imagination is truly disappointing sometimes." I sighed.

"That's not what you said earlier," he replied smugly. "I'm pretty sure you said something about how my use of that high-backed chair had been *truly* inspired."

For a second, my brain went offline as the memory of being perched on that chair while Connor slammed into me over and over again at the absolute perfect angle took over, echoes of the pleasure he'd ripped from my body rippling through me.

"That's not playing fair, prince." I scowled at him. "You won't distract me with your nefarious ways."

"I won't be a prince for much longer, so you'll have to come up with some other nickname." He narrowed his eyes at me. "Preferably one I don't hate. And you like my nefarious ways. They're your favorite thing about me."

"True." I nodded, a coy smile playing across my lips as I batted my eyelashes at him. "But you'll always be *my* prince."

"I'm not sure if it's possible to drown a mermaid," he half-heartedly growled, "but I'm willing to try."

"So touchy." I laughed before turning my attention back to the sky. "See the two lines of stars that look like they're weaving around each other?" I traced my finger through the air. "The dragon on the left is trying to do the old 'let me nuzzle your neck' trick."

"'Nuzzle your neck' trick?" Connor asked, amusement clear in his voice.

"You know the one." My lips quirked up into a grin. "It's when you know you're in trouble with your lover, so you brush your nose against their neck. Maybe plant a few light kisses while inhaling their scent, but don't do anything beyond that, because you want to get them worked up enough that they forget why they were mad at you in the first place."

"Wait, you did that to me last week!"

My grin blossomed into a full smile. "Sure did. Worked like a charm too."

A wave splashed across my face.

"Rude!" I sputtered, moving until I treaded water. I glared at Connor, who was still lazily floating, bobbing up and down in the gentle waves.

Some seaweed drifted by, and I seized the opportunity, summoning a wave and sending the clump of seaweed directly onto Connor's face.

I immediately dove. His roar of outrage cut off when I slipped below the surface, swimming away as fast as I could. My tail beat fast, propelling me through the water, and I nimbly wove my way around the coral reefs that decorated the shallow sea floor. I didn't dare glance behind me—I had no doubt Connor was hot on my tail.

My magic flashed at me in warning a split second before I whipped around the outside of a particularly large coral colony. Connor was suddenly there, and I squealed, sending bubbles rocketing to the surface. His hand snapped out to grab me, but I moved back fast enough to avoid his grasp and took off like a rocket towards the shore.

As soon as it was shallow enough, I shifted, my glittering blue tail giving way to legs, and after a couple of stumbles, I raced towards the sandy shoreline. Then the world tilted as strong arms wrapped around my waist. They lifted me up until I lay on a hard body, once again staring up at the night sky.

"Connor—"

Seaweed slapped me across the face, and I shrieked between laughs.

"You know I hate seaweed!" he grouched and slapped me with another slimy tendril.

"Nobody likes seaweed." I gulped for air as my laughter became hysterical and swiped the offending plant away from me. "You started it!"

"You're such a brat, Ash." His hands on my waist drifted to my sides.

"No, Connor." I struggled to get free. "Don't you dar—"

He tickled my sides just beneath my ribs, and I absolutely lost it.

"Did you just snort?" The tickling paused.

"No!" I tried to scramble away from him, but his arms wrapped around me like iron bands, my back locked against his broad chest.

"Pretty sure you did." His tone told me he was smirking.

"Did not!" I totally did.

"Awww," he cooed. "Is the big, bad, merfolk spy mad?"

"Yes!" I elbowed him in the ribs, but I was pretty sure I hurt myself more than him. Stupid muscly merfolk. "I'm mad at you!"

"Hmm." He repositioned me just enough that could I feel his hardness against my ass. Suddenly, I was feeling a lot less motivated to break free. "Well, I suppose it's lucky for me that someone explained a surefire way to get out of this." His lips brushed against my neck, and I bit back the gasp that almost escaped.

"Not going to work," I said, my husky tone undermining my declaration. "Still mad at you."

"I'll just have to work harder then." He nipped me just as one hand squeezed my breast, his thumb brushing over my hard nipple. This time, I couldn't hold back the moan, and he chuckled. "Still mad?"

"Outraged," I breathed out.

"Hmm." His legs wrapped around mine, pulling them apart, and his hand that wasn't toying with my breast painted a blazing hot trail down my stomach before dipping between my thighs. "Strange." Two fingers slid through the hot slickness, and I groaned, my hips bucking up in response. "This doesn't feel like outrage."

I whimpered. "Connor . . ."

"Yes?"

"I'll forgive you if you put that *princely* cock of yours to good use."

I yelped as his hands gripped my waist, and he easily lifted me up until I straddled him, my back to his face. Before I could mouth off again, he raised me enough to slam his cock in, all the way to the hilt, one hand wrapping around my long, blue hair and yanking it, forcing me to arch my back.

"Fuck," I let out with a strangled moan.

"You keep it up with the *prince* nonsense, and I'll find something else to fill your mouth with," he growled as he continued to pound into me.

"Promises, promises." I found his rhythm and started meeting him thrust for thrust. The fingers wrapped around my hair tightened as his other hand slipped around to toy with my clit.

"Come for me," he demanded.

"No," I panted. "I'm. Bored."

Water wrapped around my waist, yanking me off him, and my back gently landed on the sand, the watery strands shooting out to pin my hands above my head.

I could have broken them, but what would be the fun in that?

Connor grasped my legs and threw them over his shoulders before his cock slammed home in one thrust, tearing a scream from my throat.

"Still bored, love?" He gave me a cocky smile that had my pussy clenching around him.

"Sorry, are you"—a strangled moan slipped from my lips as he pulled back before burying himself even deeper inside me— "doing something?" I gasped.

"Guess I'll have to try harder."

A retort died on my lips as Connor's fingers dug into my thighs, pulling me against him in time with his hips snapping forward.

Some of the water pinning my wrists split off and raced down my body to circle my clit.

"Eyes on me," Connor demanded.

My eyes flew open; I hadn't even realized I'd closed them. Connor's moonlight-pale eyes look down at me, and I couldn't have looked away if I'd tried.

"Fuck! Fuck! Fuck!" I writhed beneath him. The water swirling around around my clit glided over it and pushed down.

I erupted and screamed up at the stars as the climax tore through me, followed by Connor's deep grunt a second later.

The water he'd been using sank into the sand. Connor gently lowered my legs and leaned over me, his broad chest poised over mine as he kissed my lips, his cock still buried inside me.

"Less mad at you now." The words came out a little breathy as I smirked up at him.

"If I promise to use my creative and nefarious skills again later, will you forgive me?" He brushed another light kiss to my lips.

"I suppose," I said solemnly, my lips twitching as I tried to stop them from widening into a smile.

"Pointy promise?" He held himself up with one arm so he could raise his other hand up, all his fingers except his pointer finger folded into a fist.

My resolve broke, and I laughed at the sight. On one of our many nights floating amongst the waves, he'd asked me what I liked so much about humans. I told him it was many things, one of which was all their bizarre customs. Pinkie promises had been mentioned, which led us to a long conversation about why that particular finger was the one used for these promises and if others could be used instead. Thumbs were too awkward, so we settled on the pointer finger.

I looped my finger with his. "Pointy promise."

His laughter joined mine, and after one final squeeze, we unlooped our fingers. Connor dropped his arm back to my side and leaned down to nuzzle my neck. "Soon, my father will be stepping down and someone new will take over. I'll be free of any duties I have to the throne then, and we can do this all the time. It'll be nice to have no ties to the throne for the first time in my life."

The warm feeling of contentment that had been coursing through my blood went ice-cold.

"Yeah," I said a little weakly. "No ties to the throne."

He nuzzled my neck one more time before pulling out of me so he could lie down and tuck me into his side.

"Lokis arguing over a bet," he declared and pointed up at a cluster of stars. I made a noise of agreement, even as my thoughts were elsewhere and my magic pulsed beneath my skin.

It wasn't fair. It wasn't fucking fair that he was my fate. He was my *everything*, but I had another fate as well, and that one was going to tear him away from me.

Chapter One

Three Years Later

"I'm going to kill him."

"No," I said again. "We're putting a temporary pause on murder."

"Just to recap," Connor said in a flat, annoyed tone. I heard that tone frequently these days. So different from the playful one he'd used around me—and only me—during those few blissful months we'd had. Before fate had forced my hand and I'd watched my world blow up in front of my face. "We managed to successfully sneak past all the guards," he continued, and I nodded along. "You secured the information you need, and all that's left is to snap the neck of this useless traitor?"

Magic pulsed from the fae kneeling on the floor as he tried to break free from the bands of water encircling his body. Eachan may have been a low-ranking sidhe in the Seelie Court, but he still belonged to one of the ancient fae families known as the Tuatha Dé Danann. His magic was formidable, and he was particularly gifted with water.

Unfortunately for him, I was the Merfolk Queen, and he was no match for me. If he were more clever, he would have tried to use fire against me. Alas, few sidhe liked to mess with the more volatile elements and therefore didn't practice with them nearly as much as they should.

"That's correct." I leafed through a few more documents on Eachan's desk.

"But I can't kill him." Not a question. An annoyed statement.

My lips curled up as I straightened the mess I'd made of Eachan's desk. Not because I particularly cared, but because I was curious if I could get actual steam to come out of Connor's ears by continuing to mess about. "Correct."

"Ashling," he growled. Eachan choked as Connor's magic joined mine and tightened the band around his neck. The fae's pale face gained a purple tint as he struggled to breathe.

"Patience," I soothed. "Just a few more minutes, then you can snap away. Honestly, you're sounding more like Nemain these days with the growling and murder hard-on."

I laughed as Connor sent me such an icy look, I was genuinely surprised the water didn't freeze.

"My uncle will kill you for this," Eachan ground out as Connor finally loosened his hold.

Seconds ticked by as I waited for him to say something else. Maybe offer some kind of deal in exchange for his life. Expand on the horrible ways I would meet my end. Instead, Eachan pursed his lips together and merely gave me a cold stare.

At barely one hundred years old, Eachan was young for a fae, only coming into his full power a few decades before. I could relate because I was only ninety-seven. Granted, nobody knew that. If the fae ever learned that their newly appointed Merfolk Queen wasn't even a century old, they'd be scandalized. Luckily for me we were an arrogant species as a whole, therefore they'd never look too closely into my murky past—it would never have occurred to most fae that they could be so easily duped.

I pondered Eachan as he continued to glower at me. Everything I'd learned about him over the previous few months implied he was a bit of a disappointment to his family and more interested in partying and bedding pretty fae females than serving in the Seelie Court.

It was all a lie. Eachan had played a role in the slaughter of tens of thousands of humans.

Unbeknownst to most people, the fae queens had quietly stolen humans from their realm over several centuries and relocated them to other realms. These backup human worlds provided extra magic, which the fae queens used to maintain the ward around the realm their brother—the exiled fae king, Balor—was locked away in.

To keep humans safe, the queens had kept the realms a closely guarded secret. They didn't have the numbers to send armies to guard all the realms, and even if they did, that would have drawn attention to their existence. Protection through obfuscation. It was actually a pretty smart plan and had worked for a long time until they'd trusted the wrong person. Now these backup human realms were being targeted, and the peaceful existence of those living in those realms had been replaced with terror . . . with no one to help them.

There was no way the queens had told Eachan directly, but they'd told someone, and that person had whispered the damning words in Eachan's ear.

He hadn't been the one to do the deed, but he'd known exactly what was going to happen. He'd known he'd signed the death warrant for all those living in the hidden human realms. As far as I was concerned, his hands were coated in blood.

I was one of the few fae who *liked* humans. Some of them

at least. They were so much less complicated than fae and found joy in the simplest of things. Most of them didn't deserve to be caught up in the machinations of the fae queens' war against their brother. But even if I didn't have sympathy for humans, the fall of those backup realms put the ward securing Balor in jeopardy, so I would have fought to protect them regardless.

My nose twitched as the memory of the vision I'd received when I'd been just five years old flitted through my mind. It was always there. A constant reminder of what was at stake. I rubbed my nose, trying to wipe away the scent of rotting corpses.

Connor's pale green eyes latched onto the movement, and I knew he was filing it away for later reference. He knew I'd been hiding something from him and he wavered between trying to figure it out and not caring. Meanwhile, I alternated between being terrified he would learn my secrets and being hurt when he switched to indifference.

Murder was so much easier.

A creak announced a door opening somewhere towards the front of the house. Eachan opened his mouth to scream, but Connor slammed a meaty fist into his jaw before slipping some water magic around the sidhe's mouth as a makeshift gag. Blood poured from his busted lip, turning the stream of water a faint pink.

Quietly, I turned to face the room's entrance and slid a dagger free from the hidden holster on my lower back. My magic nudged me, so I moved two steps to the left.

"Eachan?" a smooth, masculine voice called out from the hallway. "You better be ready. I'm not waiting on you if you're drunk off your ass again."

A slender fae with long, golden blond hair stepped into the room.

Hello, Darragh. How kind of you to join us.

His dark brown eyes widened as they fell on Eachan kneeling next to Connor. I felt the moment his magic lashed out. A second after spotting them, he saw me, and his magic clamped down around my body, cutting off my airflow.

Until the knife I'd thrown pierced his throat.

I sucked in a gasp as the airlock Darragh had placed around me fell away.

"Can I kill this one?" Connor stalked towards Darragh, who was kneeling, blood rushing out between his fingers as he clamped a hand to his throat. The wound was far from fatal, but it would take him a minute or two to fully heal from it. And it was hard to do magic when blood was pouring out of your throat.

"Yes," I rasped. Fuck, I hated air magic. Even more than fire magic. There was something so fucked up about being attacked by something I couldn't see.

Eachan struggled to get free as Connor swiped my dagger off the ground, where it had landed after Darragh had pulled it out. The blond sidhe gave up holding onto his throat and started scrambling back on the floor. I felt his attempts to wield his magic, but the blood loss was too great. Connor grabbed Darragh by the hair when he twisted and tried to surge to his feet, burying the dagger into the still-healing wound.

With one strong pull, he yanked the blade all the way through Darragh's neck, and the fae's body fell to the side as Connor tossed the head a second later, watching as it rolled.

Eachan did his best to scream through the water that still bound his mouth. I waved my hand in the air and a stream of water followed it before flattening into a disc. Then I flicked my fingers back, and it shot forward, sending another head rolling across the floor.

"See?" I smirked. "I can do it too."

Connor just gave me an unimpressed look and walked towards me, stepping around the growing pools of blood. "If you could have done that, then why bother with this?" He held my dagger out, and I took it, wiping the blood off on my pants before tucking it back into the holster.

"Darragh is—was—impossibly fast with those fucking airlocks of his." I shrugged. "A dagger is faster, and the fae never expect them."

"Now who sounds like Nemain?" he grumbled.

"You're the one who doesn't like her," I pointed out. "Personally, I think an unhinged shifter with freaky magic and a lethal set of skills is a good person to know."

"I'll remind you of that when she buries her claws into your gut and unleashes that fucked-up magic of hers." He cocked his head at Eachan's body before stalking back over to Darragh's and rummaging through the dead fae's clothes.

"Nemain loves me," I declared.

Connor stopped his search to shoot me an incredulous look.

"Okay, maybe not *loves* me." My lips curled into another smirk. "But she is obsessively curious about me after all that shit that went down with the Olympians, and at the end of the day, she is a feline."

"And?" He resumed his search.

"As long as I remain an oddity to her, I'm safe from her claws and freaky magic. Nemain is vicious, but I've already done her a favor and I have no interest in ever targeting anyone she cares about. So I'm good. You, on the other hand" —I pointed a finger at him—"are fucked. She hates you."

"Feeling's mutual." His fingers slipped under Darragh's tunic, and he pulled a silver chain free. I tried to get a look at it, but he slid it into his pocket too quickly. "Also, Nemain doesn't hate me, I hate her. She just dislikes me, and she would never seriously harm me because of Kaysea and—" His hand tightened into a fist at his side before he slowly unclenched his fingers. "Because of Kaysea."

And Myrna, I thought but had the sense not to say out loud. Nemain had been in love with Kaysea's and Connor's sister, who had loved her deeply in return. Nemain was also the reason the mermaid had died a brutal death. At least that's what both she and Connor believed, and I supposed it was at least partially true. Sebastian had only targeted Myrna to punish Nemain.

Wrong place, wrong time. I was quite familiar with how that worked, albeit for me, it was usually right place, right time.

Even if Nemain weren't best friends with Kaysea, she would never dishonor Myrna's memory by hurting her brother. For a psychotic killer, she was oddly honorable sometimes.

Connor shot one last disgusted look at Darragh's corpse before striding back towards me. My eyes dropped to the pocket he'd tucked the necklace into, and I debated asking him about it, but if he'd wanted to discuss whatever he'd found, he would have. I could have ordered him to do it—I was the bloody Merfolk Queen—but I didn't need the insight from my magic to tell me that wasn't a good idea.

I'd already pushed my luck by twisting events to my liking so Connor was indebted to me and, therefore, had to help me with this task of taking out the traitors. He would tell me when he was ready, and I almost certainly wouldn't like it.

"Let's get out of here." I swiped my bag full of the documents I'd stolen from Eachan's desk and slung it over my shoulder. He'd done a good job of covering his tracks, but I was excellent at reading between the lines. I had no doubt there were more fae secretly working to ensure the exiled king's return. Anyone with close business ties to Eachan was high on my suspect list.

Connor trailed after me as we walked through the massive house. I could fault Eachan for a lot of things, but his taste in architecture and home decor wasn't one of them. Skylights were installed throughout the house, and stars blinked down at us from a cloudless sky. Some type of vine was growing along the walls, and delicate, blue blossoms shaped like bells hung from the dark green stems.

His home was beautiful and relaxing. Too bad it'd belonged to such an ugly person.

Only our footsteps sounded as we turned down another hallway before passing through a large archway into a beautiful outdoor space. Like most sidhe houses, this one had been designed around the garden—the fae didn't like to be far from nature—which turned out to be quite the boon for us. We'd been able to use the pool in the center to bypass the wards around the house entirely.

I snuck glances at Connor as we made our way to the sparkling pool that lay in the center of the garden. His expression was closed off and his eyes were distant. Yep. A not-so-pleasant conversation was definitely in my future.

With a sigh, I dropped my bag next to the edge of the water, startling the fish that had been swimming in slow, lazy circles. Connor's frown deepened, as if a thought he didn't particularly like had just occurred to him, and he opened his mouth to say something before snapping it shut.

"Something the matter?" I slid the thin straps of my dress over my shoulders and let it fall to the ground before stepping out of it. When I looked up after tucking the dress into my bag, I found Connor's heated gaze on me. My body instantly reacted, remembering what it felt like to have his hands tangled in my hair as his teeth grazed my nipple and the way his fingers dug into my hips as he thrust inside of me.

The scent of lust filled the crisp night air, and my breathing quickened. Connor jerked his head to the side and yanked his clothes off, leaving them in a pile on the ground as he dove into the pool. As soon as he hit the water, he shifted, and I saw a flash of his green scales before he disappeared beneath the surface to the awaiting gateway.

My blood that had been burning hot a second ago cooled, and I was left with a familiar hollow ache. I walked to where he'd hastily discarded his clothing and shoved it into my bag before activating the magic so everything stayed dry.

Then I tilted my head back and looked up at the starlit sky. This was fun. Loved it. Absolutely loved having no friends because my entire past was a lie and letting people close was dangerous.

Really loved that every person who made a pass at me was only doing so for the political advantages and that the few times I'd flirted with someone for no reason other than that I'd liked them, I'd seen the same wariness flash in their eyes as they'd wondered if I'd only been using them.

But what I loved more than anything else was that I'd already met my mate and fallen in love with him. That him simply standing next to me soothed my soul in a way I hadn't thought possible, and every time he left me, it felt like a piece of me went with him.

Connor didn't know any of that though, because in the six months we'd been together, I'd never told him.

A coward wasn't something I generally considered myself, but at least now he was a part of my life, even if I'd strong-armed him into it. Connor had made it very clear he didn't want anything to do with me. If he learned we were fated mates, he'd run until a hundred realms separated us.

"Yeah." I slid the bag across my back and glanced up one last time at the stars that now seemed to mock me. "Love this life."

Chapter Two

THE SIGH I'd been holding back for the past hour rushed out as the dark red scaled tail slipped beneath the waves.

"I thought he'd never leave." Kaysea slumped in her chair, where she'd been perfectly posed during Galather's tirade. Unlike me, Kaysea was used to all of this. She'd been born a princess and had grown up surrounded by fae politics. Unlike her brother, Kaysea seemed to really enjoy it. I'd asked her once why she hadn't made a bid for the throne. Her parents would have supported her, and the merfolk families would have no doubt been thrilled about the idea.

Not because they loved Kaysea and thought she was perfect for the throne, well, some of them did, but because they mistook her kindness for weakness and therefore thought she'd be easy to manipulate. The fact that she was absolutely stunning didn't hurt either. I'd overheard countless schemes from the elite merfolk of the court about winning Kaysea's hand or proposing an engagement between one of their children and her.

Since her parents had stepped down and I had risen to the throne, Kaysea wasn't *technically* a princess anymore. But she still had plenty of political power to wield as an honorary princess, especially since she'd stepped in as my top advisor. So the offers kept coming, and she kept politely dismissing them.

Most of the time, the merfolk would let it go or try a different tactic, but some of the fools would push the matter, and then they'd find out that beneath that sweet exterior was someone with a will of iron and powerful magic.

The smart ones would realize the error of their ways and give Kaysea the respect she deserved, but some of the idiots would complain about it. Loudly. And then the rumors would start about what they had done and what they planned to do about it.

I was very good at always being in on rumors. Between my magic, snooping tendencies, and very well paid informants, there wasn't much I didn't know.

Which is why I knew that over the past fifty years, Connor had killed three merfolk who had been planning on harming Kaysea after she had so thoroughly rebuffed them. They'd been the lucky ones, because it was Nemain who had found out about the other two.

Connor loved his sister beyond reason and would kill for her in a heartbeat, but he wasn't the type to play with his food. He'd killed them quickly and disposed of their corpses. No fuss, no muss. Nemain . . . she had a lot of aggression to work out, and who better to work it out on than males who didn't understand the meaning of no?

"What are you thinking about?"

"Hmm?" I blinked rapidly, not realizing I'd zoned out a little, and looked back at Kaysea, whose light green eyes were laughing at me.

"You live a lot in your own head, don't you?"

You have no idea.

"I mean, after listening to that arrogant fuck prattle on, can you really blame me?" I gave her a knowing smirk. "And to answer your first question, I was thinking about how Nemain would react if we told how he leered at you throughout that meeting."

Kaysea scrunched her nose. "Let's not tell her that. She's a little more on edge lately, and Galather could still be useful, but he won't be if Nemain cuts him into a dozen pieces and sets him on fire."

I thought about asking what exactly had Nemain more worked up than usual, but decided against it. Kaysea had started as my advisor, but we'd gradually drifted into friend territory. That was mostly her doing, but I wasn't complaining. I'd never really had a friend before. Granted, Kaysea didn't know the real me. Just this version of myself I had built up over the years.

Which to be fair… was becoming the real me? If you lived a lie long enough… didn't that make it the truth eventually?

Ugh. I was too tired for philosophical bullshit. Being friends with Kaysea—built on on a lie or not—was strange, but in a good way.

Still, I was under no illusions about where I stood with Kaysea compared to Nemain. The shifter was her best friend, and I didn't want to put her in an awkward spot by asking questions about Nemain's personal life. Though things had also changed between me and the newly minted Unseelie Knight.

I snorted. Still wild to think that Nemain was the freaking Unseelie Knight. Even my magic hadn't seen that one coming.

More than once, Kaysea had dragged me to the Inferno to get drinks with her and Zareen, only for Nemain and her motley crew of psychopaths to show up. I wasn't exactly in their little inner circle—yet—but I was…adjacent to it?

I mean, I did go with them to a realm to kill a bunch of asshole gods. That's quality bonding time right there. Maybe when I was done with the current crisis, I'd dig into what was going on with Nemain. See if there was something I could do to help.

I was aware of the prophecy around Finn potentially ending all the realms and Nemain being the one to keep him off his dark path. I'd never had the privilege of having that particular vision myself, but plenty of others had. Kaysea's had simply been the most recent.

The queens had a hidden room full of documented visions. I'd perused it on more than one occasion—not to their knowledge, of course—just to make sure they didn't know anything about me. So far, they were ignorant of my foresight magic and lineage, but I'd learned quite a few fun things during my breaking and entering visits.

All of my attention was on preventing the future I had seen in my vision from coming to pass. I'd just have to hope that Nemain could keep her shit together enough for her role in all this. Although, even if she did manage to keep Finn from devolving into the stuff of nightmares . . . every other vision around that kid suggested there was nothing but chaos in his future.

Gods. It would have been really nice if the realms could not be in jeopardy for a while. Maybe then, I could actually enjoy being queen, because to my surprise . . . I did enjoy it. A little less on days I had to deal with people like Galather, but the rest of it was fun.

For the most part, the merfolk realm ran itself. Trade agreements with the other fae realms had been in place for thousands of years. They rarely changed.

Dealing with the daemons was a little newer, but even then, most negotiations had been settled centuries ago.

I didn't spend my time on tedious arguments like the price of grain. Instead, I had to convince my people that, no, they could not slaughter an entire bloodline over a perceived slight. Some people might have found that exhausting to deal with, but I'd always enjoyed learning what made people tick . . . and then manipulating them with that knowledge.

Well, I usually enjoyed it.

"This feud between Galather and Elmon is getting tiresome." I stretched as I rose from my throne. I'd crafted it myself from driftwood and adorned it with shells. It was a stunning design that I was quite proud of—but comfortable, it was not. Maybe I could hide some cushions in its design somehow. "Honestly, I don't know how your parents didn't lose their minds dealing with it."

Kaysea chuckled and joined me where the waves were gently lapping at the shore. I had a larger, much more grandiose throne room deep beneath the waves in the most grand of our underwater cities, Naewynn. It was a beautiful space that rivaled that of the fae queens, but I preferred to conduct most of my affairs in this simple cove. The island was located in Mag Cíuin, which was technically an Unseelie realm, but this particular realm was mostly water, and I'd claimed the island for my own.

"The only time I've ever seen my mother lose her temper was when she was dealing with him," Kaysea admitted. My brows rose because Queen Fiodh was one of the kindest, most even-tempered individuals I'd ever met. Kaysea caught my expression and snickered. "She threatened to ban him from every ocean . . . and might have suggested she'd cut off body parts if he complained again. My father calmed her down, but Galather treaded carefully after that." She released a long sigh. "He's probably excited about a new queen because now he has a clean slate to be totally unhinged again."

"Great." Clear, turquoise waves rushed around my feet and I wiggled my toes. "Anything else that requires my attention?"

"Why?" Kaysea slid me an amused glance. "Gonna disappear with my brother again?"

To my surprise, Kaysea had always been supportive of me

being with her brother and thought we balanced each other out well. I hadn't told her that I'd essentially blackmailed him into helping me, which was the only reason he'd been in my company so much lately.

That would have led to questions I couldn't or wouldn't answer.

"We're not back together." I tried to ignore the pang in my chest as I remembered how quickly Connor had left after we'd finished our mission the night before.

"If you say so." The corners of her lips quirked up, and I hated that I was giving her false hope. "Nemain has been driving me nuts with her questions about you two."

My eyebrows rose. "I had no idea she was so invested in my love life."

Freaking feline shifters and their curiosity. Although, of all the things for Nemain to ask about, this was probably one of the least harmful ones. It wasn't like she'd be able to detect the mate bond.

"Oh, she doesn't give a shit about you," Kaysea interrupted my pondering. "I mean, she's definitely curious about you but only because of your deal with Connor. She grilled me about you after everything went down with the Greek gods, and I might have mentioned that you and my brother have a history."

"Of course you did." I rolled my eyes.

"Sorry." Kaysea had the decency to wince. "It's just that I tell Nemain everything, and she . . . ." Melancholy settled into her features, and it looked so out of place on her usually cheerful face. She swallowed. "Nemain and my brother will never be friends, and she'll never admit this, but I think she wants him to be happy. For Myrna's sake."

I had no idea what to say to that, especially knowing there was a very real chance Connor would be walking away from me permanently soon. Kaysea seemed to sense my inner turmoil, because she didn't say anything else on the matter. We both looked out over the water. She was good at this—being at peace in the moment.

"How's Zareen doing?" I asked to change the subject. I'd only met Kaysea's daemon girlfriend a few times in passing, and she'd seemed kind and completely devoted to Kaysea. Their relationship was adorable and uncomplicated. *Must be nice.*

"Pele fired her."

"What?" My head jerked to the side so I could face Kaysea again. She was smiling broadly as she watched some large, serpentine creatures playfully leap out of the water, their purple scales glistening in the sun.

"Zareen has been talking about opening up a bakery for years, but when she signed the contract to work for Pele, it was for a century. She was only twenty years into it."

I nodded. The hundred-year contract thing was typical for young daemons when taking their first apprenticeship or job, especially when it was for a high-ranking daemon like Pele who didn't want to deal with training new people and wanted to cultivate loyalty amongst those who worked for her.

"It's not unheard of for daemons to renegotiate though," I pointed out. "Did she not talk to Pele about it?" The future ruler of the Daemon Assembly could be difficult to read, but I'd always got the impression that she treated those who worked for her with respect and consideration.

"Zareen thinks Pele walks on water." Kaysea laughed. "She was going to tough it out and wait."

"Ah." I grinned as understanding dawned. Pele had a tendency to take a direct approach, and she was nearly as good at information gathering as me. I had no doubt she was aware of Zareen's dream. She'd probably decided to wait an allotted amount of time to see if her employee would come to her, and when she hadn't, she'd taken matters into her own hands. "So how much has Pele already set up for Zareen?"

"She reached out to me a few months ago and asked for my assistance." Kaysea's lips twitched. "Between me, Pele, and Asmodeus, we found the perfect location in Meenri for the shop and also a smaller front to set up in Emerald Bay just down the street from The Inferno. Asmodeus helped establish a gateway between the two locations so everything can be baked in Meenri and easily stocked in Emerald Bay."

"That sounds perfect." I smiled. Kaysea and Zareen were so kind to everyone; they deserved this.

"It is," she agreed. "The grand opening will be in a couple of weeks. You should come."

"I'd like that."

The creatures that had been dancing amongst the waves slipped beneath the surface and didn't appear again. Playtime was over.

I sighed as the many problems I needed to solve crashed back into me. "Anything else that requires my attention?"

A crease formed between Kaysea's brows, which was never a good sign.

"The fae queens are hosting a celebration."

My magic flared. Something about this was important. "What type of celebration?"

"They're commemorating five millennia of rule. The Tuatha families and some select others have been invited to stay at their palace in Tír na mBeo for the week. Culminating in a renewal ceremony where they'll reenact the transference ritual."

I frowned. That wasn't right. They were over five thousand years old, probably closer to six, but they hadn't banished their brother until roughly 2500 BCE, so they were still five centuries short of their five millennia.

Not that there was anyone to call bullshit on them. The

queens were the oldest of the fae by far. Most fae lived for one to two thousand years, depending on how much magic they possessed. The queens' lifespans were extended because their magic was tied to the fae realms.

All the fae who had been alive back then had passed or were locked away in the realm with Balor—the devourer magic running through their veins had extended their lifespans.

The queens were using the five millennia claim as an excuse.

"They're putting on a show of power," I murmured.

Kaysea nodded. "The rumors about their magic fading have been growing."

"Fuck." I rubbed my forehead.

I didn't particularly like the fae queens, but they were the only reason the ward around Balor's realm was holding. The loss of some of their backup realms had impacted them greatly, as they'd relied on the magic boost from those humans to supplement their power.

How much exactly, I had no idea. That was one piece of information I hadn't been able to uncover.

"The Tuatha aren't particularly happy about it. While they always enjoy a good party, the invitation was very clearly an order." Kaysea snorted. "Those snobby assholes hate being told what to do."

My head snapped to Kaysea. "*All* the Tuatha Dé Danann have been ordered to attend?"

She looked at me for a long moment, clearly not under-standing the urgency in my tone before nodding slowly. "Yes."

With both Darragh and Eachan taken care of, all my remaining targets would be in one location and likely distracted by the festivities. My magic hummed beneath my skin, radi-ating satisfaction.

"Did I get an invitation?"

The crease between her brows deepened as Kaysea gave

me a peculiar look. "Of course. You actually want to go? I'm sure the invitation was only sent out of politeness, not actual obligation like it is for the Tuatha."

Given that I rarely attended anything where the fae queens were in attendance unless I absolutely had to, I wasn't surprised Kaysea was taken aback at my inquiry, but this was too good an opportunity to pass up, and my magic clearly agreed with me.

Kaysea didn't know any of my ulterior motives, and as much as I wanted to tell her, I couldn't. She would absolutely tell Nemain, who may or may not tell the Unseelie Queen. Even if she didn't tell Elvinia, Nemain would probably insert herself into my business, and while Nemain was exceptional at killing things . . . she didn't exactly do it subtly.

Once I took care of this traitor business, I wanted to continue living my life. There was no way for me to know how the fae queens would react if I killed several of their subjects. At the very least, they would scrutinize me more, but I couldn't let them learn the truth of my bloodline, not if I wanted to continue breathing.

"It's been a while since I've visited the fae realms for anything other than a quick business chat," I said casually. "I'm overdue for some quality time there. Plus, the queens throw the best parties."

Kaysea squinted at me. "Who are you, and what have you done with my queen?"

"Hilarious." A plan started to come together. One Connor really wouldn't like. "Kaysea . . . did that invite include a plus-one?"

Chapter Three

"CONNOR!" Kaysea called as her brother stepped out from the waves beneath the darkening sky hours later. I'd felt him as soon as he'd passed through the gateway just off the shore. Technically, it wasn't the official gateway to this realm—that one was on the other side of the island. This gateway was the one I'd snagged from Nemain when I'd helped her with the kraken situation.

Still couldn't believe there actually *was* a kraken and I'd met him.

As long as the gateway remained in the water, I could change where it led to. I could also set up wards around it so no one else could see it, which was what I did when I was in my little hidey-hole realm.

I'd asked Nemain if I could keep it after the battle with Artemis and the rest of the Olympians—mostly because I was worried she would close it at an inopportune time, leaving me stranded somewhere.

I did know how to create gateways on my own, but it required time, complicated magic, and they couldn't be moved. Nemain's gateways were unique, and if I had more free time,

I'd love to study them to see if I could unravel what made hers different from the less flexible ones created by fae and daemon magic.

There was also the fact that Nemain didn't seem all that concerned about breaking down how her magic worked. I'd briefly questioned her about it when asking if I could keep the gateway, and I'd literally watched her eyes glaze over when I'd started talking about magic theory. The only other person I knew who had anything like it was her mother, Badb, and I definitely would not be asking her about it.

Few people scared me, and Badb was absolutely one of them. Kalen, Badb's mate and Nemain's father, was up there too. I still remembered when Kaysea had dragged me to a party hosted by the Unseelie Queen. There had been this space around Badb and Kalen. Even the Unseelie Court members were wary of the queen's assassins.

Meanwhile, Kaysea had practically squealed at seeing them and ran up to wrap her arms around them. The look of surprise on their faces would forever be etched into my mind, a memory I would cherish always. Kaysea was a hugger, and apparently that even applied to Badb, the Great Battle Crow, and the Erlking.

The Notorious Hugger barely gave her brother enough time to grab one of the towels we kept stacked on a nearby bench before throwing herself at him. I was a glutton for punishment, because I'd been sneaking glances at him as he'd strode out of the waves completely naked, and now I was hoping that towel would slip.

It did not.

"What are you doing here?" Kaysea asked, giving him one final squeeze before releasing him and stepping back. I rose from where I'd been sitting on the ground, leaning against my throne with a bunch of paperwork spread out around me, and moved to stand next to her.

Connor smiled at his sister before looking at me with an unreadable expression. "I have some things to discuss with Queen Ashling."

Ugh. Him using my title meant he was really peeved off about something.

"I always have time to chat with a *prince* of our realm."

Connor's eyes narrowed, and I gave him a pleasant smile in return. He hated being referred to as a prince.

You're the one who wanted to title drop, I thought. My smile widened as his expression grew more annoyed.

I could almost hear him thinking, *You're such a petty asshole.*

Kaysea's gaze bounded back and forth between us. I knew she was collecting as much information as possible and would probably be sharing it with Pele and Nemain. Given the way Connor was now eying his sister suspiciously, he was thinking the same.

"We were actually just wrapping up here," I said smoothly. "Would you mind escorting me home, Connor? I'm happy to discuss whatever you need there."

"Of course, My Queen."

He said it in a flat tone, but my mind conjured up a dream I'd had where he'd purred those words in my ear as his fingers slid inside me.

Heat pooled between my thighs, and Connor stiffened, his light eyes drifting down my body possessively for a few seconds before he caught himself and looked away.

Kaysea cleared her throat. "Well, I'll be going then. Do have fun *discussing* whatever it is you two need to talk about."

"Kaysea," Connor warned, but his sister just gave him an innocent look before turning to me.

"Would you mind switching the gateway to Emerald Bay?"

"Sure." I concentrated on the water, letting my magic slip through it. "Done."

"Thanks! I'll be there for the foreseeable future. Let me know if you need anything!"

Kaysea walked over to the bench and pulled off her wrap dress, then folded it and tucked it into a basket beneath the bench before practically skipping off to the waves. She dove in, and a glittering green tail rose out of the water and slapped the surface once before disappearing. I waited a few seconds to give her time to swim through the gateway and then switched it to my realm.

Connor watched me, his expression carefully blank. Yep. He was definitely pissed off at me.

"See you on the other side." I gestured towards the gateway, and he jerked his head in a nod before striding back towards the water. The towel slipped from his waist, giving me a view of the world's best ass—I might have been biased—and he tossed it towards the bench before slipping beneath the waves.

I slid my own wrap dress off and tucked it into the basket next to Kaysea's before diving into the water. With barely a thought, my form shifted, pale legs becoming a bright blue tail, and the same glittering blue scales extended up my body in swirling patterns to cover my breasts.

The clear water flowed over my skin, and it felt like I was being welcomed home. Between my duties as queen and my dedication to preventing my vision from coming true, I spent most of my time on land, but there was always something so freeing about returning to this form.

As much as I wanted to keep swimming, I had matters to attend to. Connor was already grumpy; it'd only get worse if I made him wait, and convincing him to go along with my plan was going to be challenging enough as it was.

A few strong beats of my tail had me soaring through the gateway, then I let my magic wrap around it to prevent anyone else from swimming through and discovering my secrets.

I broke the surface, greeted by purple and green swirls dancing across the night sky as I swam to shore. The beautiful display was one of the reasons I had chosen this realm for my secret home away from home. It was a grander version of the northern lights found in the human realm, and I'd never tire of gazing up at it.

I trudged out of the calm ocean waves towards the cottage resting on a grassy hill. It was far less grand than the castle I technically now owned in Naewynn, but I loved it because it was mine and it was the one place I could be myself. Mostly.

An open door greeted me, and I bit back my sigh as I headed inside. Connor stood with his back to me, wearing one of the many pairs of sweatpants I kept here. He'd never commented on me having some in his size. At well over six feet tall and built like a mountain, he was considerably bigger than me. If I'd tried to wear those sweats, they would have instantly slid off my petite frame.

I headed into the small bedroom at the back of the cottage to get dressed.

When I slipped back into the main room, Connor was still staring at what I'd affectionately dubbed the Murder Wall.

He didn't look at me as I sidled up next to him and struggled with wrestling my curly blue hair into a bun. Still without looking at me, Connor pulled the necklace from his pocket and held it between us.

The silver charm flickered against the soft yellow fae lanterns lighting the space. It looked like a stylized lock and key.

"It's a pass-through charm. Only someone who held one of these would have been able to get past Eachan's ward." He pinned the necklace to the wall between the sketches I'd made of Eachan and Darragh. "These charms only work as long as the ward owner is alive. If I had killed Eachan last night when

I'd wanted to, it would have alerted Darragh that something was wrong."

I fought back the scowl I wanted to make at the necklace. Something would have given away my foresight magic eventually, but still. If he hadn't found the damn thing, I might have been able to keep the charade up a little longer.

Hey, babe. You know how we broke up because I hid something major from you and basically lied to your face for six months? Well, I never stopped lying to you. I can see the future. Sometimes. It's quirky. I didn't tell you because I knew you'd ask about what else I had seen. It's that we're fated mates. Well, technically fated mates aren't a thing. Not like in all those romance books your sisters reads. By the way, I know you steal them to read when you think no one is looking.

Anyways, my magic strongly implied that if I'm going to succeed in preventing this end-of-the-realms vision from coming true, I need your help. But that same magic also told me that we're destined to be mates. Huh. Maybe fated mates are a thing? This might need more philosophical reflection. I'm putting a pin in that to get drunk and discuss with Kaysea some night.

The bond started to snap into place when we were together and I've been suppressing it so that you don't feel it. Because my magic implied that if I told you about the whole mate thing, you might walk away from us— from me. Or not. It chose that fucking moment to not be clear.

Peachy?

"Good thing you didn't kill him then," I said lightly, glancing at Connor out of the corner of my eye.

"You moved just before Darragh entered the room," he continued, keeping his eyes fixed to the board as the muscles along his jaw flexed. "If you hadn't, he would have seen you immediately and put you in the airlock just as he did me. Changing your position bought you a few extra seconds— enough time to throw a dagger."

"Lucky I moved then," I said in the same casual tone. This was exactly why I didn't have any friends or long-lasting relationships. If anyone spent any extended period of time with me, my foresight magic would become obvious quickly.

Connor's temper snapped, and he twisted to look at me, his pale eyes practically glowing. They were a green so light, depending on the lighting, they looked white. Most people found them hard to read and a little frightening, but it wasn't hard to see what he was feeling right now. The only other time I'd seen him this pissed was when we'd been standing in the throne room and it had been announced that I would be the next queen. He'd looked at me like the declaration had been a betrayal, which it had been.

I'd listened to him pour his heart out for months about how much he hated the throne, and never once had I told him that I'd been working for years to ensure I'd become the new Merfolk Queen.

I should have told him about my intentions from the start but was selfish and wanted whatever time with him I could get. Part of me also thought I'd be able to uncover why Connor had been so determined to walk away from the throne when his parents had stepped down and use that information to figure out a compromise, but I still had no idea.

"We were able to take out Taillte because she got in a fight with her lover and stormed off without the half dozen guards she typically has with her," Connor kept going, clearly having ruminated about this for a while.

Might as well let him get it all out. My eyes flitted away to the drawing of the pretty fae female with long, auburn locks. She had been instrumental in building the alliance between the seraphim and Lir thanks to her penchant for cruelty. One of the favorite pastimes of the seraphim was hunting down human children. Taillte was particularly gifted with earth magic, and she would use it to trip the children up just for fun if it seemed like they might get away.

We hadn't given her an easy death.

"There is no way you could have planned for that exact scenario," Connor said, and I met his accusatory stare once more. "I can list dozens of other times when we coincidentally happened to be in the perfect place at just the right moment."

"Maybe I'm just lucky." Laughter started to bubble up my throat, but I strangled it back down. Lucky was not something I had ever been.

"You're a seer." He threw out the declaration like a challenge. "That's the only explanation. What I don't understand is why you would hide this from everyone? It's not that uncommon of a gift. Everyone knows Kaysea is one."

"Bit more complicated than that," I hedged. He'd have to be told something, but I couldn't tell him everything. If Connor learned we were fated mates and I'd been hiding it all this time, he might walk away—and stay away. That was an uncertainty my magic refused to answer. It was, however, quite clear that without his help, I would fail in my task.

He narrowed his eyes. "Explain."

"For someone who was adamant about not wanting the throne or any type of leadership position, you sure do love to give orders," I said dryly before walking over to my couch and plopping down.

Connor followed and parked himself right in front of me, crossing his arms as he glared down at me. It was probably supposed to be intimidating, but it mostly just drew attention to how muscular his arms were and his impressively broad chest. Or maybe that was just me and my poor neglected libido.

He wasn't going to let this go, and he'd already figured it out anyway. I couldn't risk telling him we were fated mates, but I could at least clarify how my magic worked.

"It's true that I am a seer, but I actually rarely get visions," I admitted. "My magic works a little differently. Instead of clear visions, I usually just get . . . hunches."

"You get hunches," he repeated in a flat, unimpressed tone.

I scowled up at him. "Do you want me to explain, or do you want to act all haughty?"

His lips twitched, and for a second, I saw the Connor that nobody else saw. The one who had laughed with me as we'd floated on our backs and stared up at the stars, making up more and more ridiculously named constellations.

"Sorry," he said, some of the hardness leaking out of his eyes. "I just feel like every time I think I know you, more secrets come out."

Oh.

"I'm sorry," I rasped, the words bitter on my tongue because I still had some secrets he would likely hate me for.

His arms dropped to his sides before he sat on the other end of the couch—as far away from me as he could get. My couch was small, so it was only a couple of feet, but somehow, the distance felt far greater.

"I know," he said tiredly. "Things may not have worked out between us, but I could handle it better. There's just a lot going on in my life right now, and I take my frustrations out on you."

His father, the previous Merfolk King, was entering the last stages of his life. I didn't have any family anymore, and even when some of them had been alive, things had been complicated, but Connor's family was full of love and support. I knew for a fact that his father hadn't blinked an eye when Connor had told him he didn't want to follow in his footsteps and take over the crown. He only wanted his son to be happy.

If someone had explained that concept to my mother, she would have laughed in their face.

"I should have told you about my intentions to claim the throne sooner." My head dropped back against the soft cushion. "You made it clear you were looking forward to starting a new life away from all the politics you'd grown up in. It was an asshole move on my part not to say anything."

He snorted, and I flopped my head to the side just in time

to see the half smile curl his lips. "Definitely an asshole move." Those fathomless eyes of his slid to meet mine. "Some might say that entrapping me in this bargain to help you was also an asshole move."

"Some might," I acknowledged, "but I needed help, and it had to be someone who wasn't squeamish about ending lives and who I could trust. The first isn't hard to find, but the second is quite challenging. And both together? It's a short list, my friend."

"I'm glad you did." He looked away from me to study the Murder Wall once more. Four names were crossed out. Five remained. "I may have no interest in ruling, but I still care about our people. Balor cannot be allowed to return. He was a conqueror once, and all evidence suggests his need to instill his rule has only increased."

Decaying bodies. Crows cawing. Rotting flesh tearing. Grief-stricken wailing.

I squeezed my eyes shut and waited until the vision faded, sinking to the bottom of my mind like a stone cast into a pond. It would rise again, it always did, and it was still just as crystal clear as it had been ninety years ago.

When I opened my eyes, I found Connor scrutinizing me, his brows furrowed in concern. I smoothed away any hint of anxiety on my face, and he frowned. "Is there anything else you need to tell me?"

"No." Lie.

He stared at me.

"You know everything that's relevant."

Another lie. More staring.

"I know there's something else."

In the near future, you and I are going to be standing on a rooftop, and I'm going to tell you that I love you and that you and I are mates. No amount of begging my magic has given me any insight as to what your response will be. I think there's a significant chance you'll walk away—again—and I've been living with that dread for years now.

I kept the thought to myself, even as I waited a few seconds to see if my magic would chime in on any of this, maybe let me know if I could tell him now and everything would be fine? Even better, give me a visual of us having celebratory sex for getting all our shit figured out, but as usual, it decided to remain silent. Argh.

"There's nothing else," I said evenly, "aside from queen business that I can't share with you. Unless you've reconsidered my offer?" I arched an eyebrow at him and gave him a salacious grin.

Connor just rolled his eyes. "Still not being your consort."

"Ah, come on." I pushed my bottom lip out into a dramatic mock pout. "You wouldn't have any responsibilities aside from looking pretty and *servicing* me."

He shook his head ruefully. "You're impossible. I can't believe you're queen."

"Rude." I stuck my tongue out at him. "I did kill a god, you know."

"I loosened him up for you."

"It's not like he was a can waiting to be opened."

Connor let out a deep, rumbling laugh, and my toes curled at the sound. I really was hopeless and on a collision course with heartbreak.

"I've missed you," he confessed. "I've missed this. Just being with you."

My throat tightened at the admission. After we'd broken up, Connor had avoided me as much as possible. Even after he'd agreed to help me, we hadn't spoken about our past relationship once. "I've missed you too."

He brushed his wet hair away from his face and let out a deep sigh. "I need more time."

I nodded, not trusting myself to speak right now. Tears

built in my eyes, and I looked away from him, staring at the floor and willing myself to hold it together.

"But"—my head snapped up at that one word to meet his gaze, hope blooming inside my chest—"maybe we can give it another shot in the future?"

"I'd like that," I croaked.

"If you get another brilliant idea to manipulate me into helping you . . ." A wry smile spread across his face. "I'd advise you to rethink your strategy. Being strong-armed into doing things makes me cranky."

"Everything makes you cranky." I grinned back at him. "But duly noted."

"And, Ash?"

"Yes?"

"No more lies between us." The good humor drained from his face and was replaced with a solemn expression. "You said you've told me everything I should know, and I'm going to believe you. Don't betray that trust again."

Tell him. Tell him now! I shushed the voice inside my head because there was no way I could pull off the rest of this mission on my own, and there was a very real chance that Connor would walk away from me if I told him the truth. The fate of the realms depended on me. I couldn't risk it. Plus, maybe something would change and my vision wouldn't come true, in which case there was no point in telling him anyway.

It was weak and desperate logic on both counts, but when it came to Connor, *weak and desperate* basically summed up how I was feeling these days. I just needed a little more time to figure it all out.

"I promise." I gave him an easy smile that I hated myself for. "There's nothing else."

He held my gaze for a long moment before nodding. "Okay then. Care to make another attempt at explaining your magic, and I'll try to keep the asshole commentary to a minimum?"

"Sure," I said, happy to be moving on to another topic. "I've only received a handful of visions in my life. One of them was when I was five years old." I swallowed and shifted on the sofa until my feet were tucked under me before I twisted to face Connor. "I saw Balor striding through a battlefield. Even in the vision, I could *feel* the magic dripping off him. The ground was littered with rotting corpses. Thousands upon thousands of dead fae, daemons, and others. An army of all species rallied to fight against the exiled fae king . . . and failed to defeat him."

"Do you know when this happens?" His expression was that of a fae warrior who had served his realm for centuries. Serious, calm, and resolute.

"No." I shook my head. "But I do know that all of them"—I pointed to the sketches pinned on the wall—"are lynchpins in it coming to pass."

"Lynchpins?"

"No futures are completely set in stone. But some . . ." I frown as I look for the right word. "Some are more wobbly than others."

"Is *wobbly* a technical term for this type of thing?" His tone remained steady and professional, but his eyes sparked with amusement.

My gaze narrowed. "What happened to no asshole commentary?"

"I implied limited assholery, to be fair." A playful grin stretched across his mouth. "It's the little details that matter."

"You can take the fae prince out of the court, but you can't take the court out of the prince." I smiled back at him.

"Exactly."

"Perhaps because I'm merfolk and water is in my nature, I often think of fate like a river," I explained. Excitement bubbled up my throat as the words spilled forth. Aside from my mother and a few other now dead family members, I'd never been able to talk about my magic to anyone. "Sometimes that river is raging, and it's difficult to divert its path. Any attempts might be overridden by its current."

Connor nodded in understanding.

"But sometimes the current is slower, and that river splits into a dozen smaller ones. Some of those smaller ones might eventually lead to the same place, but others might head in completely different directions."

"I'm guessing those fates are easier to change?"

"Yes and no." I bopped my head from side to side and pointed to the wall. "Take our fun Murder Wall. Each one of those Tuatha Dé Danann represents a split from the same river, but they end up at the same place. So they all need to be cut off. If even one is missed, it will return to its original path and the river will proceed in the same direction."

"So if even one of them survives, Balor will return." Connor looked at the board before glancing back at me curiously. "Is that normal, or are there some fates that are certain?"

"No fates are absolutely certain." I shrugged. "Everything is the result of a choice. Either yours or someone else's. Oftentimes, it's one choice building on another. The fae up on the board could choose to walk away at any moment and everything would change."

Connor's brows furrowed. "So nothing is certain, anything could change, but also the fate of our realms relies on this?"

"Exactly." I let out a long breath.

"Fun," he deadpanned, and I snickered.

"This is where intelligence gathering blends in with my magic." I leaned forward on the couch, closing the distance between us a little. "My magic gives me nudges. They're typically vague feelings, like *go here* or *this person is important*. This is why I'm so fanatic about gathering up every little detail I can about everyone and everything. It helps fill in the gaps."

Connor gave me a shrewd look. "This explains how you rose through the ranks so quickly to be such a strong contender for the throne."

And the fact that I'd blackmailed and murdered a few people. Bad people who'd had it coming . . . or at least would have had it coming based on the seriously fucked-up vibes I'd gotten from them.

"I got mad skills."

He looked at me for a long moment, and I knew I wouldn't like whatever he was going to ask next.

"Has your magic ever told you anything about us?"

Nope. Didn't like that question. It was the one I'd known would come when he learned about my magic, and it meant I had to lie to his face. Again.

"Connor, if my magic had given me anything about our relationship, don't you think it would have gone better," I smoothly misdirected, "instead of blowing up in my face?"

"True," he mused, and I couldn't quite tell if he believed me. Time to change the topic.

"We've taken out the four easy targets." I waved a hand towards the crossed-out sketches of Ferris, Taillte, Eachan, and Darragh. "The remaining five are going to be considerably harder."

We stared at the wall, where four drawings were pinned around an image of a fae female with glittering auburn hair and yellow eyes that shone like gems against her perfect porcelain skin. Maeve. The would-be fae queen.

"Lughán, Coireall, Rowan, and Aoife do whatever Maeve tells them to, so if she's involved, it makes sense that they are." He frowned at the pretty Tuatha Dé Danann. "I'm a little surprised Maeve chose to back Balor. It's no secret how much she lusts after the fae queens' thrones, but she has to know that Balor doesn't share power and already has a queen."

"Maybe she thinks she can make Siofra disappear and slide into her place."

"I've read through all the documents about Balor," Connor said, still studying Maeve's portrait as if it would give him the answers he was seeking. "By all accounts, he is completely devoted to Siofra and she to him. They have skill sets that complement each other's perfectly for conquering realms. He's the brute magical force, and she's the always plotting general."

I made a noise of agreement. "Best I can guess, Maeve thinks she can use Balor's resources to take out the fae queens and then backstab him."

"That would be a sidhe thing to do."

"I'm surprised you asked Pele to let you review all the information she's gathered." I glanced away from the wall to give him a rueful smile. "That daemon isn't exactly known for sharing, and she plays nicely with the fae because she has to, but she doesn't like us."

"I didn't—Kaysea told me. Pele wouldn't have given me the time of day even if I'd asked." He grimaced like he'd just bitten into a rotten fruit. "She pretends she's above it all, but Pele is petty as fuck. I tried to drown Nemain one time, and she's still bent out of shape about it."

"What?" I choked on air. "You tried to *drown* Nemain? And you're still alive?"

"Long story." He rubbed his throat like he was remembering whatever had happened. Knowing Nemain, she'd had a knife against it. Despite the fact that he was still here in front of me, a panicked dread flashed through me at the thought I could have lost him in that moment if the feline shifter had retaliated. "I might have said some asshole things."

"Shocking," I shook my head. Connor's dickish ways could have gotten him killed.

"And she . . ." The smallest amount of pity flashed across his face. "Nemain was different back then. This was only a few years ago, not long after Magos rescued her from that murdering bastard, Sebastian. I've known Nemain for a long time. She's always been this fierce—albeit slightly unhinged—force of nature, but she was truly broken for a while, and if Kaysea hadn't intervened, I might have died."

"Saved by baby sister." He huffed but didn't disagree. I thought about everything I knew about Nemain—past, present, and future. "If anything ever happens to Mikhail, I think we'll all see a whole new level of unhinged Nemain."

I only had a split-second warning, a sudden adrenaline rush like I was falling, before the vision consumed me. Thousands of tormented screams filled my head as if they'd come from my very soul. I slammed my eyelids shut as fire burned so hot and bright, I was pretty sure it seared my retinas. Blue flames mixed with orange. There was no escaping the piercing death cries as the fire devoured them whole. Then I felt a warm liquid run out of my ears and drip down my neck. My entire body had gone rigid as it experienced the brutal death of thousands.

"Ash!"

Gradually, the shrieking faded until there was just a low ringing between my ears. I slowly opened my eyes and blinked. Something soft was touching my fingers. The area rug that stretched across the living room.

Floor. I was on the floor. Something warm and hard was behind me.

Connor loosened his arms slightly from my waist, and I realized I was sitting between his legs with my back to his chest. I winced when I looked down and saw I'd dug my nails into the flesh of his forearms.

"Sorry." Carefully, I raised my hands, leaving behind tiny droplets of blood before the wounds healed.

"It's fine," he murmured. "I've seen Kaysea have visions before. I know how intense they can get sometimes."

"That's one word for it." I brushed my fingers beneath my ears, and they came back bloody. Great. At least the faint ringing was fading. Fae healing for the win.

"What did you see?" he asked gently, his arms still loose around me like he wasn't ready to let go quite yet, which was good because I'd missed feeling him against me like this— suffering through a vision had been worth it.

Was I taking advantage of his concern for me? Yes.

Did I care? Nope.

I leaned further into his embrace, letting the feel of him ground me in the now. "Nemain. Rage. Pain. Desperation. I think she killed a lot of people."

"Given Nemain's history, that's not surprising," he grunted. The feline shifter had carved a bloody path across the human realm after her parents had been killed and again after Myrna. Nemain did have a bit of a reputation. "Were you able to tell what set her off in your vision?"

"Not sure." I concentrated, trying to draw any useful information from what I'd seen, but it was too chaotic. "Given what we were talking about, I think something happened to Mikhail."

"Fuck."

"Yeah." I turned my head slightly so my cheek was against his chest. "Fuck."

"Any suggestions on how we avoid that? Nemain isn't my favorite person, but there's a very real chance she would bring Kaysea down with her."

She wouldn't. I felt it in my bones. No matter how far gone Nemain was, she would protect Kaysea, but Connor wouldn't believe me, and I supposed it didn't really matter. Whether or not Nemain intended to, Kaysea could come to harm because of her actions.

"That's a problem for future us." Reluctantly, I pulled away and got to my feet. Connor rose as well, walking over to my small kitchen area and getting a wet washcloth to help me clean up. "Thanks." I wiped the blood off my ears and neck. "Honestly, Kaysea is more in tune with Nemain. She might be able to get a vision with more information."

Connor frowned, clearly not liking this idea.

"We can't control our visions." I shrugged. "But Kaysea is a far more powerful seer than I am. Whatever I saw, I don't think it will happen soon. Taking care of the traitor Tuatha needs to remain our priority."

"Alright." Connor ran a hand through his hair. "Has your magic given you any ideas on how to approach the remaining five? They're all incredibly paranoid. Breaking into their territory will be challenging."

I smiled, the last of the headache from the vision finally fading away. "About that . . . Want to be my date for an epic fae party?"

Chapter Four

"Welcome to Cathair na Réaltaí, Queen Ashling." Kalen greeted me with a bow when I stepped away from the gateway that had brought me to the grand palace of the fae queens. He nodded respectfully to Connor, who stepped through after me. "And welcome to you, prince."

A muscle in Connor's jaw ticked. I grabbed his hand and smiled at Kalen. "Thank you for having us. We are delighted to be here this week to celebrate the long reign of the queens."

"Allow me to show you where you will be staying so you can get settled before the opening party tonight." Kalen gestured towards the door, and the three of us started walking.

I'd been to this palace at least a dozen times, even before I'd become queen, when I'd been working for the previous king and queen. I'd been a fairly regular visitor here, but this was the first time I'd been in this wing and the first time I'd stay here. All the other times, I'd only been to the throne room or the outdoor gardens, where the queens often held meetings. Cool earth brushed my skin with each step—Connor and I had packed shoes, but we'd opted to not wear them out of politeness. The queen's palace, like many fae structures, had been built with a connection to nature in mind. The floor was bare, a subtle amount of earth magic at play to ensure dust and dirt didn't spread, and it was common courtesy to go barefoot.

Fae orchids grew along the walls that resembled bark. The flowers were far larger than the ones commonly found in the human realm and had a sweet smell to them. I also knew from experience that they were slightly moody about being touched. I had no desire to break out in a rash, so I walked down the center of the hallway.

Of course the sidhe wouldn't bat an eye at mildly poisonous plants growing randomly throughout their home. There were many fae realms, but they were divided up amongst the Seelie and Unseelie. Only Tír na mBeo was jointly ruled by both queens, and it was where they conducted most of their political business with outsiders. I was an outsider of sorts; all of the merfolk were. We might be fae, but we had our own realm and our own throne.

"Kaysea sent along your belongings this morning, and I had them brought to your quarters," Kalen said as I admired the plants from afar.

"My apologies if she overpacked." I winced slightly. "I told her we didn't need much, but I'm fairly certain she packed every single gown I own."

"She definitely used this as an excuse to buy me a new wardrobe," Connor grumbled as he tugged at his long-sleeve, dark green shirt. The fabric was stretchy and practically molded to his body, showing off his broad chest and shoulders. I was fairly certain I could even make out his back muscles if I stared hard enough. Connor probably thought his sister had picked out clothes to torture him, but I knew the truth.

The brat had done this to tease me—I'd barely been able to keep the drool inside my mouth all morning.

"Oh, we are used to Kaysea and her overpacking ways," a cheerful voice announced.

I looked over my shoulder to see Olwen, the Seelie Knight, striding down the hallway. Where Kalen dressed just like his daughter—always in dark clothing, ever prepared to slip into the shadows and murder someone—Olwen favored bright clothing. I thought they represented her chaotic nature quite well.

Today, she wore a daffodil yellow dress that flowed down to her ankles. Her dark silver hair was in a thick braid that rested over her shoulder and fell to her waist. She was like a ray of sunshine against Kalen's glittering darkness.

"You're late, Olwen," Kalen chided, but there was no real heat to it, and the smile he gave Olwen was genuine. Based on my own research, despite the tension between Kalen and the Seelie Queen, he seemed to consider her Knight a friend. I knew for a fact that Olwen and Badb went out drinking at least once a month and tended to get hammered each time.

They were such an odd group.

Kalen and Olwen chatted away as we went up a flight of stairs and then down another hallway, this one with some type of climbing rose on the walls. Connor was to my left and Olwen to my right with Kalen on Connor's other side. I gave polite responses here and there while Connor was like a silent, broody shadow at my side. If he kept this up, he was going to blow our plan before we even started.

"I'm sorry if we seem a bit out of sorts." I patted Connor's shoulder before looping my arm into his. "We were up late last night and could probably use a few hours of rest before the party."

"No worries," Kalen said smoothly. "You'll have plenty of time to relax."

Olwen sped up so she was a few steps ahead of us and then

spun around to walk backwards. "So when did you two start fucking again?" My arm tightened around Connor's in warning. His mouth flattened into a hard line, but at least he didn't burst out in instant denial or a weak explanation. I was excellent at spinning lies. Connor . . . not so much. There was nothing I could do about the glare he shot at Olwen though.

"Olwen," Kalen said with a sigh.

"Oh, don't pretend like you weren't thinking the same thing." Olwen snorted.

The Seelie Knight slid a glance at Nemain's father. "If Badb were here, she would have asked the same thing."

"That is one of the many reasons my beloved is *not* here," Kalen replied, a faint grin on his face.

"Shouldn't Nemain be attending?" Connor asked in a clipped tone. "Given that she *is* the Unseelie Knight and everyone who belongs to the court was ordered to be here?"

I bit back a groan. Why couldn't he just keep that gorgeous mouth of his shut?

In a blink, Kalen turned from polite representative of the Unseelie Court to something else. My body instantly tensed as the predator who walked amongst us revealed himself. Kalen's obsidian eyes gained a depthless edge, and dark, cold magic rolled off him in waves. Ghostlike flames splashed against the walls, and the temperature in the hallway dropped ten degrees. "My daughter is none of your concern."

"What my esteemed colleague means to say is that Nemain is indisposed at the moment," Olwen smoothly cut in as she slid between Kalen and Connor. If she was concerned about her safety, she didn't show it, but she had also known Kalen for centuries, so this was probably nothing new to her. Besides, I was pretty sure Olwen was a little crazy. "And everyone agreed that her being around arrogant fae is probably not a good idea right now. Unless we want to thin the population of the courts."

"Not the worst idea," I muttered. Connor sent me a chastising look, and I rolled my eyes. It wasn't like he hadn't been thinking the same thing.

"Here we are." Olwen stopped in front of two large, silver doors. "As you are a queen in your own right, we thought it best that you have this entire wing to yourself. It is heavily warded so no one can pass through other than the fae queens and a select few others such as myself, Kalen, and staff, who we handpicked ourselves. Feel free to add more wards inside."

"Any tentacled monsters I need to worry about?" I gave Olwen a pointed look.

She snorted. "Is Nemain still complaining about that?"

"Yes," Connor, Kalen, and I all said at once.

"Gods." Olwen laughed and lightly punched Kalen's shoulder. "Really holds a grudge, doesn't she? The apple didn't fall too far from the tree despite you and your psycho mate not raising her, eh?"

Kalen's black eyes glittered at Olwen, but she just cackled some more before striding off down the hallway with her hands in her pockets.

Crazy bitch.

"The opening festivities will begin an hour after sunset." Kalen looked away from Olwen to glance at me. "Do you require an escort?"

"I don't know," I drawled. "Is someone planning on killing us between here and the ballroom?"

The Erlking's gaze slid to Connor, and blue flames danced across his shoulders before the magic he'd been leaking across the room pulled back into his body until I could barely feel it. Death still lurked in his eyes though, and it occurred to me that he likely knew about the time Connor had tried to drown his daughter.

Subtly, I dropped my hand towards my hip, where I had

fastened a small, poisoned blade. Connor was holding Kalen's gaze, not directly challenging him but also not backing down.

A smile that was more a baring of teeth flashed across Kalen's face before he looked at me once more. "You're a queen, Ashling. Someone is always trying to kill you."

"COULD you maybe not antagonize Kalen while we're here?" I leaned against the silver doors inside our quarters. "We have enough to worry about without you getting your dumb ass murdered because you can't stop talking shit about his daughter."

"I don't understand why everyone keeps making allowances for her," he grumbled. "Nemain's the fucking Unseelie Knight, a title many would kill for, and she can't even be bothered to show up to a party and drink for a few hours."

"You're being an asshole." I shook a finger at him. "I distinctly remember you promising not to be one here."

"Try." Connor's lips quirked up at the corners. "I said I would *try* to not be an asshole."

I let out a low laugh and pushed off the door to further examine the rooms we would be staying in. Several couches with large, fluffy cushions were situated around the center of the room, and a table made of a gorgeous reddish-brown wood, large enough to seat six people, was at the other end. We were on the second level of the castle, which meant the floor was stone and not dirt, but the walls consisted of that same bark-like matter.

Green vines with fluffy, white blossoms scattered amongst the long leaves grew up the walls and across the ceiling. A shallow stream carved its way across the floor, mostly following the wall before flowing through an archway into another room, which was likely the bedroom. It wasn't the same as being close to the sea, but I appreciated the gesture all the same.

I trailed my fingers across the back of a couch before walking past Connor and into the bedroom. The green vines continued to grow along the walls here, but the flowers had changed to a vivid purple shade. A deep pool with floating lilies took up almost a third of the room to the right, fed by the stream that flowed in through the small archway. I admired the beauty for a few seconds before turning my attention to the large bed against the back wall.

The *only* bed.

Connor stepped up to my side and stared at the bed with an unreadable expression. It wasn't like we hadn't known this would be the sleeping arrangement. I had made it clear when I'd accepted the invitation that Connor would be coming as my lover. He'd protested and said he could come as my guard, but that would have drawn attention to us in a way I didn't want.

It wasn't that I never had guards with me—depending on the situation, sometimes I would bring half a dozen warriors I trusted. But this was a social event hosted by the fae queens themselves. Nobody had guards because the queens guaranteed everyone's safety.

Not to say that deaths never occurred at these events, I'm sure they had in the past, but they were always hidden away in the shadows. The use of escorts was normal when traveling between events, but they were usually provided by the queens, and if I'd said I'd wanted Connor here as a guard, it wouldn't have made sense for him to stay in my room with me. In my bed.

Speaking of which . . .

I flicked my hand towards the pool, and water flowed out in a steady stream towards me. Fae could not only see magic, we could directly interact with it. Daemons, witches, dragons, and most other species had to use spells or artifacts to bend magic to their will. All we had to do was ask.

Okay, maybe it was a little more complicated than that. I let my vision sharpen, focusing on the dark blue glowing specks in the water. The color of magic varied based on what it was infused with. Raw magic was a kaleidoscope, so beautiful, it still stole my breath away, but magic also soaked into elements and people, and its color adapted with it. The magic inherent in all elements was what allowed sidhe to interact with them.

Despite the sidhe blood running through my veins, it was my merfolk side that reigned supreme—the only element I could control was water, and while I could feel the magic in other elements, I couldn't do anything with it. But I was far more gifted at manipulating water than any sidhe could hope to be. Technically, I could manipulate raw magic too, but that required pulling it from water, which was difficult. Magic loved to be infused with elements and would fight you when you tried to separate it. There really wasn't any reason to do that when I could just manipulate the water itself.

The stream swirled around me, and a wave of my hand sent it towards the bed. It encircled the entire frame and hovered a few inches over the floor. My own magic poured out of me, carrying with it my intention, and it intertwined itself with the magic in the water. The glowing blue specks merged with my silvery blue ones until they became luminescent strands. I wasn't particularly skilled at crafting wards that phys-ically kept people out, but making small zones where no sound could escape, I was *very* gifted at creating.

Half a thought had the water lowering to the floor and soaking into the stone. A glimmery circle shone brightly around the bed, and I stepped over it before flopping onto the dark blue covers. When Connor failed to follow me, I sat up and curled a finger several times, beckoning him forth.

Hesitantly, he stepped forward before finally crossing the

circle and sitting on the edge of the bed a foot away from me. His back was stiff, as if he was ready to bolt at the slightest movement.

"Connor," I purred. Slowly, he twisted to face me. When I reached out to grab his shirt and tug him forward, he only resisted a moment before going where I'd directed him. A few seconds later, he was lying flat on his back in the center of the bed and I was straddling him.

He didn't make a move to touch me, but I didn't miss the way his fingers curled into the mattress like he was struggling not to. Nor did I miss the hard length straining against his pants. Unfortunately, the fact that he still looked ready to bolt was kind of a mood killer.

"Relax, Connor." I placed one hand on his chest and the other next to his head as I leaned down to whisper in his ear. "I promised that I would respect your wishes. This is all pretend."

"This"—he glanced down at where my body was practically molded to his—"doesn't feel like *pretend*."

"Do you know how I managed to claw my way to power?" I lifted my hand from his chest to toy with a lock of his hair. "I embraced my paranoia. You never know when someone is watching. I'm relatively positive this room is safe currently, but I doubt it will stay that way once more people know I'm here. I rose from relative obscurity to a position of power in the fae realms. Nobody knows anything about me . . . but they all *want* to."

He shifted slightly beneath me, and I had to bite back a groan as his erection rubbed against my center, causing a delicious amount of friction. Connor froze, his eyes darkening with want and need before his expression went carefully blank.

Fuck. In all my scheming, I hadn't thought about how awkward it would be for us to pretend to be together. Connor might have hated me after I'd risen as queen, but that didn't mean he had stopped wanting me. On the rare occasions he couldn't avoid me, I'd seen his eyes fill with desire before he'd squashed it. He'd been riding that fine line between love and hate, whereas I had just been pining.

And now here we were, with so many unresolved things between us and the possibility of maybe trying again when all this was done—if fate didn't blow everything up in my face again. We had to pretend we'd rekindled things and were madly in love. In order to sell that, Connor would need to get used to me touching him.

We just had to make sure we didn't blur the lines between what was fake and what was real. Easy peasy. Definitely not a recipe for emotional damage.

"Unless I'm in my secret home or my heavily warded wing of the palace in Naewynn, I assume anyone could be watching or listening at any given moment."

Connor's gaze softened. "That sounds lonely and exhausting."

"It is," I agreed, letting his hair fall from my fingers. "But I knew what I was signing up for when I pursued the throne."

"I suppose you did." It was my turn to go still as Connor raised his hand and ran his fingers along my jawline. Nobody had touched me like this since him, and I'd forgotten what it felt like. Apparently, we were both going to have to work on our reactions to being touched by the other. "I'll make sure I do a convincing job pretending to be your lover so people don't question it. I won't fail you."

"You could never fail me." *But I'm failing you now by not telling you the truth.* An ache formed in my chest even as I leaned into his touch more. "The ward I placed around the bed will prevent anyone from hearing us, I'm quite confident in that, but if someone does manage to spy in this room, it'll look strange if we're just sitting on the bed talking to each other."

"Hence the touching." His fingers trailed down my neck, and I shivered at the touch.

"Yes," I breathed out. "Hence the touching."

"So what's the plan for tonight?" Connor's pale eyes followed the path his fingers traced across my collarbone. "Opening festivities for long events like this tend to be pretty casual—it will probably be the best opportunity to mingle and get the lay of the land."

"Agreed. I'll need to spend at least some time talking to the queens." My breathing quickened when Connor's fingers lightly skimmed across the trim of my dress, his knuckles brushing the top of my breasts. "We need to keep an eye on Maeve and the others, see if there is anyone they seem particularly friendly with."

"I've met Maeve a few times." Disgust coated his voice. "She'll easily smile in your face while plotting to stab you in the back. It'll be hard to tell if she has any genuine allies outside of her inner circle."

"Any information could prove useful. Almost everything I know about her comes with a question mark at the end." Clearly, Maeve took a similar approach to me when it came to protecting her secrets. I had to admire her level of paranoia. Most of the data I'd collected about her was hearsay or guesswork. It wasn't a secret that she was power-hungry, but nothing concrete could be laid at her feet. In a thousand years of existence, she had never slipped up once.

"We'll need to be careful around Kalen and Olwen too," Connor murmured. "He is ruthlessly cunning, and Olwen hides a sharp mind behind her charming smiles and idle chatter."

"I know." Exhaustion tugged at me. We'd stayed up late the night before, hashing out a basic plan, and sitting here surrounded by Connor's warmth was starting to lull me under. His scent was everywhere too. It reminded me of the lush tropical forests that grew on the coastline of many fae realms. Strong and invigorating.

"Sleep, Ash." Connor's large hand cupped the back of my head and guided me down until I was tucked into the crook of his neck, my body still sprawled on top of him. "We have nowhere to be for a few hours. Might as well get some rest before we have to spend the night pretending to be . . . whatever this is."

I'm not pretending. This is real.

The words tried to claw their way out of my throat, but I held them back. "Sweet dreams, Connor."

Chapter Five

"THIS IS QUITE THE PARTY." I sipped my wine, enjoying the light, fruity flavor. Given how beautiful the rest of the palace was, I hadn't thought I'd be so enchanted by the ballroom, but it was magnificent.

Located in the center of the building, the room extended past the second story. A balcony wrapped around the entire room with thick canopies of blue vines draping down to the floor. Amongst the broad, flat leaves were large flowers with violet petals that slowly opened and closed. In true fae form, the floor was bare earth, but intricate lines of a glittering silver mineral ran through it, making it feel like we were walking on starlight.

And then there was the ceiling, or rather the lack of one. The entire top of the room was open, revealing a night sky filled with what felt like an impossible amount of stars. Cathair na Réaltaí.

City of Stars.

Connor stood at my side, an arm wrapped around my waist as he took in the sights with a bemused smile. I had to say I was impressed with his acting skills, because I knew he was hating every moment of this. The partygoers kept sneaking glances at him and whispering, and more than a few had come up and asked him to dance, which he'd politely declined.

Despite growing up as the Merfolk Prince and being surrounded by politics, Connor was a soldier at the end of the day. He'd much rather be fighting or even guarding entry to this room than listening to asinine chatter and false platitudes.

Kaysea, on the other hand, would've *loved* this. There was so much gossip to gather.

It hit me then just how much I'd come to like the former Merfolk Princess. Kaysea wasn't just an advisor . . . she'd become my friend. My only friend.

Gods, how sad was that?

"Shall we?" Connor extended his arm, and I looped mine around it. Tonight was more of a casual event, since many of the Tuatha were still arriving. The queens had strode into the ballroom thirty minutes before and had immediately been bombarded with members of their respective courts trying to curry favor.

As the Merfolk Queen, I could have cut ahead of the line, but I didn't want to draw attention by throwing my weight around. Instead, Connor and I had just been flitting about the room and whispering into each other's ears.

I'd even managed a silly girlish giggle. I was quite proud of that one. We'd attracted more than a few reproachful looks, and I'd had to hide my grin from those.

All fae were arrogant, but the Tuatha were so caught up in thinking themselves superior that they didn't realize how easy it made them to fool.

The queens were arrogant too, but I had no doubt they wouldn't be as easy to trick. I'd have to adjust my persona as necessary to keep them from looking too closely. Our plan hinged on us being able to wander the palace and watch our targets; I couldn't do that if the queens suspected I was here for anything other than a fun getaway with my lover.

"Greetings, Queen Áine." I smiled at the Seelie Queen with a shallow bow before doing the same to the Unseelie Queen. "And to you as well, Queen Elvinia. Thank you for inviting me."

"It's lovely to see you both again," Connor said, dropping his arm from mine to bow to both queens.

"Thank you for gracing us with your presence," Áine replied in a polite tone that rang as disingenuous. The Seelie Queen had chosen a gown the same color as her eyes, a bright green that reminded me of spring grass. Her rich, chestnut-brown skin practically glowed, and her dark brunette curls were adorned with soft white flowers. She was the image of power and health.

If Áine was the beginning of spring, then her sister, Elvinia, was the cold and brutal winter. The Unseelie Queen wore a black tunic with elegant snowflakes of silver threading. Her short, black hair fell in a dark curtain to her chin, not even a hint of a curl. Golden eyes watched those gathered around like prey as magic pulsed around her.

Both queens were reclined in thrones made of branches and leafy, green vines. The vines winding through Áine's bloomed with bright orange and red flowers, whereas Elvinia's had thorns and dark purple berries along with a yellow-scaled serpent coiled on top, occasionally flicking out its tongue to taste the scents in the air.

I kind of wanted to pet it but figured it would be weird to ask. So I kept subtly sneaking glances at it instead.

"What my sister means to say," Elvinia drawled, "is that we were surprised you bothered to show up, given how you've seemed quite happy to avoid us as much as possible."

"My apologies." I let my lips form a small, sincere, and slightly contrite smile as I placed a hand on my chest, dipping my head towards both queens. "That has not been my intention at all. I admit that while I thought I was well-prepared to take on the weight of the crown, I found myself wishing for more hours in the day almost immediately. By the time things started to settle down . . . something else began to occupy my time." I gazed almost shyly at Connor, who leaned forward to kiss me on the cheek.

"Should I apologize now too?" he said in a light, teasing tone. "For occupying so much of your time?"

A thrill raced down my spine. I hadn't been lying earlier when I'd admitted to Connor that my life was sometimes isolating and lonely. I had to assume that, at any given moment, someone was watching me, waiting for me to stumble, but that didn't mean I didn't thrive in high-stakes situations like this. Part of my public persona was real, but much of it was make-believe, and it was fun to roleplay.

Now we got to trick a room full of the most powerful fae that we were nothing more than besotted lovers. Everything between me and Connor was complicated and was absolutely going to blow up in my face, but nobody was better at compartmentalizing than I was. I shoved all those emotions and complications into a box and onto a metaphorical shelf.

I needed everyone to believe that Connor and I were in that lovey-dovey stage of being obsessed with each other. That way, they wouldn't question us sneaking off occasionally or hiding out in our room.

"I do like the way you apologize." I smirked, letting my fingers trail down Connor's chest. The laces at the top of the light cream shirt had been left undone, allowing his broad chest to peek through. More than a few fae had been giving him appreciative glances since we'd arrived. I wanted to claw their eyes out for looking at what was mine, but that wasn't the type of attention we needed.

So instead, I'd let my hands trail over him possessively and given them a few pointed looks. Mine to touch. Mine to kiss. Mine to fuck. *MINE.*

"Young love," Elvinia scoffed. "Wonderful."

"Forgive my sister," Áine said dryly. "She doesn't know the meaning of the word *love.*"

It was true. To my knowledge, Elvinia had never been in love with anyone. She didn't even take casual lovers, and if she had, she'd hid it exceptionally well. Áine had been a part of a few brief flings but nothing more from what I could tell.

"And you?" I looked at Áine with genuine curiosity. "Has love ever made a fool of you?"

"There has been no great love in my past." She shrugged and let her gaze wander over the crowd. It lingered on someone behind me for a moment, and I saw something flicker in her eyes before she moved on. "And there will be no great love in my future."

"Word of advice from two queens to another." Elvinia's golden eyes sharpened.

"Enjoy your dalliances—" Áine's eyes flicked to Connor and back to me.

"But know that it is just one more thing for you to lose," Elvinia finished.

Both queens rose from their thrones, and Elvinia held out her arm. The yellow serpent slithered up to rest along her shoulders, its tail wrapped around her throat. Connor and I stepped to the side so they could walk past us towards where Kalen and Olwen were speaking. I stared thoughtfully at Olwen. She had been behind me . . . Was she who Áine had been staring at in that small window of vulnerability?

I filed away that tidbit to contemplate later.

"Care to do a turn about the room with me?" I batted my eyelashes at Connor.

He laughed under his breath, and it was the genuine one he'd always done around me when I was being ridiculous—

before things got all messed up between us. "'A turn about the room?' What does that even mean?"

I looped my arm through his. "They always say that in some historical romance drama Kaysea makes me watch. It's just a fancy way of saying 'walk around and talk to people.'"

"Then why not just say that?" Connor stepped forward towards the nearest group of Tuatha, and I moved along with him, my hand resting on his forearm.

"Because it sounds classier the other way."

"Queen Ashling," an older fae female greeted us as we approached. Most of the sidhe naturally leaned towards androgyny. Both sexes tended to be tall with slender builds, and they all shared features that made me think of grace and elegance: high cheekbones, dainty, turned-up noses, and full lips.

The sidhe always had an otherworldly beauty to them, but none more so than the Tuatha Dé Danann.

The Tuatha before me was no exception. Her willowy frame towered above my barely five and a half feet, and her platinum blonde hair flowed down her soft pink dress to below her waist. Flowers the same pink shade as her dress wound about her hair, held there by nothing more than her magic, which was practically dripping off her.

That was the other thing about the Tuatha Dé Danann— their beauty was nothing more than a distraction from the amount of magic they wielded. Power was all they cared about; they simply hid their lust for it behind pretty smiles and false platitudes.

I smiled broadly. "Rosalind." I held her gaze until she dipped her head in acknowledgement. I might be queen of the merfolk, but the Tuatha Dé Danann didn't particularly care. I wasn't their queen after all.

Next to Rosalind, a sidhe male with auburn hair pulled back into a bun that somehow still looked fancy passed a silver coin to the male standing beside him. "Well," he drawled, "looks like you win your favor after all, Slyvian."

"Told you she'd come." The Tuatha male who'd accepted the coin winked at me. "Anyone with half a mind for politics would be here. Just look at all this power in one room." He waved a hand around the grand ballroom. "Think of how many political deals can be made this week! So many opportunities for negotiation . . ." His honey-brown eyes trailed up my body, gaining heat as they went.

My fingers curled at my sides before I forced them to relax. I didn't know this male, and him outright ogling me like this was a clear insult. He didn't respect me as queen. I was nothing more than a potential plaything to him. I could show him just how wrong he was, but that would draw too much attention.

I also didn't want to appear weak in a room full of sharks.

"It's strange, Slyvian," Connor drawled as he gave the fae a bored look. "I could have sworn you valued having your eyes in your head, given the conversation we had the last time you looked at someone I was escorting like that, but if you've changed your mind . . ." Faster than I could track, Connor had a small blade in his hand, the point resting against the corner of Slyvian's left eye. "I can fix that for you."

Rosalind just sipped her wine and watched the scene unfold with a detached expression, like she didn't care one way or another how this played out. The auburn-haired Tuatha, however, clearly found this all incredibly entertaining because he chuckled, his hazel eyes lighting up.

"Ah, yes." He slapped a hand against his thigh and gave me a wide smile. "This was before you became queen, my lady. Our beautiful but not-so-bright Slyvian here got a little too drunk and made a pass at Kaysea."

"A pass?" Rosalind snorted. "He asked how much she would charge to wrap her thighs around his head and then held up two silver coins."

"Wow." I peered at Slyvian, who was still holding perfectly still while Connor pressed the blade a little harder into his skin. "Honestly, kind of impressed you're still alive."

"I keep telling him he owes Kaysea a life debt." The Tuatha male, whose name I still didn't know, chuckled. "Connor was ready to carve out his eyes and cut out his tongue, but Kaysea laughed off the situation and pulled her brother away."

"I apologize," Slyvian said tightly, sliding his panicked gaze to me. "I meant no offense."

"Yes, you did." I rested a hand on Connor's forearm. "Let it go, Connor. We both know he'll squirm and scream if you cut his eyes out, and I don't want to get any blood on my dress."

"Slyvian has a woefully low pain tolerance. He'd definitely scream," the other male confirmed.

Rosalind rolled her eyes. "Honestly, I don't know why I hang out with the two of you."

"Because I'm your favorite cousin, and you have the unfortunate burden of being Slyvian's sister."

"Evander." She sighed and looked at the auburn-haired Tuatha. "If you have to constantly remind me you're my favorite cousin, it's probably not true. I'm going to go drink until I forget I'm related to the both of you." With that, Rosalind strode off.

Her self-appointed favorite cousin, Evander, winked at me. "It is a lovely dress. Enjoy the party, Queen Ashling." Then he walked away towards a group of boisterous, young sidhe males, no doubt to instigate more trouble.

Connor leaned forward until his face was only a few inches away from Slyvian's. "You have three seconds to get out of my sight, then I'm not going to worry about how messy things get."

As soon as Connor pulled the dagger away, Slyvian bolted

like his ass was on fire. I followed his fleeing form across the ballroom until my eyes locked with a pair of citrine yellow ones. Malevolence swirled in their depths, surrounded by a face of impossible beauty. Her lips were painted a vibrant red that matched her hair and shone brightly against her pale skin.

Hello, Maeve.

I broke our stare-off and wrapped my arms around Connor, leaning into his hard body. He tucked the blade behind him and pulled me against himself, one of his hands trailing down my back to stop just above the curve of my ass. I had to tilt my head back to properly look at him, and he had to duck his head down. Our lips stopped a hair's breadth from each other, and I felt like my heart was beating too loudly and far too quickly.

"Ready for the main event?" I whispered against his lips.

"You lead, I'll follow." A thousand dirty thoughts exploded in my mind, and he must have seen it on my face, because his lips curled into the barest hint of a smirk. He kissed the corners of my mouth before brushing a kiss against my lips and then grazed his nose along my jawline so he could nuzzle my neck. "I'll still make you kneel in the bedroom though."

Fuck. Me. Sideways.

Connor pulled that haughty, arrogant expression back onto his face as he stepped back. Smoothly, I unwound my arms from around his neck and took the arm he extended to me. I knew my cheeks were on fire. Despite not being an easy blusher, Connor always managed to get me. Most likely because he didn't look like he'd be such a dirty talker with his usually polished exterior. Pushing all filthy thoughts aside for now, I let my typical, bemused smile play across my lips as we walked through the crowded space.

The ballroom was enormous, but I was pretty sure almost every member of the Tuatha Dé Danann was here. Some of them might not have agreed with the fae queens, but that didn't mean they would dare ignore a summons. Neither Áine nor Elvinia cared about being liked—they knew it was impossible to appease all in their respective courts.

The fae were fickle, and their loyalty could change easily, but no one had ever doubted the power of the Seelie and Unseelie Queens . . . until recently. I suspected many had come here for this event not only because they were too scared not to, but also because they wanted to see for themselves if the queens were truly still as powerful as they had always been, or if the rumors were true and they were slipping.

As little as I cared for the fae queens, we were in deep shit if they faltered now. They had a role to play in the end, and I needed to make sure they got there. If I uncovered any plots against them while I was doing my own mission here, I'd have to make sure they caught wind of them. Preferably without the queens knowing it'd come from me because then they would want to know how exactly I'd found out about it.

Another thrill ran down my spine. The stakes didn't get higher than this.

Tuatha parted to make room for us as we weaved our way towards Maeve, who was still holding her own little mini-court with all her sycophants. As much as I wanted to believe the Tuatha got out of our way because they respected me as the Merfolk Queen, I was pretty sure it had more to do with Connor strolling by my side. If any of them showed the slightest hesitation, Connor would smile at them as if daring them to hold their ground.

None of them did.

Maeve's jewel-like, yellow eyes tracked our progress. If she was the cunning wolf watching us approach, the four sidhe fanned out around her were the hungry pack waiting for scraps.

Lughán and Aoife stood to her left, whispering to each other, the former in his trademark black tunic and pants while

Aoife's red dress stood out vividly against her deep brown skin. Of the five Tuatha, those two were the closest. The occasional lovers had been friends for a long time and were just bad news all around. Both were petty and cruel, even more so when they were together.

To Maeve's right were the two I was really concerned about. Coireall stood there stoically, his lithe frame wrapped in a bright turquoise tunic and light brown pants, and his long, golden blond hair was braided away from his face. While the fae didn't follow human fashion, they had modernized their clothing throughout the centuries. Not Coireall though. He believed strongly that the fae had been at their mightiest a thousand years ago and he chose to dress like they had back then.

Disgust flickered in his eyes as he took me in. Coireall firmly believed the merfolk were beneath the sidhe and had advocated several times over his long life that the merfolk were undeserving of having their own realm.

I smiled broadly at him before letting my gaze slide to the final member of Maeve's quintet. In a well-tailored, navy blue suit that would have made Pele envious, Rowan studied me with cool detachment. Other than Maeve, she was the one I knew the least about—something that greatly bothered me—but I did know she was basically Maeve's right hand, which meant she had to be powerful. Not only to impress Maeve enough to choose her but to keep the other three from stabbing her in the back and taking the position.

My cheeks hurt a little from smiling so much, but I really needed to sell this performance.

"Maeve!" I said a little too cheerfully, like I'd had too much wine. "You look absolutely stunning!"

It wasn't a lie. The gilded gown hugged her slender curves as if liquid gold had been poured over it. Every time she moved, the fae lanterns made it light up. The dress radiated beauty and strength; I could practically imagine a crown on her head.

"Thank you, Queen Ashling," she said in a low, throaty tone. "You look"—those golden eyes trailed down my body as she tilted her head back and forth, deciding on a word—"nice."

It physically hurt to keep my eyes from rolling.

"Oh, thank you." I ran a hand down the pale green material. The simple satin dress wasn't flashy like her metallic gold gown, but it flowed over my skin like water, and based on the few times I'd caught Connor staring, it clearly did absolute wonders for my ass. I hadn't only chosen it for its flattering cut though. I leaned a little more into Connor, whose arrogant mask hadn't slipped once, although his arm had tightened around mine at Maeve's slight. "I saw it a few weeks ago while walking through Naewynn and couldn't resist." I let a shy smile flash across my face, here and gone in a blink, but I knew none of the predators in front of me would miss it. "It matches Connor's eyes."

Underestimate me, I willed. *I'm just the weak Merfolk Queen besotted by a new lover.*

"I think you look stunning." Connor bent down and kissed my cheek. I didn't even have to fake the blush that spread over my cheeks, because his arrogant mask had slipped for a moment, and I knew he'd meant it.

"Well, aren't you two adorable," Lughán drawled while Aoife snickered at his side.

"How are you finding the party so far, Queen Ashling?" Maeve asked. Her eyes hadn't slipped from my face once, which was a little unnerving.

"It's wonderful. Things have been very busy since I ascended the throne." I stood a little straighter as if I was trying to make it clear I was standing on my own and not relying on Connor's strength. "This week will be a nice respite and allow me to spend some more time with the fae queens . . . in addition to giving Connor and me some alone time."

"How is Tír fo Thuinn these days?" Rowan asked, casually brushing a dark brown curl behind her ear as her bright green eyes continued to study me. "It's been a while since I've been."

"It's just as lovely as ever. You should come visit Naewynn. I think the queens have inspired me to host a ball of my own." I laughed and gestured around the room before waving my hand towards all five of them. "All of you would be welcome of course."

"We would certainly try to attend," Maeve said breezily. I could tell she was losing interest in this conversation. We'd never met, and while my quick ascension to the throne was interesting to many, and probably to Maeve herself, I was still just a merfolk in her eyes. Crown or not.

Aoife sent me a calculating look. "I hear you've been associating a lot lately with the Unseelie Knight. You rarely set foot in the fae realms, and yet you run off with *her* as if it's nothing."

"Still can't believe that devourer shifter mutt is an official member of our court." Lughán shook his head and grinned at Coireall. "You must be happy her parents got thrown out of the Seelie Court; otherwise, you might have a disgraceful Knight as well."

Coireall snorted, his agreement with Lughán's words clear on his face as he sipped his wine.

I thought about pointing out that Badb had never belonged to the Seelie Court and that Kalen hadn't been thrown out, he'd fled to be with his love, but that wouldn't serve my purpose here, and it's not like those two would give a shit about me defending their honor. They'd probably laugh at the idea.

"Not that Olwen is much better," Aoife muttered.

"Olwen is at least a pure-blooded sidhe," Coireall said mildly. "Even if she does leave something to be desired."

Someone's bitter at being repeatedly turned down. I smiled inwardly. For beings that were well over five hundred years old, they were a petty lot.

"Do you have any plans while you're here?" I asked politely, even as I gave Connor an adoring glance, as if I was only keeping up appearances until I could politely excuse myself from the festivities. Connor's lips curled into a smile, and my heart quickening had nothing to do with my acting skills. He wrapped his arm around my shoulders and tugged me into his side.

I snuggled a little into his embrace before turning back to Maeve. "Sorry." I let out a breathless giggle. "We sometimes get caught up in each other."

Maeve's upper lip trembled like she was fighting back a sneer. I was a little impressed she didn't just embrace it, but she probably didn't want to risk outright insulting me in such a way. She may not respect me at all, but I was still a queen, and she wasn't the type to write off potential political connections so easily. Though her distaste meant she was buying the love-struck fool act we were putting on.

"No plans. The queens beckoned, and we came," Maeve said, her tone walking the line between mockery and indifference. "We are loyal subjects after all."

"Of course," I murmured.

"Speaking of . . ." Maeve passed her now empty wine glass to Lughán, who took it from her like a good servant but not before I saw a flicker of annoyance flash across his handsome features. "We should go pay our respect to the queens."

"It was nice speaking with you." I nodded to Maeve, then blinked up at Connor. "Perhaps we should retire for the evening? This is only the opening night, and I'm feeling rather tired."

"Then let's return to our room and make use of that wading pool." His deep voice promised all kinds of wicked things as he let his arm slide down until it was wrapped around my waist. The thought of spending the next few hours with Connor in that gorgeous pool sounded like heaven.

Suddenly, my mind decided I'd had enough daydreaming and reality crashed back in. We were only pretending. Things weren't all fixed between us. He didn't know he was my mate, and when he found out I had lied to him again, he would hate me for it. I wasn't here to flirt and enjoy myself anyway. I was here to figure out how to kill five of the most powerful fae in all the realms before they ushered in the end.

"Enjoy your evening, Queen Ashling." Maeve swept by me, the others falling in line behind her like the obedient wolves they were.

"Let's go," I said quietly to Connor. "I'm ready to get the fuck out of here."

Chapter Six

"I DON'T LIKE THIS PLAN," Connor said flatly.

Really? I had no idea. You've only spent the last thirty minutes detailing every single reason you don't like it.

"Your opinion has been duly noted, but as queen, I over-rule you." Before he could start his disapproving lecture again, I rolled out of bed, stepping past my privacy ward.

The party was just getting going, and Maeve would likely be there for at least another couple of hours. As the Merfolk Queen, it had been a little faux pas for me to leave so early, but it would play into our cover of being enamored with each other.

Connor and I would still have to sell that though, even in our rooms.

As soon as I'd stepped into our guest quarters, I'd keyed in on the white, fluffy flowers that were now blooming on the green vines racing across the ceiling. The magic radiating off them was subtle, but I still recognized it.

Queen Áine had cast a cute little spying enchantment on the flowers. The magic of the fae queens had unique signatures

—Áine's had a lighter and more crisp feeling to it than Elvinia's dark and spicy magic.

Whether she could see through the flowers or just hear, I wasn't sure, but I was confident in the ward I'd placed around the bed. The queens could break it easily, but they wouldn't. That wasn't how these games were played. I would pretend I didn't know about the magic emanating from the white flowers, and Áine would pretend like she didn't care about what exactly I was hiding behind the privacy spell.

A large part of fae politics was just moving pieces around a board to see how your opponent would react.

I loved it. Connor claimed to hate it, but he was quite good at it when he wanted to be.

Connor slid off the bed, and I glanced over my shoulder at him, letting my eyes linger on his face before dropping to his chest. I'd made sure to mess up his hair when we'd been arguing in bed and had further unlaced his shirt.

"Come back to bed." He deepened his voice, adding a wolfish quality to it. His words and tone very much promised all sorts of wicked things, but his eyes were hard and pissed off.

I let out a husky laugh that said I'd welcome such wicked things even as I arched a challenging brow that said he wasn't going to win this argument.

"Seems a shame to have this pool and not make use of it." I winked at him before turning away and striding forward, slipping the straps of my dress off and letting it fall to the ground between one step and the next.

A sharp exhale sounded from behind me, and I smiled because I was pretty sure that had been a genuine response.

Pleasantly warm water greeted me as I stepped onto the shallow steps and made my way down. I moved further into the pool until I was treading water. Delicate lilies floated around me, their soft blue flowers releasing a light, sweet fragrance into the air.

It really was lovely, not a replacement for the ocean but still relaxing. The sides and bottom of the pool were made from a smooth, dark grey stone. Despite being contained inside a building, it felt like we had a natural spring all to ourselves.

I heard Connor step into the water behind me but waited a few seconds to turn around.

It was my turn to let out a sharp exhale as he waded towards me. He was so tall that I got an excellent view of his broad, muscled chest before he made it to the deep end. The lighting was softer in the bedroom, so between that and the dark colors of the stone that made up the pool, it was hard to see below the surface.

But I had no doubt Connor was every bit as naked as I was.

We were merfolk, nakedness was nothing new, but context was everything, and being alone—aside from the spying flowers —with Connor in a pool like this was different from the casual nudity on display when we dropped our glamoured two-legged form for scales and a tail.

Connor swam over to me, and I found myself drifting backwards. The lower part of my body bumped into something, and I glanced behind me, realizing there were seats carved out of the stone walls.

"Ashling," Connor purred, and I jolted my attention forward only to find myself boxed in by his large frame. "I wasn't finished with our *conversation*."

The amount of innuendo he sank into that word made me realize I might have been a little cocky getting into this pool. I'd needed to get out of bed because I'd been sick of arguing and we'd just been going around in circles, but I'd figured that I would hold the power here.

Connor was willing to go along with our cover story of being lovers again, and I had assumed he'd let me lead. So in my head, I'd thought we'd get into this pool, maybe make out a bit with some heavy petting, and he'd match whatever I did but nothing more.

I'd failed to remember that Connor had been the Merfolk Prince for longer than I'd been alive. While he might have preferred the life of a soldier, he could slip into the role of an arrogant and cunning prince like it was nothing.

And princes did not like to be defied.

"I was growing tired of it," I said, trying to keep my voice light and casual even as my heart raced. "Thought a change of scenery would be nice."

"Hmm." Connor pushed farther into my space, forcing me to scoot up onto the bench, then immediately seized the space between my thighs and planted his palms down on either side of my body. If I'd thought I'd been trapped before, I really was now. "This puts me in a rather difficult position."

I thought about raising my hand and volunteering to be put in a *difficult position.*

"How unfortunate for you"—I smiled at him—"prince."

Heat flared in his eyes before he leaned forward to whisper in my ear, the words so low, I had to strain to hear them. "I had to walk you around that ballroom while dozens of fae looked at you—in that fucking dress—like they owned you."

I blinked. I hadn't even noticed. My priority had been keeping track of the fae queens and watching out for Maeve.

"Then you had the audacity," Connor continued his angry whisper, "to slide that dress off yourself instead of letting me do it. I need to do something to take the edge off. Do not think this makes me any less pissed off at you."

When he pulled back, his light eyes had a devious glint to them. I felt the moment he dropped his glamour. Dark green scales shimmered beneath the surface, and lighter scales trailed up his torso before thinning out.

I frowned. What was he doing?

His hands gripped my ass, yanking me forward on the seat,

and I let out an undignified yelp, my hands shooting back to grip the ledge of the pool to keep my head from slamming into the hard surface. With how I was precariously perched, I would hit my head if I let go, which meant I was entirely at his mercy.

I could use magic to get myself out of this position, Connor was well aware of that.

Do I want to? Hmm . . . let me think. Kidding. Obviously I'm forgetting that I even know what magic is.

We might have been pretending now, and somewhere in the back of my mind, a voice was whispering that playing this game with all the shit between us was a bad idea, but a much louder voice was screaming, *In his merfolk form, he can breathe underwater, you idiot!*

No. He couldn't possibly mean to—

Connor's head ducked, his arms wrapped around my thighs, pulling them farther apart.

"Oh, fuck!" I clung harder to the ledge.

I felt Connor's hair floating in the water as he moved his head between my thighs and halted, giving me a chance to object. If I gave him a signal that I wasn't okay with this, he would stay down there and not touch me. I could do my best porn impersonation and we'd give Áine a good show.

That would be the smart and responsible thing to do.

Making sure my grip was tight on the rocky surface, I widened my legs.

Who said a little spite-fueled eating out wasn't healthy?

Connor didn't waste another second. He didn't hesitate or start with a few gentle licks. Oh, no. The bastard just shoved his entire face directly into my pussy and speared me with his tongue.

My back was already bowed thanks to the position, but I still managed to arch it more as I let out a half moan, half scream. One of Connor's hands slid further up my thigh before dipping down so he could play with my clit while he continued to devour me.

I could feel my orgasm building with every stroke, and my hips bucked forward when he pushed down with his fingers while fucking me with his clever tongue.

Close. So fucking close.

Connor's fingers vanished from my clit only to thrust inside my needy pussy.

Damn it! The sensitive bundle of nerves throbbed, desperate for attention. I'd been right fucking there!

His tongue darted in, licking as his fingers continued to fuck me roughly. *Fine, I'll do it myself.* I tightened my grip on the ledge with my left hand before letting go with my right, but a stream of water shot out and pinned it back to the ledge.

Fuck that. My magic reached out to break his hold. Almost there—

"Oww!" The asshole bit me! And fucking hard too based on the way my inner thigh throbbed.

Before I could retaliate, his mouth was on my clit and a scream was tearing from my throat. The pleasure he'd denied me before came hurtling back, and this time, Connor didn't pull away.

His lips and tongue continued to lick, suck, and nip at my clit while he thrust three fingers back inside my pussy.

I cried out as he fucked me through my orgasm, not giving me a second to just revel in it. As soon as he wrung the last cry out of me, he moved again, fingers slipping free to be replaced by his tongue.

He kept it up for thirty minutes—sometimes letting me come, sometimes denying me. If I tried to break free, water would shoot out like a rope to pin me down again.

"Connor!" I screamed when he finally let me come again after teasing me for what had felt like an eternity. My vision went white for a second as the climax that had been building exploded. Connor's fingers dug into my thigh while he sucked on my throbbing clit.

I was still trembling when he released me after one more long, claiming lick and surfaced. His dark green hair was plastered to his skin, drawing more attention to his chiseled features.

My heart was pounding, and I didn't think I was capable of stringing more than two words together as he picked me up off the ledge and swam to the stairs, dropping his glamour into place so he could carry me back to bed.

This time, I didn't argue.

Chapter Seven

THE NO ARGUING thing didn't last.

"You're not coming, Connor, and that's final," I snapped as I reached under the covers, searching for the mask I'd stashed there before we'd left for the party. I'd already put on my outfit for this portion of the evening—the mask was the last piece I needed. "It'll be far easier for me to sneak around on my own. You have your skills and I have mine, mo chroí."

My love. It had slipped out before I could think better of it. Fuck. All those orgasms had really addled my brain.

Worth it.

It was difficult to make out Connor's expression in the dimness. On our way back to bed, Connor had used his magic to snuff out all the lights in the bedroom. Only the faint moonlight reflecting off the pool from where it slipped in from the windows provided any light. I thought I saw his lips part and those pale eyes of his spark a little. Still . . . he did not reach for me or call me the name I missed so much.

My fingers closed around smooth fabric. Finally.

As soon as we'd returned to bed, Connor had put a careful distance between us. We'd both lay down, and it looked like we were whispering sweet nothings to each other through the shimmery, opaque veil, but in reality, there was almost a foot of distance between us that felt like a canyon.

What had happened in the pool was a mistake; I think we both realized that now. It complicated our already messy situation.

The emotions swirling within my chest were too much. Longing. Fear. Desperation. I needed to lose myself in the mission and my magic for a while to calm my mind. Being calm and centered was something I was usually quite good at, but Connor had always managed to shatter that, and the ticking clock of him rejecting me on that rooftop constantly lingered in my thoughts.

I sat up so I was kneeling on the bed and started to tug the mask over my head. Before I finished pulling it down, I felt the bed dip. My eyes were covered, so I couldn't see anything, but I felt Connor's presence in front of me. Strong fingers gripped my chin, and I went completely still as I felt his breath mingling with mine.

"Do not take any unnecessary risks, Ash. Surveillance and nothing more. Promise me."

"I promise," I breathed out. The grip on my chin tightened, and I could practically feel his indecision.

"Fuck it." Then his lips crashed against mine.

The kiss was nothing like the light grazes he'd given me at the party, nor was the feeling behind it the same challenging anger he'd been holding on to in the pool. This kiss was demanding and claiming, and I didn't even try to resist it.

One hand moved to the back of my head, and the other cupped my ass, pulling me closer to him. My lips parted, and his tongue slipped inside, hungrily exploring. I could still taste myself on him, and it drove me wild.

I miss you. I want you. I love you.

So many words unspoken between us, and yet that thread

between our souls that felt like a live wire sparked. I kissed him back like he was my entire world, because he was. The throne and this mission . . . those were duties, things I felt obligated to do because of the magic and knowledge I possessed. I didn't want them and would have been more than happy to give them away if there were someone else to pick up the mantle.

Connor was my everything.

After a couple of minutes, he pulled away from me enough to tug the mask down so I could finally see, and I wished he hadn't, because now I could see the distance in his pale eyes.

"I'm sorry." Gently, he lifted my hands away and scooted back on the bed, creating space between us again. "This is hard," he admitted. "Being around you. Doing things with you." His gaze briefly darted to the pool. "Pretending to be with you but not *actually* being with you. The lines are getting blurred, and it's hard to keep my emotions in check because I do want you, Ashling. I want us, but I need time to think through everything. It's not just about everything that happened between us. You're the Merfolk Queen and there is no separating you from the throne, which means if I'm with you, there is no separating me from it either, and that comes with a lot of baggage that I need time to work through."

"If it helps"—I swallowed and gave him a weak smile—"I always figured you'd be more of a pretty figurehead by my side." He stared at me, and even with the mask and the dim lighting, I could make out his exasperated expression. "Okay, fine," I conceded. "Handsome figurehead. That vampire hottie Nemain runs around with is pretty. You've got this whole aggressive masculine thing going on."

"You're so ridiculous. I can't believe you're our queen." He laughed and then moved forward to rest his forehead against mine, the tension that had been coursing through me easing a little. "Go do what you need to and then come back to me."

"Nothing would keep me from coming back to you."

Daemons made good shit. As a fae, it was practically sacrilegious for me to think such a thing—the rivalry between fae and daemons had started as soon as the latter had escaped the daemon realm. The daemons didn't have our natural ability to interact with magic; instead, they had to craft spells and use amulets and other devices to bend magic to their will. There were some bloodlines that had specific abilities though. Fire daemons like Pele were rare, but telepathy and telekinetic abilities were common.

My gloved hands brushed against the wall as I quickly made my way down the hallway. When I'd started searching for a daemon who could create this suit for me, it had become clear it was Kali I needed. She was considered to be the best crafter in all the daemon realm and specialized in complicated and unusual requests, and this suit definitely qualified as both of those things.

Illusion magic was woven into the silky, black fabric that hugged my skin. As soon as I put it on, the color shifted to match the environment around me, taking into account both lighting and physical objects. On top of that, it also had magic that was similar to a fae look-away ward. Even if someone did look directly at me, the magic within the suit would gently push their eyes elsewhere and make them forget. For all intents and purposes, I was invisible.

Someone would have to be in physical contact with me and concentrate very hard to be able to keep their attention on me. Between the suit and my magic, it made sneaking around in places I wasn't supposed to be practically a cakewalk.

Granted, I'd never tried in the queen's palace before or spying on someone as powerful as Maeve, but what was life without a little danger?

The suit had other fun capabilities as well. Despite every

inch of my body being covered, I could feel anything I touched as if there was no fabric separating us. My scent was fully contained, and even my footsteps were silenced. Kali's creation was truly a work of art and worth the three unspecified favors I'd had to promise in exchange for such a masterpiece.

It had been an unusual request, but not because she'd asked for favors over money—that was always how Kali accepted payment. She had plenty of money after being alive for over a thousand years and owning several lucrative businesses in the daemon realm, but at the time, I'd been a nobody rising up in the merfolk ranks.

I'd expected her to demand a task to be completed immediately in exchange for the suit or maybe to have to fetch some rare artifact from the fae realm or something. I'd never been able to prove it, but I suspected Kali had some type of premonition ability, because wanting three unspecified future favors from an unknown fae didn't make any sense. However, wanting those same favors from the future Merfolk Queen . . .

I paused at the end of the dimly lit hallway. The outer wall was to my right, its large, arched windows letting in the moonlight, and blue fae lanterns flickered on the left wall. As far as I could tell, Connor and I had this entire wing to ourselves, but as soon as I went down the stairs around the corner, things would get more crowded. It was early enough that most of the fae were likely still enjoying themselves at the party. Hopefully Maeve was one of them. Getting into her rooms would be far easier if she wasn't already in them, but I could adjust if necessary.

I was nothing if not adaptable.

My magic rolled beneath my skin, as steady as the tides, and I let myself fall into the pull of it. Most of the time, I kept my magic dampened. It was the only way to stay sane. Getting constant nudges throughout the day over often minor things was exhausting. After a lot of trial and error when I'd been younger, I had figured out how to allow only the major ones to come through and put the rest on silent.

But for times like this, I needed every edge I could get, so I let myself fall into the magic.

My vision shifted until I could see the magic pulsing in the air, shimmering specks of what felt like infinite colors drifting around me along with the vivid green of the earth magic weaving through the vines on the wall. All fae could see magic, some with more skill than others, but similar to the way I'd learned to manage my foresight, we learned how to turn it off.

I likely wasn't the only one examining the magic floating around this evening. With this many powerful fae here, it was useful to see what everyone was up to. My fancy suit not only physically hid me from sight, but it contained my magic from others as well.

I slipped down the stairwell, staying in tune with my magic. My steps were as quiet as my mind. All that existed was the next hint or gentle nudge.

Pause. Wait, my magic seemed to whisper.

The sound of three fae moving up the stairwell drifted to my ears, and the mental space I'd fallen into faded away enough for me to think. They couldn't see me, but they could touch me, and there was nowhere for me to go but back up the stairs. Or . . .

My eyes darted up, and I grinned before crouching and leaping straight up. I snapped my legs and palms out, planting them against the walls on either side of the stairs. I may not have had brute strength, but that didn't mean I was a slouch by any means. My core muscles tightened as I held myself above the fae while they walked beneath me, waiting until the sounds of them faded away.

Either they were staying somewhere else on the second floor, or they were doing their own snooping. That was the other reason I'd wanted Connor to stay behind in our rooms tonight. I was curious if anyone would come around, and I knew he could handle himself. The way those three had been feeling each other up though made me believe they were just seeking out their own bed.

I dropped to the floor and let myself sink back into the magic.

Someone like Maeve would want to be on the ground floor. Not only because she wouldn't want to be removed from earth magic, which was something she specialized in, but it was a status thing. She would want to be on the same level as the fae queens because she considered herself their equal. Aside from that, I had nothing to go on, so I let my magic guide me.

Once I exited the stairwell, I hugged the wall as much as possible. I could hear the celebration still raging and the band playing louder, the air thick with magic. The party had indeed extended past the ballroom, and drunken fae were stumbling around. I made my way down hallway after hallway, trusting my suit to keep prying eyes off me.

Stop, my magic nudged me. I froze. A second later, the door I'd been about to slink past flung open. Two sidhe walked through with long, purposeful strides before vanishing down the hallway.

I hurried forward, weaving my way through various groups before my magic poked me again.

A large group staggered down the hallway just I started to duck into an alcove. Abruptly, it felt like someone reached into my center and jerked me by a rib.

Okay, not that alcove. *No reason to be so fucking rude, magic.* Gracefully, I spun around and slid into the alcove directly across from it.

The intoxicated group ducked into the alcove I had originally chosen, their clothes flying off as they raced to get their hands on each other. I'd been very close to being in the middle of an impromptu fae orgy.

More's the pity.

Silently chuckling to myself, I continued onward. My magic seemed to be prodding me to the far west wing, which made sense. Based on my knowledge of the palace, that was an older wing with smaller guest quarters than the one I was in, but they were part of the original building and therefore considered to be places of privilege.

The only hiccup I'd encountered before reaching my destination had been running into Kalen. He'd been strolling through the hall, hands in his pockets as if he hadn't had a care in the world. I'd flattened myself against the wall and held my breath even though he wouldn't have been able to hear it with the suit on. The terrifying bastard had stopped directly in front of me and turned his head slowly to stare at the spot I was standing.

Those black obsidian eyes had burrowed into my soul for several seconds before he'd quietly said, "Full of surprises, aren't you, banríon farraige? Your tricks will not fool the fae queens. Don't make any unwise decisions tonight, lest you want me and my love to come hunting."

Then he'd just continued on his way like nothing had happened.

I'd be the first to admit that I was a bit of an adrenaline junkie. There had been numerous times when I'd been spying or stalking someone and almost gotten caught, and that thrill of nearly being discovered had only made it more fun.

If I could never have the Erlking casually threaten to hunt me with the Morrigan at his side again, that would be amazing. I decided to make it a life goal.

When I got the sudden urge to enter a room with large, silver doors, I didn't hesitate. The door was locked, but I easily pulled water from the air and used the thin strands of liquid-like lockpicks while my magic created an opening in the ward placed over the door. It was a good ward, but the beauty of water-based magic was that it was slippery and hard to pin down. In the split second my magic created an opening, I leapt through and quietly shut the door behind me, engaging the lock once more.

Then I frowned as I looked around. This didn't look like it would have been Maeve's room. It was nice but didn't seem grand enough for her. Though my magic had been quite insistent that I should be in here, now that I was, it had fallen silent. As much as I didn't want to wait around, that seemed the best course of action. The space was a combination of a bedroom and a sitting area, with the canopy bed taking up a huge chunk of one corner. I glanced up and saw rafters. Perfect.

With a running start, I leapt straight at the wall closest to the bed, twisting midair so my feet landed flat against the surface, knees bent, and my entire body coiled like a spring. Then I pushed off and landed on the railing of the tall canopy frame over the bed and raced along the top before jumping off the end. My fingers gripped one of the narrow wood beams near the ceiling, and I let my momentum swing me forward, releasing at the apex. I arched through the air before landing on the balls of my feet on another beam, crouching instantly.

Kind of a shame Connor wasn't here to see my skills in action. He would have made some double entendre about my spryness with a completely straight face. I would have answered in kind, and we would have traded lines back and forth until one of us broke and cracked a smile or laughed.

I scanned the rafters from this new vantage point and moved until I was on one towards the middle, which gave me a good view of everything and was also in a bright spot. More than once, I'd been in a similar situation, and the person I'd been spying on had launched knives or magic at the dark spots of the room just to be safe. I had complete faith in Kali's suit to keep me hidden, even in the light.

Less than an hour later, the faint sound of footsteps came

from the hallway outside the room. I'd been standing to stretch my legs but instantly moved back to a crouched position and watched as Coireall entered followed by Rowan. The two of them stalked around the room, surveying everything, including the rafters above them. I kept my breathing even when Rowan's gaze washed over me before moving along.

Maeve walked in seconds after them, cooly studying the room while Lughán and Aoife sauntered in, immediately went to the chairs, and collapsed into them.

"It's not fair that we have here," Aoife complained. "Those two get their own rooms."

"Somebody had to stay in this room," Rowan said as she took a seat on the couch across from the other two. "It's not like you two weren't going to end up in the same bed anyway." Her pert nose wrinkled in distaste.

"And none of us wanted to listen to that," Coireall added as he took a seat on the couch at the opposite end of Rowan.

"Quiet, all of you," Maeve ordered, and everyone shut up. Then she moved to where they were all seated but remained standing. "She'll be here soon."

I perked up a little. Who was this 'she' Maeve was expecting? Maybe the same person who had instructed them to stay in this room?

A small nudge from my magic had me spinning around on the beam to look at the wall behind me. Unlike the other walls, this one was smooth with a beautiful painting of a vibrant forest. In the center of the painting was a large tree, its branches stretching out so they touched both sides of the wall. I blinked when a portion of the tree trunk vanished, revealing a secret passage and a tall fae female with golden blonde hair and lightly tanned skin. She moved with a lethal grace towards Maeve, the wall snapping back into place behind her.

"Syndra." Maeve bowed to the woman, and my eyebrows crept up. Whoever this person was, Maeve either feared or respected them enough to not engage in a power struggle. I focused on the magic of the newcomer. She was definitely sidhe, but the black, iridescent streaks of magic that wound around her revealed the rest of her nature—devourer.

One of Balor's minions then. Rationally, I knew I should have been at least a little scared. I was in a room with five powerful Tuatha and a fae with devourer magic. There was zero chance of me winning in a fight against them if I was discovered, but all I could think about was the information I was going to glean from this meeting.

I wasn't frightened at all; instead, I was fucking giddy.

"Do you have good news for me?" Syndra's voice matched her movements, smooth and powerful. She was such a stark contrast to the Tuatha before her with their fine clothing and perfectly styled hair. Syndra wore dark brown fighting leathers, and I could tell by the creases that they were well broken in. Dual swords were strapped to her back, and multiple daggers adorned her thighs and waist.

Nemain, eat your heart out.

Given her clothing and her perfectly balanced stride, I had no doubt Syndra could use each one of those weapons with lethal precision on top of the deadly magic she was packing. That was what made fighting any of Balor's followers so dangerous. Most of the fae these days relied on their magic in a fight. There were exceptions like Connor and Kalen, but for the most part, fights were magic-based, which was why the fae were particularly vulnerable to devourers, because devourers were immune to magical attacks.

The devourer fae had keen advantages over other fae: they shared the same immunity to magic that all devourers had while also possessing strong magic of their own. On top of that, they also believed strongly in training with weapons.

Syndra was the first one I'd seen in person, and I was dying to know more about her. As far as I knew, most of Nemain's encounters had been with someone named Lir, who was high-ranking amongst Balor's army. Was Syndra under Lir's command? Or was she a rival?

"My plan is falling perfectly into place, just as I promised," Maeve said confidently. "We've made sure rumors of the queens' weakening powers have spread throughout the courts for the last six months. They've summoned us all here for a show of power, and the main event will be three days from now when they renew their vows to the throne."

Why was that significant? I furrowed my brows. Being the ruler of the fae realms was more than just a title. Whoever was seated on the throne had a direct connection to all the magic within the fae realms. It was why the queens were so much more powerful than all the Tuatha and why they never aged. Fae lived a long time, but we did have a limit. The usual life-span was around two thousand years, give or take a few centuries. I'd gotten a minor power boost from the merfolk throne, but nothing compared to that of the fae queens.

The renewal of vows was just a ceremonial event. There was no magical exchange of any kind, and it had nothing to do with the queens' existing power.

"Excellent." Syndra flicked her fingers, and a book appeared on the low table between all of them. "Follow the instructions for the transference casting. The glyph you'll need to carve into both trees must be exact, and there are some other key parts of the ritual, but I trust you can follow instructions well." A muscle in Maeve's jaw ticked, but she kept her mouth shut, and Syndra smiled at her like she was a pet that had done something particularly amusing. "You'll be the new queen of the fae realms. Do not fail in this, and do not even think of betraying us. You will be queen only because Balor allows it."

Oh fuck. The thrill I'd felt about learning more about my enemy vanished, replaced by outright panic. My magic wasn't nudging me; it was practically screaming at me. Three days. I had to stop Maeve and the other four before they did that ritual. Killing them had always been my plan, but I'd assumed if I couldn't pull it off this week, I'd have more time to figure something out.

My magic and the information before me were making it very clear that I did not.

"I will not fail." Maeve raised her chin. "Balor will see he has chosen his new queen well."

"Word of advice . . ." Syndra chuckled. "Don't ever refer to yourself as *his* queen again. You are his pawn, nothing more. Be grateful you are even that." With those parting words, Syndra spun on her heel and left through the same secret passage.

"I'm not sure it was wise to make a deal with her instead of Lir." Rowan stared at the wall where Syndra had disappeared. "I think she's just as likely to try to kill us all as soon as you've cut the queens off from the throne."

"There are too many eyes on Lir." Maeve's jaw hardened as derision filled her expression. "Plus, he's already lowered himself to working with the vampires and warlocks. He's not worth my time." Rowan and Coireall shared a look that said they weren't convinced of this but didn't say anything else. "The rest of you return to the party." Maeve picked up the book Syndra had left behind. "I'll be in my quarters."

I waited several minutes after they'd all left to jump down from the rafters before walking over to the section of the wall Syndra had used to make her getaway. My fingers ran along the wall, but I felt no magic. How in the hell had this passage remained hidden from everyone all this time? I doubted the queens knew about it, because they wouldn't have allowed such a vulnerability to exist in their stronghold.

"Three bricks up and to the left is a switch."

I whirled around, pulling my one and only dagger free even

as water flowed out of the pouch on my thigh to coil around my hand like a whip. No one. The room lay empty, but someone had definitely spoken. I continued scanning, waiting for my magic to chime in.

It gave me nothing, but someone was definitely here . . . Why hadn't it warned me?

Between one blink and the next, a large, cloaked figure appeared in front of me. I jerked back. Shit. There was nowhere to go.

I tried to dart past him, but he slammed me against the wall. My body angled slightly so it was my side that hit the wall, trapping one arm. My assailant caught my free hand—the one holding the dagger—and wrapped his other around my throat.

The water that had been swirling around my hand instantly crashed to the floor as my magic was snuffed out.

Okay. Not a great position to be in. I awarded myself no points for this round.

A mix of terror and adrenaline coursed through my veins. He released my throat long enough to rip the mask from my face before digging his claws back into soft flesh.

"Mmm." He leaned forward, smelling my neck. "Salty and sweet. It's been a long time since I've feasted on your kind, mermaid."

Chapter Eight

"Fuck," I rasped. "Was the creepy . . . comment . . . necessary?"

He cocked his head, and the hood of his cloak slipped back enough for me to get a good look at him, something that I definitely regretted. Sickly yellow eyes with four distinct pupils surveyed me from a face that seemed to be a mishmash of parts. His nose was flat with large slits that flared each time he breathed, and the lower half of his face was narrow and too long. It was like someone had taken a fae face and stretched it out. Thin, barely there, black lips framed a mouth full of pointed teeth.

What the ever-loving fuck was he?

"Pretty, aren't I?" He laughed, and I felt claws pierce my neck and wrist once more before he flung me across the room. Air whooshed out of my lungs as I crashed onto the ground, forcing me to inhale violently as I struggled to get to my feet. The dagger had flown out of my hand when I'd landed, and I had no idea where it'd gone. I stretched my right hand out, summoning the water that had pooled on the floor when he'd surprised me, but nothing happened.

"No magic for you, my pretty little mermaid." My freaky attacker pulled his hood all the way back, revealing a shaved head and a greyish skin tone. Slowly, he stalked towards me, like he was savoring every fearful breath I took. From his point of view, I was helpless, a weak fae who relied too much on magic and had no skills with a blade.

I let my fear ramp up for one more moment so he could see it on my face, then I shoved it aside because it wasn't useful. People had underestimated me and tried to beat me down my entire life. In the end, they'd all choked on their own pride. This fucker would too.

"Wha–what are you?" I added an extra tremor to my voice and then darted my eyes around the room nervously like I was looking for an escape, but really, I was looking for that gods-damn dagger I'd dropped.

"Hungry." He licked his lips as all four of his pupils greedily drank me in. "And bored. I was excited when Syn told me I was coming here because I thought it meant I'd get to fill my stomach every day on what had become of the fae." A thin, black tongue darted out of his mouth, and the shiver that ran through me wasn't faked. "Instead, I've been on fucking guard duty for months," he growled.

"You've been here this whole time?" I intentionally made my voice high-pitched as I took a step back from him. *Tell me your secrets, pretty boy.*

"I've been all sorts of places." He took another step towards me. "Keeping tabs on my liege's traitorous sisters, watching that snake, Lir, as he preens in the seraphim realm, even visiting that psycho shifter. Although, she's a tricky one." His mouth stretched into a wide smile, showing off rows of jagged teeth. "I think she can somehow sense me, so I have to keep my distance, but there are so many tasty morsels in her home by the sea. Their flesh calls to me."

"Impossible." I shook my head violently and took another

step back. His smile gained a predatory edge, and I let a tremble slip into my limbs. "Someone would sense you."

"You didn't." He shrugged.

"Were you a sidhe? What did Balor do to you?" I forced a hint of pity into my expression. "Why would you serve someone who mistreated you like this?"

He threw back his head and laughed, and I used his momentary distraction to quickly scan the area by the couch. The edge of my dagger's black handle poked out from the right side less than six feet from me. I just needed to carefully close the distance. My gaze snapped back to him as his laughter died off, and I took a small step to the left, towards the couch.

"The sidhe were just one type of fae that roamed our realms before those who followed the true king were banished. Even back then, they looked down on us."

My body went rigid as he vanished from sight once more. I focused on the magic in the room, trying to detect him, but there was nothing to see or feel. Even if I'd been able to access my magic, I suspected I would get no helpful nudges here, considering he'd been in this room before he'd revealed himself and I'd had no idea.

I forced myself to remain calm even though every part of me wanted to lunge for that dagger. It was unlikely I would make it. I knew an apex predator when I saw one, and the strange fae in the room with me was very much that. Without my magic, I was at a severe disadvantage. I needed to bide my time.

"My liege never looked down on us—the dofheicthe. He saw our potential even before he blended our magic with that of devourers. We excelled at remaining unseen before, but now"—he let out that chilling laugh again—"nobody sees us unless we want to be seen."

When he snapped into existence in front of me, I screamed

and fell down, scrambling away from him until my back hit the couch . . . and my hand closed around the cool handle of my poisoned blade.

His nostrils flared as he stalked closer to me. "Your fear is delicious; it'll make your flesh taste even better." Claws dug into my upper arms as he jerked me up, and I almost stabbed myself as I tucked the dagger flush against my skin, hiding it from his view. Things would definitely go from bad to worse if I pricked myself with it. "Tell me why you were here, and I promise I'll only take a few nibbles before delivering you to Syn."

"Sy—Syyy—Synnn?" I blubbered as tears streamed down my cheeks. His thin lips flattened as some mucus mixed in with my tears. Apparently, a little snot was too much for him. *Come on, fucker, tell me a little more.*

"Syndra." He said her name clearly, and I could hear the reverence in his voice. "The lieutenant of our true queen, Siofra."

Siofra, Balor's love and apparently his queen. Maeve would be so disappointed.

"I thought . . . I thought that was Lir?" I painted a confused expression on my face and let out a hiss of pain when his claws dug deeper into my skin. They must have been coated with something because I could feel the blood running down my arms but it didn't hurt the way it should. Instead, I felt a little numb. That wasn't good. I twitched my fingers, realizing I could still move them, but they felt sluggish.

Shit, I needed to end this quickly before I actually did become a snack.

"Lir serves my king." His tongue snapped out and licked the side of my neck. "He's a pompous ass. Once Syn brings the imposter queens down, Balor will see this." Another lick, and he closed his eyes briefly before popping them open to stare at me hungrily. "It's time for me to get more of a taste, my delicious little mermaid."

Two things happened at once. His head dove to the crease between my neck and shoulder, dozens of sharp teeth piercing my flesh, and I snapped the blade forward, slicing his forearm. He reared back, four pupils blinking at me in surprise, and then he held up his arm, scrutinizing the shallow cut, before looking back at the small blade in my hand and meeting my eyes again.

"You had the element of surprise and that's all you used it for?" he sneered. "Should have at least tried to bury that pathetic little knife into my throat. As soon as Syn is done with you, I'm going to ask her to give you to me. I'll start carving you apart while you're still alive. We'll see how long you last."

Then he flung me across the room, and I crashed into the bed frame before staggering to my feet. Once again, I'd lost the dagger, but it didn't matter. I'd done what I'd needed to do, now all that was left was staying alive for the next two minutes.

Note to self: get faster-acting poison.

A flicker of surprise flashed across his monstrous eyes as he took me in. Gone was the cowering and fearful mermaid. We were past that performance being useful. Knocking him off his game would help me survive now, so I shed one mask and easily slid into another, the calm, confident mask of a queen.

"Thank you for chatting with me," I said smoothly. "You really filled in a few gaps. Although I have to admit, I've never heard of the dofheicthe before. Tell me, did your kind do the whole eating other fae thing before you were banished? Or is this a new habit you formed while locked away with your second-rate king?"

"It was generally frowned upon to eat other fae back then." He took a step towards me, and I wondered if he noticed that his gait had lost some of that predatory grace. "But merfolk?" He snapped his teeth in my direction. "Nobody gave a shit about you back then. You were under Balor's control—none of this Tír fo Thuinn realm bullshit. When Balor returns, he'll kill your queen and put the merfolk back under his thumb. Maybe he'll even declare open season on them so me and mine can go hunting."

"Good thing the Merfolk Queen has plans to ensure Balor never sets foot outside of his realm then," I said lightly.

"Who are you, little mermaid?" He took another step before halting and shaking his head, his eyes narrowing on me but quickly losing focus. Then he jerked his head again as if trying to clear it. "Wh-what did you do to me?"

"Poisoned you. Obviously." I started to shrug but killed the movement when pain shot through my shoulder where he'd bitten me.

"You fucking bitch!" he snarled and lunged for me, but I slipped to the side and he slammed into the bed instead. He grasped the bedpost, struggling to remain standing, and I held my breath, hoping he would pass the fuck out already.

But of course luck was not on my side, because he used his magic to disappear again.

"Fuck," I hissed a second before he crashed into my side. Something sharp tore through my suit, and I screamed before bringing down my elbow as hard as I could. A growl tore out of the dofheicthe, and he blinked back into existence. He'd been biting me, and my elbow had connected with his ear, knocking him aside.

"I'm going to drag your barely alive body back to Syn, and as soon as she's done with you, I'm going to pull out your intestines and eat them in front of you." His claws slammed into my side where he'd bitten me and tore through flesh. I screamed and gripped his hand, trying to keep him from doing more damage, and we rolled around on the floor, him biting and clawing at me while I did everything I could to stay the fuck alive.

After what felt like hours but was probably less than a minute, his attacks weakened before he slumped on top of me. I could hear him breathing, so he was still alive—as expected. The poison wasn't meant to be lethal, but there was always the chance someone would have a bad reaction to it.

Every part of my body hurt, but it was mostly my side that felt like it was on fire. My head was swimming, probably thanks to blood loss and being hit against the floor in our tussle. I shoved the fae bastard off me and forced myself to my feet, one hand pressed against the wound on my side.

There had to have been something in his bite that nullified magic, because when I briefly pulled my hand away from the wound, blood gushed out. I slapped it back over with a grimace. Was this what not having healing magic was like? Because it fucking sucked.

The room spun around me, and I gripped the back of the couch for support. I didn't have much time before I passed out or the poison from the dagger wore off and the dofheicthe woke up. He wouldn't remember anything from the last thirty minutes though, which was the true beauty of the poisoned blade.

It had taken a lot of trial and error on my part to develop a poison that could knock someone out and also erase their memories, but it was incredibly useful since I spent a good chunk of my time interrogating others for information. Sometimes killing someone was too complicated or would lead to questions being asked about their disappearance. Knock someone out, erase their memories, maybe leave an empty couple of bottles of wine, and I had a pretty damn good cover.

Unfortunately, I doubted this asshole would believe he'd gotten drunk and passed out, but at least he wouldn't remember me and would be confused about what had happened. Given how much he respected and almost idolized this Syn person, there was also a good chance he wouldn't mention it to her because he'd be ashamed of his failure.

The loyal and honorable type tended to fess up immediately. But the loyal and arrogant—which is the category I placed my pointy-toothed friend in—almost always tried to fix their self-perceived screwups before they were found out.

Assuming I was right, it would mean he'd be hunting for an answer around the palace. And I had no way of detecting when the fucker was in the room with me. That was definitely a problem.

I frowned and debated just killing him and stashing his body somewhere but shook my head. That would draw too much attention and alert Maeve that someone was on to her.

I limped over to the chair across from the couch and grabbed the light throw blanket that had been draped over the back, wiping my blood from the dofheicthe's claws. Luckily, it didn't look like any of my blood had gotten onto his clothes and there were only a few spots of it on the floor, which I also wiped up. I had no idea how good a dofheicthe's sense of smell was, but generally, that wasn't a trait amongst the fae, so I had to hope it was the case here. I also hoped that Syn wasn't working with the vampires like Lir, because they would have no trouble detecting my blood in this room.

This was so much sloppier than I preferred to work. My mind was already making a list of all the ways this could backfire on me, but as my vision started to darken around the edges, I had to accept that I'd done enough.

The dofheicthe would wake up in less than ten minutes. He'd likely been ordered to stay in this room for the meeting to spy on Maeve and the others, so I'd been a surprise for him. His focus would hopefully be on them since they were the most obvious suspects for what had happened to him.

I briefly lifted my hand from my side and stuffed the blanket over my wound before pushing my hand back on it.

My suit was still intact enough to hide me from sight, but without my magic to give me tips, it would be harder to make it back to my room from here. Plus, there was a very real chance I would pass out.

Stumbling towards the wall with the hidden door, I swiped my mask off the ground and shoved it into my pocket.

"Three bricks up and to the left is a switch," is what he'd said right before he'd attacked me. My fingers traced the surface close to where I'd been searching for a mechanism when he'd surprised me, and I felt the slightly upraised portion of the mural.

"Thanks, friend," I tossed over my shoulder as I pushed on the wall.

Silently, the secret opening gave way, and I slipped into the hidden passage, allowing myself one second to appreciate the simplicity of it. There was no magic—it really was just a mechanical door disguised by the painting. The queens had likely searched for traps or hidden passages with magic after they'd ousted their brother, but this left no magical trace.

Darkness enveloped me as the door closed. Fae lanterns would have been detectable by magic, which would have ruined the whole point of the mechanical door. Thinking was getting difficult between the pain and light-headedness. I'd never been more grateful for my natural sense of direction as I set off towards my suite, using the wall for support.

Occasionally, I had to stop to reorientate myself or just to give my body a brief break so I didn't pass out. The stairs in particular were a real pain in the ass, and I'd almost landed flat on my face when I'd tripped over them. There was a very real chance that if I blacked out, I'd bleed to death alone in the dark. On the plus side, if that happened, I wouldn't have to worry about having my heart crushed by Connor as he walked away from me when he discovered I was still lying to him. *Always look on the bright side.*

Finally, I made it to the section where I was pretty sure my suite was on the other side. I laid my palm against the wall and concentrated. My magic was still gone, but the beginnings of the mate bond was there, hovering in this temporary state of being neither accepted nor rejected. This was a risky move to take. I'd been actively suppressing the bond this whole time because I didn't want Connor to sense it and freak out, but I needed to know if I'd reached the right room. Just a little tug. He probably wouldn't even feel it.

Closing my eyes, I let myself reach for the living thread I felt between us. It was so fragile, I was almost afraid to touch it. Okay, I was scared to interact with it for a multitude of reasons, but I carefully followed the thread that led to the soul that called to my own.

I let out a relieved breath. Here. He was here. Now the problem was that I didn't know if a door existed to get into the room. I suspected it didn't, because based on the conversation I'd overheard, Maeve had been told to specifically request that room, which implied that while the secret passage might run all throughout the palace, there were a limited number of entry points. It made sense—the doors were the riskiest part because they most definitely would give away the existence of the passage.

This meant that there was a very thick wall between me and the person who could save my life.

"Connor," I rasped, but it wasn't loud enough. Fuck it. "Connor!" I screamed and slammed my fist against the wall, sending pain ratcheting throughout my body. I fell to my knees, gasping. Blood leaked through the blanket I had pressed to my side and coated my fingers in its warmth. Well, that wasn't good. "Fuck," I panted, then tried to catch my breath so I could yell again.

"Ash?" a panicked, muffled voice came from the other side of the wall. "What the fuck is going on?"

Answering was beyond me, and the pain was fading, replaced by a cold numbness. I must have blacked out for a few seconds, because suddenly, I was lying on my back in a pool of my own blood.

With the last lingering remnants of my strength, I kicked the wall several times in a deliberate, rhythmic pattern before darkness claimed me.

Chapter Nine

MY EYES SNAPPED OPEN, and the only thing keeping me from bolting upright was the warm arm slung around my waist, pinning me against a hard body. Even before his scent hit me, I instinctively relaxed, as if my body recognized Connor before my mind did. Despite feeling confused and a little out of it, I knew I was safe because I was lying in his arms.

I took stock of my body, wiggling my toes and fingers a little. No pain at all. Not even any stiffness or lingering fatigue. All fae could heal themselves—if some asshole hadn't nullified their magic, that is—but some were talented at healing others. Kaysea was an amazing healer, and while Connor wasn't quite as good as she was, he was still very gifted.

"Oh, good. You're awake," he said in a low, deep tone that had me wincing. It was the one he used when he was beyond pissed off. "I can strangle you now."

"No kinky stuff before coffee." I snuggled deeper into his embrace.

"There's no coffee here," he said dryly. "I think you're the only fae in existence who sneaks coffee out of the human realm."

"Not true. Kaysea does as well."

He sighed. "That's Nemain's influence."

I twisted in his arms so I was on my back and looking up at him. He propped himself up on an elbow so he could glower at me properly. Given the way his other arm was still protectively wrapped around my middle, however, it didn't quite have the effect he was going for.

Do I ask the question and ruin the moment? Or milk this a little bit longer? Choices, choices.

A muscle ticked along Connor's jawline. I knew that tick. It meant I had approximately ten seconds until he imploded.

Goodbye, delicious cuddle. I hardly knew thee.

"What happened?" I asked in a carefree tone. Maybe I could somehow will Connor into a good mood.

"Oh, you mean after you passed out from a wound that appeared to be from something with claws trying to rip out your intestines? In a fucking secret passage that I'm pretty confident nobody knows about, including the godsdamn fae queens?"

Oh shit! My eyes darted to the wall I'd been pounding on before I'd passed out. It was perfectly intact. My brow furrowed. How had he gotten me out?

Connor growled as he saw where my attention had gone. "I was going to tear down the wall, but I knew you'd yell at me for it later, so I carved a tunnel through the floor using water from the pool. All the floors in this place are at least ten feet thick because they grow fucking trees on some of the levels."

I opened my mouth to ask more questions but clicked it shut when he growled again. Somebody was touchy.

"And let's not forget the fact that you were only bleeding to death because you had no fucking magic?" Connor continued. He really was on a roll. "How in the ever-loving fuck did you lose your access to magic?"

"Maeve is working directly with one of the devourer fae,

someone named Syndra. Apparently, she serves Balor's queen, Siofra."

Connor's scowl deepened, and my lips curled into a small smile. He was still annoyed as fuck at me, but now he was curious, which meant I was close to being off the hook instead of having to deal with him being a crabby asshole all day. I didn't even know how much time had passed. There was sunlight filtering in from the windows, but I couldn't tell if it was early morning or midafternoon. If I asked Connor that, it would just redirect his thoughts back to being pissed off at me.

"This Syndra is the one who attacked you?"

"No." I shook my head. "She left after giving Maeve a book, which I'll get to in a moment, and then everyone else left. I went to inspect the wall that led to the secret passageway Syndra had used, and that's when I got jumped. Have you ever heard of a dofheicthe? Apparently they're a type of fae."

"Doesn't sound familiar." He frowned. "But I'd never heard of the sciatháin before Niall either."

"True." I leaned my head back into the soft mattress and stared up at the ceiling, resting one hand over his forearm that was slung across my stomach. "Well, I've only met the one sciatháin, but I've got to say, I like them a whole bunch more than the dofheicthe so far. I'll take pretty wings over freaky eyes and teeth any day."

Connor stiffened. "You think Niall's wings are pretty?"

Niall's wings were gorgeous. Blueish black feathers that gleamed in the sunlight. Unlike valkyrie wings, they were soft too. He had let me pet them when I'd asked, but I'd had to do it quickly before Sigrun saw and gutted me.

"They're fine. Nothing special," I lied. "Maybe we can ask Niall about the dofheicthe. He might be able to tell us something useful about them or even about this Syndra character. What I do know is that the dofheicthe who attacked me also has devourer magic. His bite nullified my powers almost imme-diately." I raised a hand and tried to summon some water from the wading pool. No dice. I could feel my magic stirring though, so at least it was coming back. "That's why I couldn't heal."

"Niall is away with Sigrun," Connor said. "They're trying to rescue another group of kids from the seraphim realm."

"Damn." I chewed on my bottom lip. "Dealing with the dofheicthe is definitely going to complicate things."

I launched into an overview of what I'd overheard and how the dofheicthe had attacked me.

"So we have three days to take out Maeve and her crew while also dealing with an invisible fae, who belongs to a species we're not familiar with and who has devourer magic." He rolled to his back beside me so we were both staring up at the ceiling. "Anything else you want to lay on me?"

We're fated mates.

"No, I think that about covers it." I popped up so I was leaning on my elbow and could see his face. "We should keep a close eye on Maeve and the others today. Look for any signs that they think something is amiss. I think I covered the evidence of the attack well enough, but there's a chance I missed something."

"Given that you were half dead when I found you, I think that's likely." Connor's eyes remained fixed to the ceiling, but there was a hollowness to his words that alarmed me.

"Hey." I trailed my fingers down his jawline before pulling his chin in my direction, forcing him to look at me. There was a haunted look in his eyes I didn't like one bit. "I'm fine. You saved me."

"I know." He swallowed. "But seeing you like that, your chest covered in blood and lying there so still and pale . . . it was like finding my sister all over again."

"Fuck." I squeezed my eyes shut for a moment before refocusing on him. "I'm so sorry, Connor. I didn't know you were the one to . . . find her."

That sounded like such an inadequate way to describe discovering the body of your beloved sister with her heart ripped from her chest, but I didn't know what else to say.

"Technically, it was Nemain who found her," he said numbly. "It was Nemain's birthday. I got there late because there were some sidhe causing problems for my father, and I prioritized the merfolk throne over my sister. She had personally requested me to be there for Nemain's birthday. It was important to her, I knew that, but even before everything happened, I didn't like Nemain. She was the reason my sister was spending so much time on land instead of the sea. So I got there hours too late." His jaw hardened beneath my touch, and my heart ached for him. "If I'd gotten there when she'd told me to, I would have been there when Sebastian came for her. I could have stopped it."

"No," I said softly. "Sebastian was powerful. He would have killed you too."

"A warlock is no match for me," he sneered.

"He gave Nemain a run for her money," I pointed out. "A lot of people underestimated Sebastian, and they lost their lives over it."

"It doesn't matter." He looked away from me. "I was too late. Kaysea arrived before me and was trying to calm Nemain down. She was on the beach screaming, covered in Myrna's blood. I ran to the cottage they shared and found my sister. Read the note that fucker had left. My sister died because of Nemain's bullshit." His eyes snapped back to mine. "And because I prioritized the throne over her."

His reasons for never wanting to wear the merfolk crown or have anything to do with it made so much sense now. All this time, I'd assumed he'd solely blamed Nemain for Myrna's death, but that wasn't true, he held himself responsible too. Nemain was just a convenient target for his rage.

"Based on everything Kaysea has told me about your sister," I said carefully, "she would never blame you for anything that happened, and she'd want you to let it go."

"I'm their older brother. It's my job to keep them safe. I failed Myrna. I won't fail Kaysea." He paused for a moment, something like regret or shame flashing across his face. "I took her body."

"What?"

"While Nemain was losing her mind on that beach, I took Myrna's body back into the sea. We buried her in Tír fo Thuinn . . . and refused to allow Nemain to visit the grave."

Gods, he'd been in so much pain, they all had, and instead of coming together to grieve the person they'd all loved, Connor had lashed out and Nemain had sought retribution . . . at any cost. From what I'd pieced together from talking to Kaysea and others, the feline shifter had almost lost her life getting revenge against Sebastian.

"I'm surprised you were able to keep her away," I said honestly.

"I told her my parents forbade it and that if she tried, the might of the Merfolk King would fall upon her."

"Nemain doesn't really respond to threats well." My eyebrows crept up to my forehead. "If anything, they only encourage her."

"True," he agreed, "but she wasn't willing to attack Myrna's parents. Even after my sister's death, Nemain's devotion to her never ended."

Which was probably the only reason Connor was still alive after telling Nemain she couldn't visit her beloved's final resting place. Frankly, I was impressed and thankful Nemain had been able to control her temper enough to not tear Connor's head off his shoulders.

"Did your parents really declare Nemain couldn't visit Myrna's grave?" I already suspected the answer. Connor's parents were just and kind. They would have mourned their daughter and probably not been Nemain's biggest fans, but they wouldn't have denied her that.

"No," he rasped. "That was all me. I wanted her to suffer."

"And suffer she did." Another flash of shame came across Connor's face. I didn't know what to say to comfort him, and I didn't think he would admit out loud to feeling guilty about what he'd done. Grief could be such a complicated emotion. I moved down so my head rested on his chest and my hand was over his heart. "This is why me being queen is such a problem for you, isn't it?"

"I can't fail Kaysea the way I did Myrna," he said roughly. "If you and I . . . if we pursue this . . . the merfolk throne will once again be my priority because I'll do whatever I have to do to keep you safe, but if something happens to my sister and I'm not there to help—" He cut himself off and took a deep breath. "I can't lose her."

"I understand," I said quietly, even as I questioned my own answer. Did I really understand that kind of love? Myrna had died fifty years ago, and Connor was still carrying around this open wound. When my mother had taken her final breath a decade ago, I hadn't mourned her. Instead, I'd let out a breath of relief. I was no longer beholden to her desires. Every time someone in my family had died, I'd felt a little lighter, like I was that much closer to being free.

"What are you thinking?"

"How do you know I'm thinking about something?" I tilted my head on his chest so my chin was resting on it and I could gaze up at him.

"You're tracing the same pattern over and over again." His hand fell on mine, where I had indeed been idly tracing the infinity pattern on his skin.

"I guess it never really occurred to me until now just how fucked up things were with my family—with my mother in particular."

"How so?" He looked at me curiously, and I bit the inside of my cheek while I thought about how to answer. It wasn't that I wanted to hide anything from him, more that I suddenly felt a little self-conscious. His family was full of so much love and adoration . . . while mine was the opposite.

"Growing up in my family was like performing in a play." I frowned. "Scratch that, it was like getting ready to perform in a play. Constantly memorizing lines and cues. Practicing over and over again. It was like that from the moment I had my first vision at five years old. There was no playtime or even a night off to be . . . well . . . just be me."

"That's why you enjoy floating in the water so much, isn't it?" Connor raised the hand he'd placed over mine and started playing with the ends of my curly hair. "I don't think I've ever seen you as at peace as you are beneath a starry night sky while you drift amongst the tides."

"It's my favorite place to be. Just me and the stars, and all the secrets they know." I smiled. "And sometimes you grace me with your presence."

I felt his heartbeat race a little faster beneath me. "Thank you for sharing it with me."

My own heart started to speed up, trying to match his pace. "I like being alone with you."

His arms closed around me, pulling me tighter against his chest. "I like being alone with you too."

A stream of fire flew towards me before splashing against an invisible wall and spiraling up to the sky. Appreciative murmuring rose in the crowd as the young sidhe who had created the wall of fire bowed to the queens. Áine didn't look particularly impressed, but Elvinia gave the boy a small nod. His hazel eyes lit up as if she had just declared him the most impressive fae she had ever met, and he practically skipped back to his family.

Connor and I had arrived late to the demonstration, which was basically the Tuatha families trotting out the young members of their family who had just come into their magic. The sidhe were vain when it came to beauty and liked to cover themselves in elegant clothing and fine jewelry, but what they truly cared about was how much magic someone had and how skilled they were at using it.

Being the most powerful of the sidhe, the Tuatha took this to a whole other level.

It was rare, but occasionally, a child would be born into a Tuatha family with little magic. They would wait until the young fae went through puberty, in hopes that they were a late bloomer, but if they failed to impress the rest of the family, they were usually disowned and forbidden from using the family name.

The Tuatha were real assholes and represented everything I hated about the sidhe, but I kept that off my face and instead fixed a polite smile on it as the next sidhe stepped forward. She was a few years older than the boy and had straight black hair that fell to her waist. Her tanned skin had an olive tone to it that made her yellow eyes stand out. I recognized the Tuatha bloodline immediately—Valrel. They had been one of two families given the task of hunting down and killing mine.

Like the Tuatha boy who had performed before her, the young Valrel called forth fire and put on an impressive display. Unlike the brute force that he had displayed, she created a tree out of the flames, and it even had thousands of individual leaves that flickered with a lighter yellow shade.

I wondered if she knew this pretty fire she wielded so easily had once burned children to death. Probably not. As far as the queens and the rest of the fae were concerned, my bloodline had died out over a thousand years ago. This girl was likely in her early twenties and had no idea my family had ever existed. That didn't stop her from sneering in my direction though. Not because she recognized my bloodline, but because I was the Merfolk Queen. Her family had probably told her I didn't belong here, so she was obediently falling in line.

How boring.

She created several birds out of fire and sent them flying around the garden. A few of them flew over the stream that ran in front of me—it was on the other side of the ward that the queens had erected to protect the bystanders. My fingers itched at my side, but I kept the pleasant smile on my face . . . until the girl sneered at me once more.

A six-foot-long serpentine fish made of water leapt straight up into the air and swallowed the three birds.

The remaining fire birds broke apart like ashes on the wind, and the girl stared at me from in front of her fiery tree.

"Careful." I gave her a wolfish smile. "All kinds of wicked things live beneath the surface, and many of us have sharp teeth."

The girl blanched, and my gaze followed her as she retreated back to her family. I looked away only to find Maeve's gaze on me.

Those cunning, yellow eyes of hers studied me thoughtfully, and I mentally slapped myself for doing something to gain her attention. We'd come to this event not only because it was expected of us, but also because I wanted to get a read on Maeve to see if there had been any fallout from the events of last night. I should have been more focused on continuing the lovestruck idiot persona, not schooling pretentious young sidhe.

"Perhaps we should give the next generation a break," Elvinia drawled before tilting her head as her lips curved into a mocking grin. "It has been a while since our courts have seen a demonstration from the ruling crown of Tír fo Thuinn."

Shit.

Maeve still studied me with interest. Did they know something had happened after they'd left that room? Had the devourer fae waited for them to return and demanded an explanation for his missing memories? Had I missed something in my fast cleanup of the scene?

I couldn't refuse Elvinia. She would no doubt force the issue if I tried, and then I'd likely have to do an even greater demonstration of power to appease her, but I also didn't want Maeve and the rest of them to know just how dangerous of a shark was swimming in their waters.

Why in the fuck did I have to go after those fire birds? I should have just smiled and let it be.

Connor's fingers tightened around mine, and an idea started to take root. I could still spin this to my advantage.

"I would be delighted." I dipped my head in acknowledge-ment to Elvinia and stepped forward, tugging Connor with me. "If you don't mind, the prince will be helping me." I let a slight blush color my cheeks. "The mantle of power is still settling within me, and I admit that I haven't been getting much sleep the last few weeks."

"Fine." Elvinia waved a hand, but a faint sneer rose on Áine's face along with most of the Tuatha. A queen who had to rely on the powers of someone else for a simple display was unthinkable to them. I gave myself a mental high five for not giving a shit about dick-measuring contests. I also sent out a silent thanks to the universe that the fae were so arrogant, they wouldn't even entertain the idea of appearing as less than they were.

Connor scowled at the crowd before facing me. In the light, his pale green eyes appeared even lighter, almost white. He slipped into the patient and steady expression that I'd so often seen him wear in the Merfolk Court, but I didn't miss the slight uptilt of his lips. He knew exactly what I was doing.

"Ready when you are, love," he said softly. My heart skipped a beat at the nickname, even knowing that he was putting on a show, just like me.

I closed my eyes and concentrated. The trick was to do something that required some power and skill, but not blow them away. If I did something too obviously simple, it would raise suspicions that I was deliberately hiding my power. I didn't like the way Maeve was watching me, and I definitely couldn't afford for the queens to take an interest in me.

Raising my hands, I called the water from the nearby stream and felt it flow above my head. I pictured one of my favorite places in all of Tír fo Thuinn. On an island, surrounded by endless turquoise water, there was a hidden cove. Sheer cliffs rose up on either side of it, and sparkling blue water plummeted two hundred feet from the top to the awaiting water below. My mother had taken me there for my eighth birthday. I had no idea why she had done it. It was the first and last time she'd done anything for one of my birthdays, but I'd appreciated it all the same.

Still holding the image in the front of my mind, I opened my eyes and guided the water so that it formed the two walls of the cove. Next, I pulled more water from the stream and used this to shape the waterfall, gathering the water in a pool between the two walls I'd already constructed and holding it several feet above the ground.

I glanced at Connor, and his magic brushed against mine to hold onto the pool without me even needing to ask. He would handle the part of this that required brunt power, and I would do all the delicate touches. Technically, I could do both without breaking a sweat, but we had our parts to play.

Connor effortlessly held the growing pool of water as I created a whirlpool towards the back that sucked water in before shooting it up to feed the waterfall. After some fine-tuning to ensure the water was falling the way I wanted it to, I focused on the other details. What I had was already impressive, we were holding hundreds of gallons of water above the ground and manipulating it into a moving liquid sculpture, but this wasn't enough to impress the queens or the Tuatha. I needed to add a little more awe to what we had.

With delicate care, I sent tendrils of magic to gather up the water lilies from the stream and carry them to the sides of my canyon walls. I twisted the magic so the water held them in place like vines, and the large, white blossoms floated perfectly against the light blue water.

The next part was a little more complicated, but it was the last piece I needed to pull this off. Focusing on the top of the waterfall, I slowly nudged the small water molecules that were rising where the drop started and pulled them forward until they rose like a misty wall above everything else, directly in front of the sun shining into the garden.

A faint gasp rose from somewhere in the crowd as the water droplets danced in the air, catching the sunlight until half a dozen rainbows reflected off the water, shimmering in and out of existence.

Finally satisfied, I turned to the queens. "Apologies for the simple display, but I hope the beauty of Tír fo Thuinn brings you some joy regardless."

"It is lovely," Elvinia said, her eyes still on the waterfall. I was a little surprised that she seemed to genuinely like it. My gaze flicked to Áine, and I found her focus still on the waterfall as well. The sisters finally looked away to meet each other's gaze, something unspoken passing between them. I was dying to know what it was, because I had expected them to be bored with my display and offer some backhanded compliments.

"Yes," Maeve said, drawing my attention to her. Like the queens, she was also thoughtfully staring at the waterfall.

Something inside me tensed. I didn't know why, but somehow, I knew that using my memory of this cove had been a mistake. "Truly"—Maeve's gaze snapped to mine—"a gift from the sea."

Before I could try to figure out what she meant by that or misdirect what I had done, a familiar form rushed into the garden.

"Ash—My Queen!" Kaysea dashed around the gathered Tuatha to stand in front of me, her green hair still wet and soaking the light blue wrap dress she wore, giving everyone an eyeful of her curves. A few Tuatha gave her appreciative looks but quickly looked away when Connor growled at them.

"Kaysea?" I looked at my friend in confusion. "Is something wrong?"

Please don't let anything be wrong. Shit is going sideways already, and I really can't handle anything else at the moment.

"No," she said quickly. "But . . . umm . . . I need to borrow you for a bit." She bowed to the queens. "So sorry for the interruption, but a friend of ours needs some help with something that is a bit time-sensitive."

"Perhaps it can wait until—"

"It can't," she cut me off. Several of the Tuatha snickered, and even the queens looked amused at the sweet-faced Kaysea cutting off the Merfolk Queen.

"Kaysea," I tried again.

"It's Levi."

Oh. Well, shit. Kraken-related problems were never a good thing—not that Kaysea would have interrupted without a valid reason. I thought about it more—if something was going on with Levi, then Hecate would likely be there. Perhaps the ancient witch could offer some insight on how Maeve could use the transference ritual to steal the queens' powers, or at least maybe have something to help me spot the invisible dofheicthe, who, for all I knew, was here in this garden.

I definitely needed to figure out a way to deal with him.

"Once again, our apologies." I gave a shallow bow to the queens. "Connor and I shall return as soon as we've helped our friend."

Áine gave me a dismissive wave, but Elvinia smiled. "Say hi to Levi for me. He's the best boy."

Chapter Ten

TEN MINUTES LATER, we were standing on the shore of an Unseelie realm, Mag Argatnél. After we'd rescued Levi from the gods, we'd all agreed that the human realm wasn't a good place for the kraken to call home, even if that was where Hecate had originally found him. The realm of multicolored plains was the least inhabited of the Unseelie realms, and Elvinia had been fine with us bringing Levi here. Technically, the waters belonged to the merfolk, so he was in my territory, but it had still seemed polite to ask before relocating a giant sea monster here.

"He's the best boy." My brows furrowed. Had Elvinia been visiting Levi?

"What's going on?" I asked as the fae gateway behind us closed and I went to join the pacing witch on the shoreline.

Hecate's two enormous dogs eyed me and silently flashed their teeth before sitting obediently at the witch goddess' feet. Cloudy, white eyes set in an ageless face turned in my direction and I halted midstep.

"I don't know," she said uneasily, brushing back her brunette curls from the wind that was tugging them free from her bun. "But I can feel his stress and fear. I think he wants to go somewhere else, but I don't know where to move him or what he needs."

An enormous, dark tentacle rose from the water a hundred yards off the shore and slapped the surface repeatedly. Seconds later, a low, rumbling bellow sounded, and the tentacle disappeared beneath the waves.

"Let me go check it out." I tugged my dress off and tossed it to Kaysea, who caught it and went back to chewing her lip while gazing out worriedly to where Levi was waiting for us.

"You sure that's a good idea?" Connor frowned at me.

"He won't hurt me," I said confidently. "He's my buddy."

"A hundred-foot-long buddy with tentacles full of barbs and a beak-like mouth that could swallow you in one gulp."

"Exactly. That's, like, best friend material right there."

"I'm coming with you." Connor sighed and proceeded to strip. I didn't know what it said about me that, despite the fact that the world might end in three days and that I was going to go swimming with a giant monster, I still took the time to ogle him.

Because godsdamn.

"Drool over my brother later," Kaysea snapped and gave me a hard shove into the water. "Save Leviathan!"

"I'm going, I'm going," I muttered and strode out into the waves. This realm was always windy, and it caused the currents here to be extra turbulent. Connor and I pushed through the crush of the waves until it was deep enough for us to shift into our merfolk forms and dive further down, where the water was less rough.

We swam quickly towards Levi, who was hovering forty feet below the surface. I'd explored the seas of many realms and never encountered anything like him. He resembled both an octopus and a squid. Similar to an octopus, all his tentacles were the same length, but his head was a little more cone-shaped like a squid. Usually, his eight tentacles were drifting around him, curiously interacting with the environment as if they had minds of their own, but today, he had all but two wrapped up together, the free ones out to the side, keeping him upright in the water.

Strange, Connor said to me. We got a little boost in our merfolk forms when it came to telepathy, but neither of us were particularly strong, so we usually stuck to short exchanges. He swam ahead of me, the green scales of his fins disappearing on the other side of Levi's enormous form, any concern he had about me clearly gone. Given the emotions Levi was impressing on us with his own telepathic abilities, I didn't blame him.

The kraken was scared and stressed . . . but not for himself?

I was still getting used to communicating with Levi. At first, the emotions he would press upon me had been too much and had overwhelmed my ability to get anything coherent. He'd sensed that and pulled back to make it easier on me, but he wasn't pulling back now.

Waves of fear slammed into me, distracting me enough that a sudden, intense current caught me and sent me spinning in the rough waters. Levi's tentacle shot out and gently wrapped around me, pulling me back to him, and an enormous dark eye looked at me, imploring me to help. I still didn't understand what he needed though. The waters here were rough, but that shouldn't have been a problem for him, and if he dove deeper, the churning would cease.

What is it, friend? I pushed the thought towards him, knowing he wouldn't understand the words but maybe would feel the intent behind them.

Ash! Connor suddenly appeared in my field of vision, his dark green hair floating around his head and his hands tucked against his chest. *Look!*

He braced his body against Levi, who swept his other

tentacle around to hold Connor in place. I could feel his trepidation at whatever Connor held. Leaning forward as much as Levi's hold on me would allow, I looked at Connor's hands as he slowly unfolded them from his body, allowing me to peek at what was there.

Two dark purple eyes gazed up at me while extending a bright violet-colored tentacle to wrap around Connor's little finger. A baby kraken.

I squealed, sending bubbles flying up to the surface, and the baby shrunk back into Connor's protective hold. My would-be mate gave me a chiding look. *You're scaring her.*

Her? I calmed my thoughts and stretched a hand towards the cute little tentacled creature, and she carefully reached out to touch the tip of my finger. Just like with Levi, I got a flood of emotions from her. They were way more jumbled than Levi's, but the few bits I could piece out were that she was in fact a girl and she was worried about her . . . siblings.

Oh boy.

I tapped my fingers against Levi's tentacle and tried to think curious thoughts before pointing at the rest of his tentacles that he had wound up tight. He released me, and I swam a little lower to where he had twisted his remaining six tentacles together. I got as close as I could, and as soon as there was a break in the rough tug and pull of the tide, Levi created just enough of a gap for me to see inside.

You're a seahorse daddy, I thought in wonder.

Dozens of kraken babies were holding on for dear life against the waters that were trying to pull them away. In the darkness of Levi's embrace, each of them glowed slightly. They were like little brightly colored orbs of blue, purple, and green. I understood now why Levi was so panicked. There was nowhere he could let them go unless he swam far below, but all kinds of beasties dwelled down there, and they'd be more than happy to make a snack out of a baby kraken.

I swam up until I was level with one of his enormous eyes and laid my hand flat against his smooth, rubbery hide. *Safety*, I thought. *Will find safety.*

A sense of gratitude flooded me, and I patted him one more time before swimming to Connor, who was placing the baby kraken back with the others in Levi's makeshift tentacle nest. *Be right back*, I told Connor. *Help keep them safe.*

Will do. Connor's magic brushed past mine, and the waters immediately around us calmed a little. It was impossible to hold back the seas like this for long, even I couldn't do it with my considerable well of magic, so I'd have to be quick.

I spun in the water and swam quickly towards the shore, shifting as soon as I could. Kaysea held my dress out to me, but I shook my head and turned towards Hecate. "Congrats, you're now a grandmother to several dozen kraken babies."

The Mother of All Witches blinked. "Come again?"

"Levi had babies," I explained. "He's keeping them all wrapped up in his tentacles, but we need to get them to calmer waters."

"Where?" she asked immediately, concern for her friend and his offspring causing the corner of her eyes to crease.

"For now, I think the new dragon realm, Acleonia, makes sense." My gaze flicked back to Kaysea. "I need you and Hecate to go there now and explain the situation. I'm going to set my gateway to link between here and the cove just south of where they're currently building their city. If it's a problem, I'll find somewhere else to bring him, but the waters of that sea are calm, warm, and—best I can tell—mostly free of predators."

"On it," Kaysea said. "Taliesin and Lucan should be there if Cerri isn't. I'm sure they'll be fine with it. Who wouldn't want a kraken in their backyard?"

A lot of people, probably, but when you shifted into a huge-ass winged reptile that could breathe fire, you were probably less intimidated by a giant sea monster.

"Perfect. We'll meet you at the cove." I jogged back to the water and dove in, shifting as I swam. My tail beat against the currents as I plotted out the gateways I'd have to manipulate to move Levi and his babies to Acleonia.

I would have helped Levi anyway—because, come on, baby krakens—but now Hecate would be feeling extra grateful to me and would likely go above and beyond to help me. *I see your powerful fae, Maeve, and raise you an ancient goddess of witchcraft.*

<hr>

AN HOUR LATER, I was sitting on a grassy hill that overlooked the beach below, Connor to my left and Hecate to my right. Her dogs, Philo and Zephr, were playing in the waves. The dragons had been a little wary of us bringing Levi here—apparently, this cove was a favorite place for their children to swim. While adult dragons could probably hold their own against a kraken, the youngest of their children were bite-size and had a tenuous hold on their ability to breathe fire.

Unfortunately for their parents, the young dragons didn't have the same healthy fear of the giant tentacled sea monster. While we'd all been discussing it on the shore after I'd moved Levi and his offspring here, several of the children had shifted midair and jumped into the water directly where Levi was swimming because they wanted to play with the cute little baby krakens.

There had been a collective panic on the beach, and Connor and I had started sprinting towards the water, getting ready to shift, when Hecate had started laughing. Everyone froze as Levi raised several tentacles out of the water and the children raced up them before springing off the tips like diving boards to do flips and diving back beneath the calm surface.

"I told you." Hecate chuckled. "Levi is a strong empath. Your little ones just want to play, and he knows this. He won't harm them. Just tell them to be gentle with the baby krakens until everyone is used to each other."

"I'll supervise!" Kaysea announced before promptly stripping in front of everyone and swimming out to where the kids played.

Now the three of us were up here, the dragon parents still down below on the sandy beach, monitoring the situation.

It would probably take them a while to be fully comfortable with Levi here. From what I'd been told, their original realm had been overrun with devourers and they'd been fighting for survival. Cerri's father had been in charge, and he'd wielded the safety of their children like a political weapon. They'd spent centuries living in constant fear of losing not only their own lives but endangering their families as well.

I understood their hesitation, but I was happy to see them visibly relaxing. They'd gone from standing right at the shoreline to sitting a ways back. A few of them had even left and returned with food, resulting in an impromptu picnic.

It was nice. I could have stayed here all day to watch the events unfold. Sadly, time was ticking, and I needed to see if Hecate had any useful advice before heading back to deal with the fallout of my demonstration at the fae court. The queens' reaction to it had been strange, but it was Maeve who I was really worried about. My seer magic had been a little flakey since my encounter with that damn devourer fae, popping in with some gentle nudges before going silent again.

Really not the best time to be having performance issues, but whatever.

Before I'd left the garden, I'd gotten the sense that there was something there I should have been looking for. I suspected it was the tree that would be the focal point of the queens' ritual—especially since Syndra had mentioned as much. But there were a lot of trees, and I hadn't been able to find the specific one. Even if I had, there were too many people around for me to examine it without them wondering what I was doing.

I needed to find some time to look more closely without the scrutiny of watchful sidhe eyes. And I still needed to spy on Maeve and her cronies to glean more information about their plans. For all of this, I also needed a way to detect if that dofheicthe prick was there, because I really didn't want to get jumped again.

"Something on your mind, Ashling?" Hecate asked, an amused smile playing across her lips. For someone who was blind, she saw an awful lot.

I thought through a few versions of the situation to tell her, each with varying degrees of truth in them. The more information I gave her to work with, the likelier it was that she'd be able to help me. On the flip side, I didn't personally know Hecate all that well. Until a few months ago, I'd known her by reputation only. We'd bonded over helping Levi, but I wasn't sure if that was enough to tell her everything.

Connor stirred, and I glanced at him, a question in my eyes, then he shrugged. "How much will your secrets matter if it all goes to shit in a few days?"

"Well, this is intriguing." Hecate's dark eyebrows rose, and she smiled wider. "Once upon a time, people traveled thousands of miles to pray at my temples and beg me for advice. I suggest you take advantage of my undivided attention and gratitude for helping my friend, child. You may not get it again."

Pointing out that I was a queen and almost a century old probably wouldn't be impressive to the goddess who had to be over five thousand years old.

Fuck it. I decided to just lay it all out there. Connor was

right—none of this would matter if I didn't figure out a way to stop Balor returning in three days.

"For the last hundred years, I've been getting the same vision: five individuals work to bring Balor back, and he ushers in his army and wipes out everyone who opposes him. Everyone is focused on the other prophecy around Finn—nobody but me knows about this one."

I decided to just keep dropping the bad news hammer.

"The pinnacle moment happens in three days. I know which fae are involved. They're working with the devourer fae to redirect the magic from the transference ritual. I don't know how they'll do this or how to stop it aside from killing them before they do, but they're five of the most powerful sidhe, and if I miss even one of them, my vision still comes true. Also, one of the devourer fae helping them is something called a dofheic-the, and he can turn invisible. Like, completely invisible—no hint of magic around him, and my own magic can't detect him when he's cloaking himself."

I released a long sigh and leaned back on my hands to give Hecate a moment to take all that in. Then I rolled my head to the side so I could look at Connor and frowned at the strange look on his face. "What?"

"You said for the last hundred years," he said slowly.

"Okay, that's not entirely accurate. More like nine decades."

The expression on his face grew more confused. "But you said you had that vision when you were five years old?"

"Yes?" Where was he going with this?

"How old are you, Ash?" he demanded.

"Ninety-seven." I cracked a smile as his eyes widened.

"I'm five centuries older than you!"

"According to Kaysea, age gap romances are very popular."

Connor's brows bunched together to an almost comical degree. "I don't even know what that means."

"The two of you can discuss whatever weird sex thing you have going on later," Hecate said evenly. Her expression was serious, but based on the way the corners of her mouth were twitching, I suspected she was holding back a grin.

"Not a lot of sex, sadly," I muttered, even as the brief moment of levity between Connor and me slipped away and I focused back on the task at hand. "Suggestions?" I asked Hecate. "I'll happily build a temple in your honor if you can help a queen out."

"My temple days are behind me." She waved a hand and pursed her lips in thought for a moment. "Without knowing exactly what the spell is, it'll be hard to counteract it. Can you get a copy of it?"

"Unlikely." I shook my head even though she couldn't see it. "Not in time anyway. Maeve is probably keeping it on her person at all times. I'd be lucky if I could steal it within the next three days, which would give us no time to review it."

"Is there a reason you're not telling the fae queens this? If they don't do the ritual, then the spell to steal the magic from it will be moot."

"My magic is more than just visions." I rubbed my face tiredly. "It gives me hunches and feelings, and I can use that to determine the likelihood of a successful outcome."

"Interesting," she mused. "And I take it that you telling the fae queens doesn't go well?"

"No." I snorted. "Unclear on what happens exactly, but I get the impression that my life is in serious jeopardy if I take that route." Connor stiffened next to me. "My bloodline has a history with the fae queens on account of us foretelling their deaths," I explained to Hecate. "They believe they have exterminated all of my family. They don't know I'm the last one."

I felt Connor's eyes on me. He was probably miffed at me

revealing yet another secret I'd been keeping from him, but if anyone understood how painful it could be to talk about family, it was Connor.

"Fate is such a tangled web sometimes." Hecate's gaze grew more distant, and I wondered what she was seeing. I knew in addition to her skills with spellcasting and crafting poisons, she was also a gifted seer. Her brows grew more and more furrowed as the minutes ticked on, until she winced and rubbed her face. "Whatever awaits you, I cannot clearly see it, but I did get enough fragments that I understand why you have tried to accomplish this task on your own. If any of the five traitors slip away, the realms will fall. Adding more people also increases the chance of complications."

"Yes," I agreed. "Plus, I'd really love to survive all this, which will be considerably harder if the fae queens figure out who I really am."

"Three days till the end. Five fae who need to die. One tricky, invisible foe."

"You're taking all this rather calmly." Connor narrowed his eyes at the goddess.

Hecate shrugged. "I survived the demise of my realm, and I've seen visions of at least a dozen more possible endings for this one over the last few thousand years. No reason to panic over spilt milk, or potentially spilt milk as it were."

"I can't believe you're comparing Balor returning and slaughtering his way across the realms to spilt milk." Connor shook his head, and I kind of agreed with him.

"Don't be so dramatic," Hecate chided. "I still have a few helpful suggestions."

"Such as?" I slapped my palm across Connor's mouth before he could say something potentially rude.

She held her right hand out so it hovered over the wild-flowers growing around us, and with uncanny accuracy, she plucked one and held it in front of herself. Words poured from her lips as she reached into the satchel attached to the belt at her side and pulled out some crushed herbs, sprinkling them over the white flower. As soon as the herb flakes touched the petals, the flakes disappeared, and after a few seconds, the white flower became a deep orange.

"Wear this." She held the flower out to me. "Braid it into your hair or something, but keep it on you at all times."

"What does it do?" I tucked the stem into my braid and brushed my fingers against the petals. It felt oddly . . . resilient. I wondered if her spell had also strengthened the flower's delicate nature.

"You should see an outline of devourer magic while wearing it." She frowned. "I'm still tinkering with the spell, so it's a bit of a work in progress, but it's the best I can do."

"Magic doesn't work on devourers," Connor said suspiciously.

"Correct, little princeling." Hecate grinned. "The spell is constantly searching for magic, and when it finds a dead zone, it alerts you to that."

"And devourer magic creates that dead zone," he finished and gave the flower a new appreciative look.

"It's almost like I learned something after being alive for thousands of years," she said dryly. "As for the problem of taking out five powerful fae in such a short period of time"— those cloudy, white eyes that still somehow saw too much fell on me—"you happen to be on fairly friendly terms with a few people who are quite talented at killing. I understand your hesitancy to bring more people in on this, but I don't see any other way for you to be successful."

"Nemain works for the Unseelie Queen." I dropped the end of my braid that I'd been toying with. "I can't involve her or anyone in her circle."

"Please," Hecate scoffed. "Nobody holds a grudge like Nemain. She once stopped talking to me for two decades because I stepped on her tail when she was sunning on my patio in her feline form. The fact that I'm blind and literally did not see her did nothing to appease her annoyance. You think she's forgiven the Unseelie Queen for trapping her into the role of Knight? Not to mention her suspicions of the Seelie Queen playing a role in the death of her adoptive parents."

I chewed this over. Hecate made a valid point, but I still didn't love the idea of involving Nemain. Even if she didn't tell the fae queens directly, Nemain wasn't exactly discreet. For all I knew, she'd slaughter the lot of them and then parade their decapitated heads around the courts, which would lead to all kinds of questions.

Okay, maybe that was an extreme scenario, but still . . . Nemain was chaos incarnate.

"What do you think?" I turned to Connor. "You know Nemain better than I do."

"I'll be the first to point out all of Nemain's flaws—and there are many—but when it comes to killing people, there are few more talented than Nemain . . . and she happens to surround herself with a lot of them."

"I'll consider it." There was still a chance I could figure out how to pull this off without introducing the chaos of Nemain and her merry band of killers. "Thank you for the advice and the flower."

"Of course." Hecate gave me a nod of deep respect. "Thank you for helping my friend again. Not everyone would be willing to do so."

I smiled out at the water where Levi still played with the dragon children. Several of his own offspring used their tentacles to climb all over the faces of the giggling younglings. "He might be a monster, but he's our kind of monster."

Chapter Eleven

A HIGH-PITCHED GIGGLE rushed from my lips as Connor tugged me deeper into the garden. By the time we'd returned to the fae realm, the magic demonstrations had been over and the Tuatha had been mingling in the gardens. Most of them were still keeping to their respective court, Seelie or Unseelie, but Maeve and her lot were flitting between all of them.

The queens looked on from their thrones with unreadable expressions, and I wondered if something had happened when we'd been gone or if their distance was related to my show of magic. I really hoped it was the former. We'd mingled for a couple of hours, and it hadn't seemed like anything was amiss. Maeve was back to giving me dismissive looks, and when I'd briefly chatted with the queens to apologize for my abrupt departure, they had waved it off and said it was fine. I'd tried to further the conversation, but after getting nothing but one-word answers, I'd decided I was doing more harm than good by continuing. I'd just have to monitor them from afar and make sure there was no lingering damage.

Connor spun me around and pinned me to a tree. "That

laugh is ridiculous," he breathed quietly in my ear when I giggled louder.

"That's the point," I whispered back to him, running my fingers through his hair. "Did you see Rowan's expression?"

"Yes." He kissed my neck, and I leaned into him a little more. Someone could have followed us, so we were just putting on a show. That's what I kept trying to tell my heart every time it beat a little faster. "I think that giggle is the most offensive thing she's ever heard."

"I worked hard on it." I nipped his earlobe, and the grip on my waist tightened. "Kaysea helped. We watched a bunch of reality TV and these shows created for human teenagers. My giggle is a carefully honed craft."

Connor finally broke character and started laughing. He did his best to cover it up by nuzzling further into my neck though, and I had a sudden flashback to one of the last nights we'd spent together floating beneath the stars and making up constellations.

What if I had told him then? About my plan to be queen? Would it have made a difference, or would he have just left me that night instead of later?

What if I gave up the last secret I had? That we were fated mates? Was I repeating the same mistake now?

Despite my foresight magic starting to flicker back to life since that stupid devourer bite, it was being obnoxiously quiet now.

"Where did you go?" Connor pulled back and studied me with pale eyes full of concern, any hint of amusement gone from his face.

"Nowhere I want to be." Fuck it. I had to tell him. We weren't on a rooftop—he wouldn't walk away from me now. My vision had clearly taken place on a rooftop, but it'd also heavily implied that the location didn't really matter. Still… maybe if I seized the moment here, I could circumvent fate. I clung to that belief like it was the only drop of water in the middle of a barren desert. "There's something I—"

A faint outline moving in the trees across from the one we were leaning against caught my attention. Looked like our dofheicthe friend was here and Hecate's spelled flower worked. He nimbly leapt from branch to branch before settling down on one of them, clearly intent on watching us.

The question was, did he know I was the reason he had a memory blank spot? Or was he simply watching me because I was the Merfolk Queen and he was doing some recon on everyone here?

Connor cocked his head in question, and I toyed with my braid, letting my fingers brush a few times against the flower. He gave the barest nod in understanding and traced his fingers along my jawline, giving me time to figure out what to do. It would be strange if we just left—I didn't want the dofheicthe to know we could see him. This was too good an advantage to give up, which meant we needed to proceed as if we thought we were completely alone in an enchanted forest . . . and do what any lovers would do.

My hands drifted up the back of Connor's head, and I pulled him down towards me until his lips were a hairsbreadth from mine before trailing kisses up his jawline so that I could whisper in his ear, "Hope you're ready to put on a show. We've got company."

He let a hand drop to my hip while turning his face into my neck. I angled my head to the side, giving him better access as he kissed my neck and nipped my earlobe. A soft moan slipped from me that wasn't the least bit faked, and I felt him smile against my skin. "Pretty sure I'm up for it."

Another low groan rippled from my throat as he ground his hips against me and I felt just how *up for it* he was. Strong hands gripped me, lifting me up, and I automatically wrapped my legs around his waist as he pushed me harder against the tree, his large body caging me in.

When his mouth closed over mine, hungry and demanding, I forgot all about our voyeur friend. Connor's grip on my ass tightened, and I parted my lips enough for his tongue to dart inside. Time slipped away as we kissed and tasted each other. Gods, I had missed him all these years. I had missed this.

Suddenly, Connor tore his lips away from mine and stepped back from the tree, taking me with him. "Drop your legs," he ordered in a low tone that sent a bolt of heat straight through my core. I did as I was told and unwrapped my legs from his waist, and he spun me around. "Hands on the tree." I laid my hands on the smooth bark of the tree trunk, and Connor once again boxed me in, his large body covering mine as he bent down to whisper in my ear. "Our friend is going to hear you come apart on my fingers, but he doesn't get to see you."

Oh fuck.

A small voice in my mind cautioned that this was a bad idea. That things were messy between us already and blurring the lines further wasn't going to help, but then Connor was tugging my dress down while he kissed the crook of my neck. One hand roughly squeezed my breast while the other slipped beneath the fabric pooled at my waist.

"Connor," I moaned as his fingers rubbed against my silk panties, causing a wonderful friction where I so desperately needed it.

"So wet for me." His fingers pushed harder while he pinched my nipple with his other hand, causing me to arch against him. I dropped a hand from the tree and reached back to free his cock, but the hand that had been playing with my nipple grabbed it, eliciting a frustrated growl from me. "Hands stay on the tree, love. You can play with me later . . . if you're good."

"You're not the boss of me." I twisted my head enough to glare at him over my shoulder, and he just laughed before gripping a handful of hair to yank my head back. His lips crashed against mine, and I let out a half-strangled moan as his fingers tugged my underwear aside and dove into the wetness that awaited them.

He bit my lower lip enough to draw blood before pulling back, his light green eyes full of a possessive heat. "We've been over this. Anytime I'm inside you"—he added a third finger, plunging them hard and fast as I screamed, a climax exploding through me—"I *am* the boss of you."

"Oh fuck. FUCK!" I screamed as he continued to fuck me through the orgasm. All I could do was ride his hand and grip the tree for balance. When my legs started to shake, he released my hair so he could grip my waist to support me.

"We're not done yet, my queen." He chuckled darkly as he pulled his fingers free and raised them to his lips. I watched with absolute rapture as he sucked each one of them clean. "Gods, I'll never grow tired of your taste."

"I want to play with you," I breathed out and pulled my hands away from the tree again, but he made a noise of disagreement, and I planted them back onto the trunk.

"You can wrap that gorgeous mouth of yours around my cock later. In our bedroom." His hand slipped between my thighs again. "You're going to come for me again now."

"So demanding," I panted. "Once a fae prince, always a fae prince, I guess."

The arm around my waist squeezed in warning. "You're going to pay for being mouthy later."

"Promises, promises," I crooned. Whatever I'd been about to say next was interrupted by the scream that tore from my throat as Connor swirled his fingers around in my slick heat before sliding two slowly inside me while his thumb pushed down on my clit.

He groaned as my pussy clenched around his fingers, then he drew them out before sinking them back in, the entire time alternating between circling the sensitive bundle of nerves and applying pressure to it. I writhed against him as he continued to play my body like it was his favorite instrument.

"Harder!" I cried.

"Now who's demanding?" he growled but complied. The arm around my waist tightened as he thrust his fingers in and out at a faster, rougher pace. My breathing grew ragged as pleasure started to build, and whimpering sounds spilled from my lips as Connor worked me. Just when I felt like the pressure was too much, his thumb found my clit again as he buried three fingers deep inside me.

The dam burst, and I cried out as I came again all over his hand. Connor slowed the pace but kept going, wringing out every last drop of pleasure until I sagged in his arms. "Such a good queen."

Gods, this man would be the death of me.

"Who knew the Merfolk Queen made such pretty sounds?"

In an instant, Connor's fingers were gone and I was staring at his broad back. I couldn't see who had spoken, but I'd recognized the voice—Lughán, which meant Aoife was probably around here somewhere too. I fixed my dress and wrapped my hair back into a quick bun, giving me time to glance up into the trees and spot the dofheicthe. He was still perched on the same branch but had changed his angle slightly to watch Lughán.

"What the fuck do you want?" Connor growled. I darted around him so we were standing side by side, and his jaw tightened but he didn't push me back.

"So protective." Aoife laughed as she strolled under the tree the dofheicthe was perched on to stand by Lughán, then arched a perfectly sculpted dark eyebrow at Connor. "Either the little queen is an excellent actress, or the former prince has very talented fingers." She tilted her head as a sultry smile that I did not like at all stretched across her face. "For the sake of answering that question—because I hate to leave things unknown—perhaps I can have a turn against that tree now."

It was my turn to growl.

"Enough, Aoife," Maeve commanded as she, Coireall, and Rowan joined the other two. "We're here to have a civil chat, so you'll have to play your games with someone else . . . later."

Aoife's full lips morphed into a pout, and Lughán patted her on the back in consolation before leaning over to whisper in her ear. Whatever he said turned her pout into a mischievous grin. Something told me I wouldn't have liked what he'd said, so I focused on Maeve because she was the biggest threat.

Frustration raced through me as I took the five of them in. They were all right here, away from the queens and the rest of the Tuatha. If we took them out, our problems were solved. Unfortunately, it was five against two, and even as strong as Connor and I were, I didn't love our odds. Plus, the dofheicthe was still here. I didn't know if they knew of his presence or not, but I suspected he would join in on the fight if I started one, and then it would be six against two.

"Is there something you need from me, Maeve?" I leaned against Connor, who rested his hand on my lower back, where there was a gap in my dress . . . and above, a dagger in a hidden sheath along my spine. This one was spelled with a poison that would cause paralysis within minutes. Something told me that even if I asked nicely, they wouldn't hold still for us to stab them with it one by one.

"Yes, actually." Maeve stepped forward until she was standing directly in front of me, and Connor stiffened before I felt his hand slide up higher towards the dagger but then he stopped when I leaned into him harder. If Maeve had wanted to attack me, she would have done so without revealing herself first. I wanted to know what she had to say and if it had to do with her reaction to my demonstration earlier. "Why are you trying so hard to convince everyone you're nothing but a starry-eyed, daft mermaid unfit for a crown?"

I blinked and parted my lips slightly, going for a shocked expression. "What do you mea—"

"No," Maeve interrupted. "Try again."

When one mask failed, it was time for another, and I had plenty.

I ditched the naive persona and slipped into one that was just as haughty as the one Maeve typically wore. "Can you really blame me?" An arrogant, close-lipped smile played across my lips as I let a slight drawl slip into my voice. "It's the way all the sidhe view the rest of the fae, especially the merfolk. You lot make it so easy."

"To what end?" Rowan asked from over Maeve's shoulder. "You're a queen, are you not? Why bother with such tactics?"

I didn't like the calculating look in Rowan's eyes, like a wolf who had just picked up the scent of interesting prey. I'd need to give her something to satisfy her curiosity but keep her off the main trail.

"Because I'm a *new* queen. This was an opportunity I simply couldn't pass up. I wanted to see for myself who the true power players were amongst the queens' courts and where their allegiances lie. You'd be amazed what people let slip when they think you're beneath them."

Nothing I was saying was a lie; I simply wasn't saying the full truth. Hopefully it would be enough.

Maeve's wolfish eyes scrutinized my face. I couldn't tell what she was looking for exactly but kept just how unnerved I felt hidden away. Why was she looking at me like she *knew* me?

Until this event, we'd never met. I was certain of it. So why the fuck was she looking at me like this?

My magic stretched out an invisible hand and tapped my shoulder, and I turned my head just in time to see Coireall slip away between the trees, heading southeast, the devourer fae following after him.

I would have to investigate that after this.

"Well played." Maeve stepped back, the intensity gone from her eyes, and I wanted to release a relieved breath but held it in. "It seems you'll be an interesting player after all. I look forward to your next move."

"Likewise."

Maeve's gaze lingered on me for a moment as I gave her a sharp smile before she strode off in the opposite direction of where Coireall had gone, Rowan following after her.

Aoife shrugged out from underneath Lughán's arm and sauntered towards Connor, rolling her hips in a way that sent my blood boiling. "Let me know if you want to play later." She smirked at Connor's flat expression and trailed a finger down his bicep. "I'll make you work to hear me scream."

The way he was glaring at that finger told me he was a few seconds from snapping it off, but he likely didn't want to escalate the situation.

Be smart, I told myself. *She's testing you. Just say something cutting and step between them. Force her to step back. She'll stop touching him. You'll show your dominance over her. It's a win-win situation. Do. Not. Overreact.*

My magic shot forward, and Aoife's screams filled the woods as her body seized and flailed like a puppet whose strings were being violently jerked around.

"Funny," I said coldly. "Seems like you scream pretty easily."

My elemental magic might have been limited to water. But there was plenty of water in blood.

Aoife collapsed to the ground, back arching as I drew harder on her blood. Red stains leaked from her eyes, nose, and ears.

I pulled even as darkness encroached at the corners of my

vision. The barely there bond between Connor and me purred in satisfaction as more of her screams echoed through the trees.

Lughán's magic rose against mine, and I released the hold I had over Aoife's blood, the exhaustion in my limbs instant. Going after blood was difficult, because while it was mostly water, it was also loaded with a person's individual magic, which naturally fought against the manipulation. I'd only been able to hurt Aoife so badly because she hadn't been expecting it and I was so pissed off.

Mine. My mate. She'd touched my fucking mate.

Aoife panted on the forest floor, pain still wracking her pretty features, and she glared at me with a promise of death. Lughán picked her up in his arms and raced after Maeve. Probably going to tattle on me.

Pussy.

Maybe they'd make my life easier and the two of them would come after us later. We could take them out before going after the remaining three.

It was reckless of me, but I wanted them to come back. We were running out of time, and maybe perfectly laid plans weren't how we were going to win this. Maybe we did need a little chaos.

"Hey." Connor gently gripped my chin and tilted my face towards him. "You okay?" Concern and confusion filled his voice. I wasn't surprised—that had been a bit of an overreaction on my end—but it wasn't like I could actually explain why I'd felt the sudden urge to defend my mate. The urge I'd had to tell him was gone, and I couldn't drum up the courage again.

Besides, we needed to find out where Coireall had disappeared to.

"Fine," I rasped. "Coireall went that way." I pointed southeast. "The dofheicthe followed him."

Connor dropped his hand from my face, and I stepped

around him, walking across the small clearing to where Coirreall had gone.

"Ash?" I stopped and looked over my shoulder, my gaze slamming into Connor's. "Is there something that you're not telling me?"

My heart leapt into my throat, and I had to swallow it back down.

"No." I forced the word out. "There's nothing."

The lie hung between us as we walked into the dark.

Chapter Twelve

"WE NEED NEMAIN," I reluctantly admitted the following morning. Connor and I had searched the forest for Coireall and the devourer spy but hadn't been able to find any trace of either of them. My magic kept nudging me in various directions, which had only increased my frustration because whatever it had been trying to tell me, I wasn't seeing it.

We'd also checked out the tree that would be used for the ceremony, but nothing about it appeared amiss. The main event was tomorrow night, so we were out of time.

"We need Nemain," Connor agreed, but his lips tugged downward into a frown. "Don't tell her I said that."

I sighed and leaned further into the pillow, staring up at the canopy of our bed in this guest suite for likely the last time. "We need to go say goodbye to the queens. I'll make up some excuse for us having to leave again."

Connor leaned onto his side and brushed the bright blue curls off my shoulder. We hadn't spoken much after returning to our room last night. I'd crawled into bed, and Connor had folded himself around me. Frustration and tension clung to me, and I knew he could sense it. Just like he could sense there was something else I wasn't telling him.

Not because of my magic sending me nudges, not because of the frail mate bond forming between us, but because I knew him and he knew me.

I recognized the faint creases forming at the corners of his eyes, the way he tugged on the same strand of hair every few minutes, and the deliberately slow breathing, like he was trying to force himself to remain calm.

Everything was about to blow up in my face. I felt it in my soul. Not just this bullshit with Maeve but things with Connor too. I was fucking everything up, and I didn't know how to fix it in the short time I had left. I could feel each grain of sand slipping through the hourglass, and every single one that fell sounded like a death note.

This ominous cloud was hanging over me, and it was tainting the bond between us. Connor could feel it even if he didn't understand what it was yet. He hadn't asked me again if there was something I wasn't telling him. Probably because he didn't want to hear me lie to him again.

Gods, everything was so fucked. On the plus side, it wasn't like it could have gotten worse.

A knock sounded, and a second later, Olwen walked in. For once, she wasn't wearing the humorous expression that made it seem like she was on the verge of telling a dirty joke—instead, her grey eyes were . . . solemn.

That definitely wasn't a good sign.

Kalen followed in her shadow, his expression as unreadable as always, but I could have sworn he shot me a cautious look as he moved to stand beside Olwen at the foot of our bed.

"Generally, one waits for a response after they knock before entering a room," Connor growled.

"I'd advise you to watch your tone today, prince," Olwen

replied smoothly, not a hint of humor to be seen. This was definitely not good.

"The queens request your presence, Ashling," Kalen said, a hint of apology in his voice, even if his expression said there was no room for argument.

"Of course." I rolled out of bed, Connor's shirt falling almost to my knees. "Let me just toss something else on."

"Make it quick," Olwen snapped.

Connor growled and hopped off the bed to stand between me and the Seelie Knight. Olwen's eyes flashed, and I moved to intercede, but Kalen beat me to it.

"We'll wait for you outside." Then he grabbed Olwen by the arm. "Please don't take long."

I nodded gratefully at him and quickly grabbed a dress. "We'll be right there."

Connor and I didn't say anything as we dressed. Anything we had to say would be speculation, and Olwen and Kalen would overhear. This had to be related to my waterfall creation yesterday.

Gods-fucking-damn it all, I'd successfully flown under the radar all these years and just had to snap at some snobby fae and her fire birds.

When Connor and I stepped out of our suite minutes later, I was still silently fuming but made sure to keep all that off my face. Instead, I fixed my features into a mask of confidence and slight bewilderment, like a queen who demanded respect but was a little confused about why she was being summoned like this. Not exactly a lie, just hiding the anger and frustration part of what I was feeling.

Connor didn't bother hiding anything. He looked pissed off, but like me, he knew there was nothing we could do about this. We were guests of the fae queens—in their palace. If they summoned us, we had to come because if we refused, Olwen would definitely drag us there, and she was more than capable of it. Her power was often understated, but it was definitely there. She hadn't been named the Seelie Knight for nothing.

Kalen was more of a wild card. He wasn't a Knight, but for political reasons, he owed the Unseelie Queen quite a bit. She had sheltered his tainted devourer ass all this time, even after he had pissed off her sister by falling in love with Badb instead of killing her.

If there was one love story I wanted to know, it was how the cold and merciless Erlking had been sent on a mission to kill a wild and brutal feline shifter, only for the two to fall in love instead.

I wasn't sure if I would have been better or worse off if Badb were here. Kalen was more reasonable, but something told me Badb was more willing to go against the fae queens.

Connor was a silent, brooding shadow by my side as we walked through the halls. It was early enough that most of the Tuatha were probably still sleeping off their wine from the night before. A few servants gave us curious looks that would no doubt be the cause of rumors later—the Merfolk Queen being summoned from her bed before dawn.

Ten minutes later, Olwen paraded us through a set of large, silver doors, and the anxiousness I'd been feeling all morning increased. This was the throne room where the fae queens conducted all business with outsiders. For most of the week, I'd been treated like I had belonged here—at least by the queens themselves—but the message here was clear.

You are not one of us.

My magic offered no advice, but it felt like it was on edge too. I'd have to pay close attention to it during this encounter, because anything it had to offer could play a drastic role in how all this turned out.

The queens were all that awaited us in the throne room. This room was towards the back of the palace, so even though it was on the first floor, it jutted out from the rest of the building so that the ceiling was completely open to the sky. Gentle morning sun beamed down on the bare dirt floor, and the soft pink flowers that grew along the walls and pillars were twisted to face up. Everything about the environment spoke of a calm peace.

Yet that was not the vibe I was getting from the queens.

Áine was looking at us with outright suspicion and derision. Elvinia was a little harder to read, but I got the impression she was wary . . . and tired.

"You are of the Tornelis line," Áine announced as soon as the large double doors shut behind us.

Run. That was the immediate thought that came to me. *Fucking run.*

But it was far too late for that. Instead, I raised my chin as I closed the distance until I was eye level with the queens, who stood in the center of the room, their thrones—the symbols of their power—directly behind them.

"I am. Going to try and kill me the way you did my entire family?"

"Depends," Elvinia drawled. "Are you as committed to our brother as the rest of your bloodline was?"

I paused. Was this a trick? My mother and the few family members I'd known had claimed our bloodline had always been neutral, but I hadn't been born yesterday, and it wasn't outside of the realm of possibility they had lied to me. Or that they hadn't known better.

But it was equally possible that the queens were spinning their own lies to twist the narrative.

"I am committed to our realms continuing to thrive," I said slowly. "And everything I have learned about your brother leads me to believe he would be a detriment to this."

"So you claim to support us then?" Áine pushed as Elvinia continued to study me.

"I support the realms." I shrugged. "You are helpful for the moment, but your fates are already written. They always have been. You know this; I know this.”

“We slaughtered your bloodline,” Elvinia said flatly. “Had we known about you, we would have killed you.”

I felt Kalen’s attention on me from the back of the room, and I itched to turn around and meet his gaze. Had he killed some of my family? Would he have killed me?

“It would have changed nothing.” I looked each queen in the eye. “Neither of you will survive this war.”

“So certain of our fate?” Elvinia asked, as if my declaration was no more exciting than the prediction of tomorrow’s weather.

“Fate is choice,” I said evenly. “Everything is the result of a decision you make. Either yours or someone else’s. Oftentimes, it’s one choice building on another.”

Áine gave me a skeptical look, but Elvinia’s only hardened in understanding. I knew then in that moment that one sister had accepted what was to come and the other was still fighting against it.

“You will sacrifice yourselves to save Finn. It has always been likely to happen. I don’t know exactly what the choice is that you will have to make, only that you *will* choose to save him.”

“Fate can change,” Áine snarled, defiance flashing in her eyes.

“Yours will not.” I doubled down while Connor shifted uneasily next to me, but I didn’t see how changing my answer would benefit us. The queens knew who I really was and knew the prophecy my bloodline had always stood by.

“Tell us why you have been meeting with the devourer fae running around our palace?” It took my mind a second to process the change in topic as I stared blankly at Elvinia. Her golden eyes watched my face carefully. This was the real reason I was here. The truth of my bloodline certainly didn’t help, but for some reason, they thought I was working with that damn dofheicthe.

"Seems like a rude way to talk about Kalen," I said lightly, not willing to give anything away until I knew exactly what details the queens had.

Silver chains sprung from the ground and gripped my wrists, and Connor swore and dove towards them only to let out a pained hiss as blue fire wrapped around him. Kalen strolled around us and flicked his fingers, his devourer flames tugging Connor away from me but not harming him any further.

Olwen appeared in front of me, a strange, curvy, purple blade in her hands. "Answer the question."

The silver cuffs started to burn, and I glanced down at them, something written in Seelie giving off a faint red glow. Wonderful.

"The truth will set you free." Elvinia pointed at the chains. "Lies will bring you pain."

"Fae hospitality at its finest," I mouthed off before I could stop myself.

Olwen's purple blade touched my chin, and a bolt of pain shot through me where its tip pushed against my skin. I braced myself for another shot of agony, but to my horror, it was Connor's scream that filled my ears.

I could do nothing but watch as he fell to his knees. Kalen's blue flames burned brighter, and Connor's screams were abruptly cut off as devourer flames shot down his throat. Just like with Nemain's magic, the fire burned cold, and frost started to form in patches on Connor's skin and hair. Any hint of sympathy from the Erlking's face was gone, his obsidian eyes cold and heartless.

"Stop," I begged.

"Well," Áine purred, "her feelings for the prince certainly aren't fake." She stepped closer to me, and Olwen moved aside to make room as the Seelie Queen pointed a claw-tipped finger at my heart. "In fact, I think I see—"

"Maeve is working with the dofheicthe!" I blurted out before Áine could announce my mate bond. How she was able to see it, I had no idea. It was only the beginning of a bond, and without Connor's acceptance, she shouldn't have been able to sense it. Although, I really shouldn't have been surprised that the fae queens kept aspects of their powers hidden away.

Elvinia glanced at Kalen, who gave her a barely perceivable shake of his head. "How do you know what the fae is?" she asked.

"I'll tell you what I know," I bit out. "Let him go."

"You'll tell us, or we'll carve out his heart in front of you," Áine said smoothly.

Her sister didn't argue against her, but she did flick her fingers at Kalen, and he withdrew his fire from Connor's throat. A small amount of tension eased inside me as Connor sucked in gulps of air and glared at the Erlking, receiving a smile in return.

"I was spying on Maeve," I explained. "She was meeting with another fae devourer, a female sidhe named Syndra. They met in the quarters that Lughán and Aoife are sharing." I looked at each of the queens. "There are secret passages all throughout this place. There is a door in that room that leads to them."

The queens shared a look but didn't say anything, so I continued.

"Syndra gave Maeve a book that contains instructions on how to use the transference ritual to drain the magic from both of you and give Maeve the power of the fae throne, which she could then use to undo the ward you've placed around the realm where you locked away your brother."

"Do you have proof of this?" Elvinia asked.

"Only my word."

I pressed my lips into a hard line as Áine snorted. Clearly, that meant nothing to her, and Elvinia only looked disappointed.

"Tell us about the dofheicthe," Olwen demanded.

I described what it looked like, the fact that it could turn invisible, and that its magic was completely undetectable. That got a bit of reaction. Nobody liked the idea of their enemy being able to maneuver around with such freedom. I didn't mention the flower that was still braided into my hair. They would have taken it away from me, and I couldn't afford to lose it now.

"That's everything I know. I am not your enemy here."

"You'll always be our enemy," Áine said, her voice dripping with contempt.

Elvinia frowned at her sister before returning her attention to me. "I don't necessarily agree with that, but I can't trust you either. We made the mistake of believing several members of your bloodline before, and they betrayed us—nearly set our brother free before we stopped them."

"Pretty lies will not be our downfall." Resolve hardened across Áine's face.

No, I thought. *But love for your nephew will.*

But given how determined the Seelie Queen was to avoid her fated death, I didn't voice those words.

"You must know Maeve has been lusting after the throne all this time." I jingled the chains locked around my wrists. "And I told no lies." I glared at Áine. "Not even pretty ones."

"It was Maeve who gave us this information," Kalen said. "Perhaps she wanted your attention on the Merfolk Queen so she could be free to carry out her plan."

Elvinia pursed her lips and thought about it before shaking her head. "Maeve's ambitions are nothing new. The ceremony has no real power behind it. We only feed a small amount of our magic into the tree. It's symbolic and nothing more. It's just as likely that this whole thing was a trap for Ashling. For whatever reason, they might have wanted her bloodline outed. Maybe to get Maeve in good favor with us or simply to create tensions between our courts and Tír fo Thuinn."

"There doesn't have to be tension between us," I said evenly. "Whatever my family did to you, I have no interest in repeating their mistakes. I walk my own path."

"That may be," Elvinia said tiredly, "but it won't be long until rumors of your bloodline are all anyone is talking about. We cannot afford to be viewed as weak, and doing nothing after you stole the Merfolk throne from under our noses is just that."

"I didn't steal it," I argued. "Earned it fair and square." Both queens stared at me. "Mostly fair and square," I amended. "It's not like the two of you have a lot of room to speak about stealing thrones."

Olwen growled at that, but Kalen's lips twitched, and I was fairly certain he was fighting back a smile.

"My sister and I will discuss how to handle this." Elvinia smoothed the fabric of her dark blue tunic. "For now, it would be best if you left our realm."

I stiffened. "What of the ceremony?"

"It will continue as planned," Áine answered in an unconcerned tone. "We can handle anything Maeve tries."

My magic practically set off a warning bell in my mind, and I couldn't help my wince. "That's not a good id—"

"We have ruled for over five thousand years—much to the disappointment of your family," Elvinia cut me off. "Maeve isn't the first to come after our crowns, and she won't be the last. We thank you for the information, but we will handle it from here."

Something passed between Olwen and Kalen before the former walked over to a wooden arch at the side of the room and traced her fingers along a glyph carved into the top. Then the air in the space between the dark wood rippled until I saw a familiar beach on the other side.

"I trust you can find your way home from there," the Seelie Knight said in a clipped tone. She wasn't wrong. This was the beach just outside Emerald Bay, and there was a gateway beneath the waves a short distance from shore. She could have just as easily opened it directly to the fae gateway in my throne room. This was probably her way of being rude—kicking me out of the realm and forcing me to make the rest of the way home myself.

My magic seemed pleased about me heading to the small coastal town in the human realm though, so I let the slight pass. The chains fell away from my wrists and the flames vanished from around Connor. He instantly leapt to his feet and stalked towards me, clearly ready to get the fuck out of here.

I scanned his body but didn't see any lingering damage from those flames, Kalen's control over his magic was both impressive and terrifying.

Whatever Olwen had done with that purple blade still smarted on my skin, and my wrists were sore from the silver chains. But my magic was already healing it.

I raised my chin high as I walked to the gateway, Connor a hulking presence at my side. Just as I was about to step through, Olwen grabbed my arm and leaned forward, invading my space. Connor growled, but I raised my hand and he made no move to intervene as I held Olwen's sharp stare. "I don't care about the crown on your head," she said, "or what your magic whispers to you. If you come at my queen, I will fucking end you."

An image of a bloody Olwen kneeling on the ground and screaming slammed into my mind, and intense emotions pelted my soul. A desperate need. Unwavering love. Pain so raw, it stole the breath from my lungs.

"I'm so sorry," I squeezed out, closing my eyes as I panted through the vision. "But you will not get the love you seek. Only pain awaits you."

Olwen dropped my arm like it was on fire, and defiance tinged with fear reflected in her eyes. "You're wrong."

I wasn't.

"Perhaps," I lied and stepped through the gateway towards where my magic nudged me. To the shifter who lived and breathed violence and always seemed to carry the fate of the realms on her shoulders.

It was time for a little chaos, which meant I needed Nemain.

Chapter Thirteen

To my surprise, Kalen stepped through the gateway before it closed, and my hand shot out to grip Connor's shoulder as he took a step towards the Erlking.

"Don't," I warned him.

Connor's mouth hardened into a flat line, but he took a step back. Based on his expression, he was close to losing it. Our relationship might have been all kinds of fucked-up, but that didn't change the fact that Connor loved me, and he was fiercely protective of those he loved.

Watching me get chained and hurt had sent him spiraling, and then Kalen had used devourer magic on him. I just had to hope Connor would calm down before we reached Nemain, because him mouthing off to her really wasn't what we needed right now.

Kalen glanced at him. "If I didn't restrain you, the queens would have killed you in an instant. The words you're looking for are *thank you*."

"I can still feel your disgusting magic in my mouth after you shoved it down my throat," Connor growled.

"Strange." Kalen's head tilted to the side, causing his black hair to fall over his shoulder. "That didn't *sound* like thank you."

Connor ignored him and looked at me. "Where to now?"

"We just need to wait a moment," I told him, and Kalen looked at me curiously but didn't show any sign of leaving. Asking him what he was doing here would have been pointless. The Erlking did whatever the Erlking wanted, and apparently, what he wanted right now was to stick with us.

A minute ticked by, then another. Just when Connor opened his mouth to say something, the air rippled next to us and a gateway tore open. Badb stepped through, her bright green feline eyes going immediately to Kalen and ignoring us completely. "There you are. Mikhail has it sorted. There isn't anything we can do currently."

Mikhail had what sorted? My brows furrowed together, and when I glanced at Connor, he looked just as confused.

"She needs to speak to our daughter." He pointed at me.

"Him too?" Badb's gaze narrowed on Connor, and I fought the urge to step in front of him. Of all the people to attempt to kill, he just had to have done it to the person who had psychopaths for parents.

"Package deal, I'm afraid." Kalen kissed his mate on the cheek and stepped through the gateway.

She scowled at me. "Fair warning, if he comes, there is a significant chance one of us will kill him. I'm not in the mood for his bullshit, and I very much doubt Mikhail will be either."

With that warning, she stepped through the gateway as well, leaving Connor and me to follow. I looked at the sulking prince.

"Am I really that much of an asshole?" he asked a little hesitantly.

"Little bit." I held up my hand with my index and thumb almost touching. "My magic is telling me you need to come . . . but maybe mind your words a bit?"

"Honestly don't understand what everyone is so touchy about," he mumbled before we stepped through the gateway into a hot, desert-like realm. "I'm nice to most people, and it's not like Nemain doesn't give as good as she gets. Kind of what I always liked about her to be honest."

"Careful." I gave him a rueful look. "That was almost a compliment."

"If you tell Nemain I said that, I'll lie." He smiled smugly. "She'd never believe you."

"Just try not to say anything that will get you stabbed, okay?" I pushed. Kalen and Badb had walked away from us, but I could feel the tension in the air.

Connor frowned, looking around as if he could feel the threat of violence too, and then nodded. The gateway shut behind us, and it was only then that I realized I could hear the faint sounds of a fight, echoing from somewhere close.

A lean figure stood with his back to us, overlooking a cliff. Badb said something to him, and he looked over his shoulder before disappearing in a swirl of mist only to reappear directly in front of us. Wild, twilight eyes in an impossibly beautiful face took me in.

"Hello, Mikhail," I spoke calmly, as if I were speaking to a wolf and trying to convince it not to eat me. "We need to talk with Nemain."

The vampire cocked his head, and something wicked flitted in his eyes as his attention turned to Connor. Badb let out a dark chuckle, like she was relishing what was about to happen.

I sighed. "Nemain won't be happy if you attack her best friend's brother."

"What Nemain doesn't know won't hurt her." Two daggers appeared in Mikhail's hands. I had no idea where he'd drawn them from, but at least that freaky mist sword of his hadn't made an appearance. Although, on second thought, he could probably do just as much damage with those blades.

I turned to glare at Connor. "You just had to try to drown Nemain, didn't you?"

"My history with Nemain is just that—mine." Connor slid the curved blade strapped to his thigh free. "If pretty boy wants to get all pissy because of a disagreement Nemain and I had years ago, he's welcome to try something."

Shit. So much for not saying anything that would get him stabbed. I should have known better. Connor was pissed off and looking for a fight, and Mikhail appeared to be feeling the same way.

"You really think you stand a chance against me?" Mikhail smiled.

I did not like that smile, so I gave Connor a look that clearly said to shut up. "You promised to behave."

"I'm saving the last shreds of my politeness for Nemain." Connor shrugged before giving Mikhail a challenging look. "Almost drowned her, by the way. Kaysea had to save her ass. So, yeah, if I can take a shifter bitch, I'm not too worried about a vampire prick."

Fuck. I slid between my idiot mate and the terrifying vampire, whose smile had only gotten sharper. Then my magic clued me in on the other person I should have been concerned about.

I whirled around just in time to see Badb slide a dagger in between Connor's ribs and kick the backs of his legs. He let out a hiss of pain as he crashed to his knees. Badb moved with him and wrapped a clawed hand around his throat. The entire thing had taken less than two seconds, and now Connor was kneeling, his back pressed against Badb, who still had the dagger in him as blood leaked out from where her claws were digging into his skin.

"You might want to watch how you speak around us *shifter bitches*," she half growled. "Don't think I won't kill you and dump your corpse in some godsforsaken realm where it will never be found."

Fear clamped my heart. I didn't think Badb would actually kill him, but she and Mikhail seemed a little more kill-happy than normal, and that was saying something.

Please don't say anything stupid—or more stupid, I willed to Connor.

"I'm sorry," he ground out, and I released the breath I'd been holding. "It's been a shitty day, and I spoke without thinking. Nemain and I have settled things. She paid her blood debt. I would never actually harm her."

Now. That was the word he didn't say. He would never actually harm her *now*, because he had definitely tried to kill her previously and caused her harm.

Mikhail stared at him for a long moment before turning and walking back to the cliff, taking up his vigilance once more. Okay then. I glanced at Badb, who reluctantly released her hold on Connor's throat and pulled her dagger free.

He grunted and clamped a hand over the wound, waiting a few seconds for his healing to kick in. Finally, he rose slowly and bowed his head in Badb's direction. "Again, I apologize for my words. I meant no disrespect, Morrigan."

Those emerald eyes that were identical to Nemain's took his measure for a long moment before she snorted. "You always were a terrible prince." Then her gaze slid to me. "You did good in asking Kaysea to be your advisor—she at least understands how to play politics."

I thought about pointing out that Badb was also terrible when it came to politics and that she was exactly like Connor. She had a notoriously short fuse, which was why Kalen tended to handle all fae court business. The Morrigan was only called in when someone needed to die.

But everyone was calming down, so I kept my mouth shut.

"Come on." I held my hand out to Connor, and he intertwined his fingers in mine. Together, we walked towards Mikhail. He didn't say anything when I stopped next to him, Connor next to me, and Badb moving to stand at Mikhail's other side with Kalen next to her.

The four of us looked over the cliff to the valley fifty feet below. Strange tree-like structures grew out of the ground, yet no leaves adorned the pale grey, spindly appendages that stretched out from the thick trunks like bones. The branches all grew together, creating a nightmarish nest twenty feet above the ground.

Thanks to the lack of leaves though, I was able to see through the tangled mess to what held Mikhail's attention: Nemain, which wasn't a surprise, but I sucked in a harsh breath when I saw the dozen seraphim soldiers attacking her.

Their white wings were tucked in tight, useless down there thanks to the bone trees keeping them grounded. That did little to diminish their ruthless and vicious fighting skills though. These ones clearly worked in a unit, because their attacks on Nemain were well-coordinated, none of them getting in each other's ways as they tried to gut her with their swords or set her alight with their flames.

A chilling laugh echoed across the valley as Nemain dodged every sword strike and their orange fire met her shield of blue devourer flames before instantly vanishing. I quickly scanned the ground and saw several broken and bloody bodies strewn about. Nemain had been busy.

"She's getting better at using her flames as a shield," Badb noted.

"Still too slow sometimes," Kalen replied as he watched his daughter fight with a critical eye. "And she can only do the shield. She needs to learn how to make armor out of it so her back and opposite side are protected too."

"What happened?" I asked Mikhail, not taking my gaze off the death dance below us. Nemain had clearly needed to blow off some steam, and the fact that Mikhail was standing here tighter than a bowstring instead of down there helping her . . . meant it had been something bad. "Is Magos okay?"

I knew Artemis had placed a curse on him before we'd shown up. Every time he drank blood, he would lose a memory of his beloved wife, who had died centuries ago. As if that wasn't bad enough, the bitch had made sure his bloodlust would continue to rise, forcing him to choose between keeping his sanity or forgetting someone sacred to him.

The Olympians were cruel, petty assholes, and I was glad I'd gotten to gut one. He hadn't stayed dead, but at least I'd made him hurt.

I didn't know Magos all that well, more in passing than anything, but I knew he was important to Nemain and had rescued her when no one else had been able to. She couldn't stab a curse, couldn't set it on fire and burn it to ashes, and a curse from an Olympian was impossible to unravel.

Maybe murdering a bunch of seraphim was Nemain's idea of therapy.

"He's . . ." Mikhail paused, and I glanced at him, catching the way his jaw tightened. "My uncle is fine. It's Finn."

I felt Connor's gaze on me, and I met his concerned stare. Finn's fate was to bring about the end of the realms if he chose the path of darkness. According to the prophecy, the only person who could steer him towards a path of light was the one cackling maniacally beneath us while she cut apart seraphim and coated herself in blood.

"Shit," Mikhail swore before vanishing into mist. A moment later, he appeared behind Nemain, catching the sword that had been a second away from spearing her through the back. Another seraphim shot a bolt of flames directly at Mikhail's face, but Nemain's devourer flames were instantly there, gobbling it down. Instead of retreating back to her, the crystal blue flames attached themselves to Mikhail's forearm and spread out like a shield.

Interesting . . . I hadn't known she could share her magic like that.

"Do you know what happened?" I slid a glance at Badb. She tried to hide it, but I could see the hints of pain on her face as she watched her daughter take out her rage below.

"Finn hurt Elisa," she said softly.

Connor frowned. "He loves Elisa. Not only is she Bryn's girlfriend, but she dotes on both him and Isabeau."

"There was a falling out between Nemain and the two older vamp kids, Misha and Damon," Kalen said evenly. "They left, and Isabeau feels like they abandoned her. She's really upset by it."

"And if she's upset, Finn's upset." Connor sighed, and I gave him a curious look. He had clearly been keeping more tabs on Nemain and her circle than I'd thought. Then again, Kaysea had probably told him everything because that was just Kaysea's nature. She no doubt thought she could make Connor and Nemain friends eventually by sheer force of will.

"Elisa is playing peacekeeper," Kalen continued. "And the boys are trying to make Isabeau understand. They don't want to hurt her, but she refuses to speak to them. Elisa was trying to convince her to give them a chance to explain, and she started crying. Finn . . . overreacted."

"Is Elisa okay?" I asked. Vampires had excellent healing capabilities, but Finn was incredibly powerful. If he'd lashed out without thinking, he could have seriously injured Elisa.

Badb sighed. "She is now. He threw her out the window. It's unclear if he used air magic or if he solidified raw magic into something concrete and slammed that into her, but the end result was that Elisa crashed through the window from the third-floor apartment. She was impaled by multiple large shards of glass and then broke her back when she landed on the rocks below."

Holy shit.

"Only Elisa, Finn, and Isabeau were home at the time." Kalen swallowed. "Nemain got home hours later to find the three of them still on the rocky shoreline where Elisa had fallen. Finn had managed to heal her enough to keep her alive, but his control over his magic is tenuous. He was too freaked out to heal her fully."

"Bryn is away with Sigrun and Niall," he added, "which is only adding to Finn's stress levels, and now he's spiraling even more because he knows how much Elisa means to Bryn. He didn't mean to hurt her, and we've all tried to explain to him that Bryn won't be angry at him. Elisa is okay now, and she's not holding it against Finn."

"He's stopped talking to all of us." Badb's expression grew troubled. "Even Isabeau has been quiet."

"When did this happen?" It had to have been recent. Nemain probably would have called on Kaysea or Zareen to heal Elisa fully, and that's the type of thing Kaysea would have mentioned to me.

"Yesterday."

"So just to recap . . ." I rubbed my forehead. "Nemain is currently dealing with supporting her friend, who has been cursed by the gods. Which, in a roundabout way, only happened because she's being targeted for harboring an emotional fae kid with tenuous control over his insanely dangerous magic, who is wanted by the exiled fae king—a.k.a. his father. And she's also dealing with the warlocks and vampires; both of whom have a bone to pick with her. Did I get all that right?"

Badb thought about it. "Yes, that's accurate."

I looked at Connor. "We can't ask Nemain to help us. She's clearly got enough shit going on."

A scream tore out from the battle below, filled with so much frustration, pain, and rage that it made me take a step back. Mikhail appeared a second later, holding a hand to his stomach, where blood was slowly leaking out. Then a wall of blue flames shot up in a perfect cylindrical column and burned for several seconds before vanishing.

I held my hand out as frozen ashes fell from the sky—the remains of the seraphim and the bone tree forest.

Mikhail's vibrant, purplish-blue eyes met mine. "Nemain is ready to talk to you now."

<hr>

WE STOOD amongst the frozen ashes. Badb had opened a gateway to get us down to Nemain, who was still kneeling a short distance away, surrounded by the aftermath of the battle. Apparently, she needed a minute.

I squinted my eyes at Mikhail. "Did you purposely let yourself get stabbed just so Nemain would end the fight?"

He shrugged. "I thought finding some seraphim for her to slaughter would cheer her up, but it seemed to only piss her off more. Maybe whatever you've come to ask her help with will do a better job of taking her mind off things."

"And if it doesn't?"

Another shrug. "There's always someone who needs killing."

I pondered if there was a way to get group discounts on therapy sessions when Nemain finally rose. She strode towards us, a calm expression on her face, like we hadn't just watched her slaughter dozens of seraphim and then scream in rage as her magic chaotically exploded out of her.

Her emerald green eyes gave away her true mental state, ablaze with fury as she pointed a bloody sword at Mikhail.

"You let yourself get stabbed again, and I'll make you regret it."

"What are you going to do?" Mikhail grinned. "Bleed on me after I kick your ass?"

My gaze popped back and forth between the feline shifter and vampire, who were sizing each other up like they were thinking about going a round. Whether that round would be fighting or fucking, I had no idea. I wasn't entirely sure they did either.

"Is she threatening to stab him . . . for getting stabbed?" I whispered loudly as I gave Connor a wide-eyed look.

Connor mockingly whispered back, "Are you saying that logic doesn't check out?"

Nemain's head snapped towards me and Connor, her eyes darting back and forth between us. "Did Connor just make a joke?" She looked at Mikhail again. "Did I get hit on the head really hard or something? Is this a hallucination?"

"He's actually very funny," I told her.

Nemain stared at me. "Did *you* get hit on the head?"

"Nobody got hit on the head," Connor growled.

"Ah." Nemain nodded. "There's the grumpy fae prince we all know and love." Then she frowned. "Well, know and tolerate."

"Any reason you didn't just use your devourer flames to do this"—I gestured at the frozen ashes surrounding us—"in the first place?"

"I needed them to die screaming on my blade."

Okay then.

A few skeleton trees still stood, and my magic nudged me lightly, telling me to step beneath the one to my left. Weird, but whatever. I casually walked over to it like I was inspecting the trunk before turning to face Nemain again. "I need your help with something."

"Do I get to kill people?" she asked eagerly.

"Yes."

"Fantastic." She grinned—or tried to. It was really more of a baring of teeth.

"Huh." I chewed my lip for a moment. "Honestly, I thought you'd ask at least a few more questions before agreeing."

Nemain wiped her sword clean on Mikhail's black shirt, and he just rolled his eyes at her antics. "I mean, they brought you here"—she pointed her sword at her parents before sheathing it on her back—"and they always know everyone's business in the fae courts. It's annoying, really. So, clearly, they think whoever it is you're going after needs killing."

She checked her daggers that were strapped to her thighs when she found an empty sheath, and Mikhail vanished into mist before reappearing with the missing dagger in his hand. Nemain smiled at him like he'd just brought her a box of chocolates before taking the blade and sliding it into the sheath.

"But if it's someone in the fae courts," Nemain continued, "then it would be a little complicated for them to get involved, what with them belonging to the Unseelie Court and all, plus having that history with the Seelie Queen."

"Have you forgotten that you're the Unseelie Knight?" Connor arched a brow at Nemain. "You're just as tied up with the courts as they are."

"That bitch knew what she signed up for when she gave me the Knight title." Nemain shrugged.

"*That bitch* being the Unseelie Queen?" A grin tugged at Connor's mouth, and I could tell he was fighting it with every-thing he had, because gods fucking forbid he got along with Nemain for a minute.

"Yup," Nemain said with a pop. "I'm a bit of a loose cannon, which I think is just what the fae courts need. Shake things up a bit."

Kalen let his head fall back so he was gazing up at the sky. "You and your mother are going to be the death of me." Badb rubbed his back in comfort but didn't disagree.

"Maybe there is somewhere else we can go to talk over everything?" I eyed Kalen. He clearly knew what I wanted Nemain for, but he'd also helped bring us to the queens this morning, so I wasn't exactly sure how much I should trust him with our plans.

Catching my wary expression, the Erlking nodded before wrapping an arm around his mate. "We have business to attend to elsewhere."

Badb arched an eyebrow at him. "We do?"

"Yes." A wicked smile graced Kalen's lips. "We were interrupted this morning. I still owe you many things."

A laugh poured from Badb as a gateway opened behind them, revealing a castle surrounded by snowcapped mountains. She stepped through, tugging Kalen after her, and wrapped her arms around him. The two were still making out like a couple of lovestruck teenagers as the gateway closed, leaving us alone with Mikhail and Nemain.

"I honestly don't know what to make of those two," I murmured.

"Same," Connor grunted.

Nemain's expression had turned serious once more, a hint of uncertainty in her bright green eyes. "We can go to Hecate's to discuss things. She's been visiting Emerald Bay lately and rented a place just outside of town."

"Something wrong with your place?" I waved around to the half-burned-down trees. "Did it get the same treatment?"

"Do you want a preteen vampire girl to know all your secrets, Merfolk Queen?" Nemain asked tiredly. "Because there is no mind Isabeau can't waltz into."

I blanched. "Seriously?"

"Yeah," Nemain said with a sigh. "And my mind is a bit of

a mess right now. I need to get my thoughts sorted before I'm around her, because she might take something the wrong way."

"Aki should be there now." Mikhail tucked a loose strand of Nemain's ash-blonde hair behind her ear. "She'll be able to help."

"An empath only gets you so far." Nemain glanced up at the tree I stood beneath. "Even one as talented as Aki."

I vaguely remembered Kaysea mentioning a Kalari empath staying in Emerald Bay to help out Nemain's band of misfits. It made sense. The feline shifter was the reason the Kalari had their empathic magic back. And if anyone needed the help of an empath, it was that lot.

"Hecate's sounds great," I said, eager to get out of here. The place was giving me the creeps, not to mention there wasn't a drop of water anywhere near us.

"One small matter first." Nemain took a step back, her hand dropping to the dagger sheath at her thigh. "Pele asked me to test a theory next time I saw you."

Three things happened at once. My magic told me very firmly to stay where I was, a branch snapped, swinging down in front of me, close enough that I felt air whoosh over my skin, and Nemain's dagger flew through the air directly at my face—and thunked into the branch.

"You psychotic fucking bitch!" Connor snarled and leapt towards her, only for Mikhail to slide in between them, a sword with mist rolling off it in his hand.

"Well, shit." Nemain snorted. "Pele was right."

The branch finished snapping and fell to the ground before I reached down and pulled the dagger free, stepping around Connor's stare-off with Mikhail to pass it back to Nemain. "So you just threw a knife at my head because Pele told you to?"

"After all our centuries together, I mostly just do whatever Pele tells me to. It's easier, and I get rewarded for being a good shifter."

Mikhail chuckled, his sword vanishing, and stepped back to Nemain's side. "Be honest. It's her punishments you're trying to avoid."

"True," Nemain replied with a smile. "She is the queen of edging."

I knew Nemain and Pele had been in a casual relationship for centuries but hadn't been sure until now that they were still a thing with Mikhail in the picture.

"You threw a knife at my head," I repeated, the adrenaline that had been coursing through my veins wearing off enough for me to think. "You threw. A fucking knife. At my head."

"Sure did." Nemain slid the digger back into its sheath.

"What if it had killed me?" My voice took on a higher pitch, and I was starting to really appreciate Connor's opinion of Nemain being a psychopath.

And where the fuck were you? I yelled internally at my magic, because apparently Nemain had finally managed to drive me insane and I was treating it like it was capable of speaking and defending its actions. *A bit of warning would have been nice!*

Briefly, my magic churned inside me as if it could feel my irritation, but it wasn't actually sentient, so it wasn't like it could respond. Whether it hadn't warned me because it had always been inconsistent about Nemain thanks to her devourer heritage, or because it knew there wasn't truly a threat was anyone's guess.

"I mean, you probably would have been fine. It's not like I'd actually cut your head off." Nemain shrugged. "And Pele was pretty certain you had premonition magic that helps you always be in the right place at the right time. You randomly moved to stand under that tree earlier."

"That was your reasoning?" Connor snarled, and I wholeheartedly agreed with him. I doubted Pele had explicitly suggested that Nemain throw a knife at my head to prove her theory, but she'd known Nemain for centuries. She'd likely phrased things in such a way to spur Nemain on for her own amusement. By the glint in Mikhail's eye, I suspected he was going to be recounting this to Pele in great detail.

Freaking daemon.

"She's fine." Nemain waved at me. "Not even a hair out of place."

"You could have killed her!"

"Bit of an exaggeration," Mikhail drawled.

"I could have been pissed off enough to bring my complaints about the Unseelie Knight attacking me to the fae queens," I pointed out. Granted, with my current status, it wasn't like they would have cared, but Nemain didn't know all the details. "After healing from being stabbed in the fucking head!"

"Oh, then I would have definitely killed you." Nemain grinned.

Mikhail shrugged. "Can't complain if you're dead."

Chapter Fourteen

Connor was still pissy about the whole dagger-to-the-face test when we all took a seat in Hecate's garden a few minutes later. The ancient goddess was nowhere to be seen, but her magic was everywhere. Soft grass covered the ground, and tall walls of shrubs with dark purple flowers bloomed on all sides of us. I couldn't see the ocean but could smell the salt in the air and hear the waves crashing nearby. We must have been in the backyard behind her house.

The four of us sat in the center of the peaceful place, half barrels of herbs and brightly colored flowers decorating the space around us. Nemain had made it sound like this setup was new for Hecate, but she certainly hadn't wasted any time settling in. Emerald Bay was rapidly becoming a place of power in the human realm.

"I recommend not touching anything," Nemain said lightly. "Eddie got curious about those pink flowers"—she pointed to a barrel to my right—"and Vizor dared him to touch them."

"He babbled nonsense for two days and then passed out for another three." Amusement danced in Mikhail's dark eyes. "Someone has been leaving harmless pink flowers at his shop ever since. Eddie thinks it's Vizor, but I'm pretty sure it's Cerri."

"Or Lynette," Nemain mused. "She's the hidden troublemaker."

"Don't touch the flowers." I placed my hands in my lap. "Got it."

"So, who are we killing, Ashling?" Nemain took her swords out and placed them on the table between us so she could lean back in the chair. "Give us all the juicy details."

I laid everything out for them. Maeve and her inner circle. Their partnership with Syndra and the dofheicthe snooping around. My bloodline and getting kicked out of the fae queens' palace. And the fact that we had less than forty-eight hours to prevent Balor from returning and ending the realms as we knew them.

When I finished, I raised my hands and made a sweeping gesture. "So there you have it. Thoughts?"

Nemain stared at me for a long moment before her eyes drifted to Connor and back to me. Then her brows furrowed before she crossed her arms. "This is such bullshit. Why didn't I get this prophecy? I'm really good at killing people! But instead, I get the one about saving Finn and keeping him off the dark path. This is so unfair."

"My heart bleeds for you." I said dryly.

"I know you're playing fast and loose with the rules," Connor cut in, "but if the Unseelie Court learns that you helped us with this, Elvinia will be forced to punish you. She might decide to ignore your involvement if it's not widely known, but she can't allow you to flaunt your disobedience all the time. Definitely not for this."

"I can be subtle." Three pairs of eyes stared at the feline shifter covered in blood, and Nemain rolled her eyes before waving a hand at Mikhail. "He can be subtle and I'll do my best."

Mikhail smiled. "I'll keep her on task, but you said they all must die or none of this matters, correct?"

"Yes." I nodded. "So we'll either need to wait until they're all gathered in the same place, or we'll need to coordinate our attacks. We absolutely cannot afford for one of them to slip away."

Nemain rose from her chair and held a hand out to Mikhail. "Care to take a stroll around the queens' palace with me?"

He slipped his hand into hers and rose. "Sure."

"Don't do anything without us," I warned, already thinking about all the ways this could go horribly wrong.

"Just getting the lay of the land. I promise." Nemain slid her swords back into the sheaths across her back. "We need to figure out where Maeve and her friends are hanging out. They're likely lying low since they're waiting for the ceremony tomorrow. Taking them out quietly in the palace will be difficult. Maeve and Coireall are particularly nasty in a fight."

"Shouldn't you change first?" Connor looked pointedly at Nemain's torn and blood-soaked clothing.

"Nah." She grinned wide enough to show off her fangs. "The more unhinged and stab-happy the fae think I am, the better. Keeps them off my back."

"You are unhinged and stab-happy," Connor said, once again looking like he was fighting off a smile.

"I know." She winked at him, then she and Mikhail stepped through a gateway and vanished.

"Still not sure if this is the best or worst plan," I admitted.

"What's your magic say?"

"Not much. I think it's scared of Nemain," I muttered before closing my eyes and taking several deep, even breaths. After a minute, I opened them again and met Connor's questioning stare. "It's a little murky, which isn't unusual when it comes to anyone who has devourer blood, but no bright, flashing warning signs that we're about to die or anything."

"Wonderful," he said dryly. "So wait here then until they get back?"

"Yeah." I rubbed my stomach. "Maybe we can find some food since we were robbed of breakfast."

"Kaysea's probably in town. I would kill for one of Zareen's chocolate croissants right now." He looked around the garden. "There's got to be a door around here somewhere. Hecate probably has a mirror or phone inside we can contact her with."

"Plotting over pastries. You do still remember the way to my heart," I replied with a smirk.

Connor gave me a small smile. "I never forgot it."

My heart skipped a beat as he gave up searching for a way out of this fantastical garden and closed the distance between us. I watched as he gently grasped my hands and held them out so he could look at my wrists, which still bore some faint markings from the silver chains that had been wrapped around them in the queens' throne room.

"They don't hurt," I assured him. "The marks are fading fast and should be gone within the hour."

"I don't remember the last time I was that scared." He continued to stare at my wrists as he lightly grazed the marks with his thumb. "You were right there—mere feet from me—and I couldn't do anything to save you."

"Hey," I said softly, pulling one hand away from his to cup his cheek. "It's okay. We're going to survive this, and then we'll deal with the fae queens."

"Is your magic telling you that?" He turned his head to kiss my palm, and I stepped closer to him until I was leaning into his chest. Connor pulled my hand away and tucked it against his heart, his other arm wrapping around my waist and holding me close.

"I don't need my magic to tell me that." I closed my eyes and breathed in his scent. "You are mine, Connor, and I'll kill whoever I must to make sure we get a chance."

"Likewise, love." He kissed the top of my head, and I felt the mate bond between us start to rise. *Not yet*, I told it, shoving it back down. Continuing to deny the mate bond hurt, but we were so damn close. Once Nemain and Mikhail returned, we'd plan how to take out Maeve and the others, then I'd finally be free of that damn fate.

Free to actually fix things between Connor and me. To claim my fated mate.

I just needed a little more time.

The wall of greenery to our left parted, and Hecate strode through the newly formed archway. I frowned as I looked over her shoulder and saw smooth tile and an ornate railing on the other side of the shrubbery wall. The sound of crashing waves became stronger too . . . from beneath us.

This wasn't a backyard. Fear and panic clenched my heart so hard, I thought it would stop beating. We were on a rooftop.

"No having sex in my garden," Hecate said with a laugh as her hounds guided her over to one of the chairs. "I know how fae mates are in the early days, and I already gave Mikhail and Nemain the same warning. My garden is for *my* peace and enjoyment, so you'll have to find somewhere else to indulge each other's company."

Connor's body, which had been so warm and inviting under my touch a second ago, went completely rigid. Then, slowly, he dropped his arm from around my waist and took a step back to look at the witch goddess. "What did you say?"

"I can explain—"

"No." He cut me off with a betrayed look before turning back to Hecate. "What did you call us?"

The bemused expression drained from her face, and sensing the tension in the air, one of the hounds let out a low whine before resting his large head on Hecate's knee. "Perhaps I misspoke." Her brows furrowed together as she absently patted the dog's head. "It happens at my age."

"I don't think it does," Connor said as his accusatory gaze fell on me. "Are you my mate?"

This couldn't be happening. I took a step towards him and began to plead. "Just let me—"

"Are you my mate?" He bit out the words so coldly that I halted in my tracks.

"Yes," I said in a broken voice I barely recognized. It felt like the world was crumbling around me and there was no chance of me picking up the pieces this time.

"Have you always known?"

I squeezed my eyes shut and spoke the word that would damn me. "Yes."

A boom sounded as the waves crashed harder below, and my eyes flew open as I felt the spray of water. Hecate's hounds growled and rose to stand protectively around their mistress.

Connor's wintery stare drifted over to them, and his jaw tightened. "Apologies, Hecate. I mean you no harm, and I appreciate you speaking the truth."

"Perhaps the two of you should discuss this"—another wave slammed into the building, and this time, I felt it shake before droplets of seawater fell over us like rainfall—"somewhere else."

"What the Merfolk Queen does is not my concern."

"Connor—"

"I'll still help you. For the sake of the realms," he said tightly. "But I told you *no more lies*. And not only did you keep this from me, but you smiled in my face while you did it. We're done. Nemain can find me when she returns."

He turned on his heel and strode out through the archway that Hecate had come through. I raced after him. As soon as I passed through, I saw the reason the house had been shaking so much. I'd assumed Hecate's home had been built near the water, when, in fact, it'd been built over it.

The coastline jutted out on either side of the structure, forming a cove. But we were well past that. At least part of the house and this balcony extended over the water. It reminded me of the floating palace Artemis and the other Olympians called home.

Most of the time, the waves were probably gentle and rolling, but Connor's temper had gotten them riled up. I pushed my magic out, doing my best to counteract his impact on the tides.

I might be pissed off at Hecate for throwing those words out so casually, but I didn't want her damn house to get knocked down. Besides, this was all my fault. The witch had only spoken the truth I'd been too scared to say.

"Please!" I grabbed Connor's arm just as he was about to jump over the guardrail into the water below. "I love you! I have always loved you. Just let me explain!"

He whirled around to face me, and I hated that the pain and fury in his eyes was there because of me. "I asked you point-blank if there was anything else you needed to tell me. After I told you that I couldn't handle any more lies between us." His voice cracked with pain, and I felt it like a knife to the heart. "You said *no*." He looked down to where my fingers still gripped his arm before raising his gaze once more. "I felt it sometimes. This thread between us." A cold laugh spilled from his lips. "Thought I was going crazy because it would disappear almost as suddenly as I felt it. Then I would think that maybe it was just wishful thinking on my end."

A pained noise slipped from my lips when he tugged his arm free, but he didn't move away from me. I could still fix this. He hadn't walked away from me yet, which meant there was still a chance.

"Most of the visions I get are fragments." I clasped my

hands together to stop myself from reaching out to him again. "When I was twenty-five, I got a small one of me floating in the water. Nothing else. Just me floating and the sense that someone was there with me. Someone important."

Connor's pale eyes watched me, but he didn't interrupt or walk away, so I quickly plowed on.

"Years later, I got a little more: a starry night sky, then a laugh." I closed my eyes and smiled. "A laugh that lit up my soul. Those little glimpses were the only joy I had for many years. My life consisted of doing what my mother bade. To ensure that I would have the political power one day to take the merfolk throne. She only cared about me exacting vengeance against the fae queens. I never told her about the vision of Balor's return. I think some part of me knew that she might welcome it—if only because it would guarantee the deaths of the queens who had nearly exterminated our bloodline."

Slowly, I opened my eyes but kept them on my clasped hands. "The day I met you, I knew two things." My throat went dry, and I had to swallow a few times before I was able to speak again. "You were the one floating in the water with me, looking up at the stars—my fated mate . . . and I saw this moment." Finally, I raised my gaze to meet his stoic expression. "I saw us standing on a rooftop, you enraged and me pouring out my heart to you."

"What happened?" he asked in a flat, emotionless tone.

"I don't know," I rasped. "That's where the vision always ends."

"All these years." He shook his head before taking a step away from me, and something cracked inside my chest. "You knew I was your mate and lied to me about it. Was it because I didn't want the throne? Was I good enough to fuck but not be your mate?"

"No!" I screamed, my fingernails biting into my skin and

drawing blood. "I needed the power of the throne if I wanted to keep Balor from returning. My magic never wavered in steering me towards that path. You made it abundantly clear you wanted nothing to do with the throne. What the fuck was I supposed to do, Connor?" I threw my bloodied hands up. "You fucking tell me how I was supposed to choose between the fate of the realms and what I wanted! Which was you! It has always been you!"

"You could have been honest with me!" he snarled back. "I grew up in a sea of lies because everyone always wanted something from me. It was one of the many things I hated about being prince and why there are so few people I trust, but I did trust you, and if you had told me all this from the start, I would have chosen you. My hatred of the crown be damned, I would have fucking chosen you."

"And now?" My eyes burned as tears overflowed. The pain I'd felt in the visions of this moment were a pale echo compared to the real thing. Dying would have been less painful. "What do you choose now?"

"You made the choice for me when you decided to keep lying." He took another step away. "Now you get to find out how your vision ends."

A strangled sob ripped free of my throat as Connor leapt over the railing. On shaky legs, I stumbled forward and stared into the dark blue waters below, but instead of raging waves, there was only the steady pull of the tide rushing in and out.

The mate bond within me flared to life . . . and then fell apart, the pieces carried out onto the retreating tides and vanishing along with my mate.

Chapter Fifteen

THUNK. My dagger sank into the driftwood, and I stared numbly at it. The wood was chipped up from all my previous throws, but I found I wasn't interested in getting up again to retrieve the blade. After Connor had left, Hecate had come out and murmured her apologies. Apparently, she was incredibly sensitive to newly forming magic because it gave off a particular feeling. One of vast potential. To her, our mate bond had been so obvious, she'd just assumed everyone knew about it.

I'd been emotionally tapped out at that point, so I couldn't even rustle up any angry words for her. This was on me. I'd fucked up.

She'd promised to wait for Nemain and Mikhail's return so I could clear my head. While my heart might have been shredded and my will to do anything was at an all-time low, that didn't mean I got to take a break and bow out of the impending apocalypse.

"Being queen fucking sucks."

"So does being the weirdo vampire."

"What the fuck?" I leapt to my feet as my heart pounded inside my chest and looked at the wooden gazebo, whose stairs

I'd been sitting on. Apparently, despite my mental state, I was still capable of having the shit scared out of me. "Who's there?"

Between one blink and the next, a little girl appeared, standing at the top of the gazebo so she was eye level with me. It took a second to recognize her because I'd only met her once in passing when she'd been over at Kaysea and Zareen's place.

"Isabeau?" I stared at the young vampire girl. Her face was red and puffy as if she'd been crying a lot. "What are you doing here?" A cursory look up and down the beach told me nobody else was here. At least no one I could see. How the fuck had she done that? I hadn't sensed or seen any magic . . . and my own magic hadn't given me any hints to her presence either. Vampires had a lot of devourer blood in their veins, that might have been why. And Isabeau came from an Apex bloodline, so she was particularly strong . . .

Nemain's words floated through my mind just then. *"There is no mind Isabeau can't waltz into."*

Oh shit. Could she see everything in my head right now? I'd know, right? If she was in my head right now, I'd be able to feel it. Nobody was that powerful. To just drift through another person's mind without leaving some kind of—

I am.

"Fuck." She was a kid, so I shouldn't have been swearing in front of her, but fuck me, this was bad. Shit, was swearing in my head not as bad as saying it out loud? Also, why the fuck was I concerned about swearing when this kid could take a front-row seat to all the people I'd killed over the years. My memories would traumatize her.

They won't. You should see the fucked-up shit in Nemain's head. She smirked. *Honestly, I'd rather see that than the mushy stuff in Bryn's head about Elisa.*

"All the same," I said slowly, "how about maybe we don't swear and we talk out loud, okay?"

"So we can pretend I'm not the freak I really am?" She nodded, sending her curls bouncing. "Got it."

"That's not—" I sighed and rubbed my forehead. "Look, kid, you've been in my mind, you know I've had a shi—not so great day. I'm not as talented as you, and using telepathy—especially when I'm rocking legs and not a tail—is exhausting."

"You don't have to do anything though." Her dark eyebrows bunched together. "It's easy enough to pluck the thoughts from your mind and drop others in there."

"It's the principle of it. Also, why am I arguing with you?" I threw my hands up. "How old are you anyway?"

"Just turned nine." She raised her chin defiantly, but given how puffy her eyes were, it didn't quite have the impact she was going for.

"Great. Why are you here? And how did you do the invisible thing?"

"Shouldn't you be able to use your fancy magic to suss that out?" She squinted at me.

Fuck it. I summoned a stream of water from where the cove curled around the bend so she couldn't see it and dumped it on the girl. She shrieked and leapt down the stairs, sliding past me as she flung water everywhere. Apparently, if you kept your thoughts vague enough and just went for general vibes, she couldn't decipher your intentions.

"Co-co-cold!" she wailed as she tugged at her soaked sweatshirt. I rolled my eyes and flicked my fingers, summoning all the water back until her clothes were bone-dry again, then a ball of water spun next to me as a lingering threat.

Because that's what my life was now. Sitting on a beach with a mind-reading vampire kid who had boundary issues and threatening to soak her with cold seawater while waiting for my psychotic friends to return so we could kill a bunch of bad guys.

"Isabeau, I'm tired." I sank back onto the gazebo steps and

lowered the ball of water to the ground before releasing my hold on it. "And I'm not good with kids at the best of times. So how about you tell me what in all the hells you're doing here by yourself? And how exactly you're able to pull off being completely invisible?"

She glowered at me for a moment, her bottom lip jutting out in a pout, before she slumped on the stairs next to me. "I wasn't invisible," she said sullenly. "I just told your mind not to see me."

"That's it?" My eyebrows shot up.

"I'm still figuring out how it works." She shrugged. "It's harder to do in the apartment because people expect me to be there and they're looking for me. I have to concentrate more. So far, it has never worked on Nemain or Mikhail. I don't know how, but they always know. It used to never work on Magos . . . but he's been distracted lately."

"Interesting." I narrowed my eyes at her. "Did you use this ability to sneak out of the apartment and come here?"

There was zero chance they had let her wander around alone, and given what I knew about her and Finn, I was surprised the fae boy wasn't here.

She looked away from me to stare at the sand in front of her feet. Suddenly, she looked so much older than nine years old. "I'm not good for Finn," she said quietly. "He's my best friend—I only want to help him, but he hurt Elisa bad the other day because of me. And sometimes . . ." She bit her lip. "Sometimes he thinks really mean things about Damon and Misha. I'm mad at them and I don't want to see them, but I don't want them hurt either."

"So what?" I cocked my head at her. "Your plan is to run away?"

"Just create a little distance," she half growled. "Give Finn a break for a while so he can calm down. I heard Elisa talking to Nemain the other day. The Vampire Council is interested in me again because of what I did to Katrina." Cunning brown eyes that had no place on such a young kid looked at me. "My presence is a danger to everyone. There's a gateway to the merfolk realm over there." She pointed to a spot not far from the shore. "I could make that swim, and from what I gleaned from Kaysea's mind, there's an island on the other side."

"I have a very strict no-runaway-vampires rule in my realm," I said seriously.

Isabeau looked at me for a long moment. "You're making that up."

"No." I smiled at her. "I'm declaring it a rule as of now."

"I'll find somewhere else to go," she said defiantly. "I'm pretty sure I can sneak into The Inferno. Pele is hard to get past, but she's hardly there anymore. Spends most of her time in the daemon realm these days."

"Okay." I nodded. "Talk your plan through with me. Say you manage to sneak into her office where the gateway is—I think you might find using your illusion magic around the lokis a bit tricky, by the way—how will you activate the gateway? Have you ever used one before?"

I doubted she had. Why use a daemon or fae gateway when you had Nemain? Your own personal chauffeur across all the realms.

"No," she said slowly, her eyebrows furrowing together as she thought about it, then she crossed her arms and shot me yet another look of defiance. "I can figure it out."

"May we all have the confidence of a nine-year-old Apex vampire," I muttered. "Your plan needs work, kid."

"So does yours!" she snapped back.

"Rude."

Two figures rushing down the beach caught my attention, and in an instant, I stood between them and the girl.

As soon as I recognized the one on the left, I relaxed and gave Isabeau a knowing look. "You're in trouble now."

She looked around me and saw Elisa storming our way, and a bunch of colorful expletives erupted from her mouth.

"Language!" Elisa yelled. They were still a ways off, but vampire hearing was a hell of a thing.

"Who's the person with your sister?" I asked.

Isabeau sighed. "Aki. She's a Kalari and Damon's sort of girlfriend."

Ah. The strong empath Nemain had mentioned before. Good. Between her and Elisa, they should be able to handle Isabeau, because I sure as fuck had no idea what to do here.

The vampire devil child in question glanced up at me. "Do you really think the lokis would see through my illusion?"

I thought about it. "Honestly, I'm not sure. I wasn't able to detect you at all. You said it's harder when people are expecting you to be there—they wouldn't be counting on you strolling into The Inferno, so you'd have that advantage. But the lokis are also so good at crafting illusions that their magic might be able to sense yours."

"Hmm," she hummed as she tapped a finger against her lip. "I wonder if I'm part loki?"

Elisa and Aki were almost to us. "Nemain is very familiar with the lokis. If she thought that's what you were, I'm sure she would have told you."

"I guess." Isabeau let out another put-upon sigh. "Elisa is going to be so mad at me."

"Time to face the music," I agreed with her.

Once again, those sharp eyes fell on me. "Is that what you're going to do with Connor?"

"You're kind of a little shit. You know that, right?"

"Nemain tells me that regularly."

Somehow, that didn't surprise me in the least.

"Isabeau!" Elisa snarled, and her blue eyes flashed with anger. "I have been looking everywhere for you!"

"How'd you know I was here?" Isabeau leapt up from the

stairs and planted her hands on her hips, and my heart clenched when a flash of green scales caught my attention just off the shore. Connor.

Either he'd also come to this cove to seek solace, or he had followed me here because, despite his rage at me, I was still the Merfolk Queen and these were dangerous times. Something told me it was the latter. He was protective of those he loved, and I knew he still loved me, even if he had chosen to walk away from it.

From me.

"How I found you doesn't matter," Elisa snapped back. "The point is that you shouldn't have left in the first place!"

Isabeau squared off against the older vampire before glaring over her shoulder at me. "Your mate is a snitch! And snitches get stitches!"

"You can't say things like that to the Merfolk Queen!" Elisa gaped at Isabeau before sending me an apologetic look. "I'm so sorry, Queen Ashling. Thank you for watching over her."

"It's fine." I rose from the seat to stand next to Isabeau and ruffled her hair. She snapped her fangs at me, and I thought Elisa might pass out. "She's better company than most fae."

Aki snickered, then her eyes widened at something over my shoulder before she angled her body to block Isabeau's view of the very naked merfolk male walking out of the water. I knew she was looking at Connor because, even with our broken mate bond, I could still feel him. His magic was so strong and he was still pissed off, making the air feel charged.

"There are clothes in the gazebo," I said lightly, not turning to face him.

"I know," he replied in an equally light but tense tone.

Elisa knelt in front of Isabeau, not caring about getting sand all over her well-tailored dark suit. "Why did you come here, sweetie? I told you I'm not mad about what happened the other day. Kaysea healed me up. I feel fine, and I don't blame Finn or you in any way."

"You should though." Isabeau sniffled, the defiant girl from a minute ago nowhere to be seen. "Finn was upset because of me. I'm making everything worse."

"You're not." Elisa shook her head. "Nobody thinks tha—"

"Nemain is scared of me!" Isabeau blurted out. All of us looked at her in confusion, including Connor, who had found a pair of loose-fitting pants and was standing a healthy distance away from me. "She rescued us all those years ago. We live in her house, and she's responsible for Finn! I can't be there if she feels that way. I'll mess everything up for all of you!"

"There is zero chance that Nemain is frightened of you," Elisa said calmly. "The only thing that scares Nemain is running out of hot water."

"And giant worms," Aki offered. I looked at the Kalari, and she shrugged. "Long story."

"She is!" Isabeau screamed and pointed at her head. "I hear everything! She is terrified!"

"Foolish child." Aki's kind eyes fell on the girl. "You hear, but you don't listen. She isn't scared of you, she's scared for you because Nemain knows better than anyone what it's like to be viewed as a monster."

"And you are a monster, Bo." Elisa brushed away the weeping girl's tears. "You can spin illusions of our darkest thoughts and entrap us within them, no secret is safe from you, and you haven't even begun to come into your power. You are a creature of nightmares." A beautiful wolf smile stretched across Elisa's face. "I claimed you as my sister all those years ago, and I have never once doubted you. I fucking love you, kid. Always and forever."

"Language," Isabeau sobbed as she threw her arms around Elisa.

"Damon and Misha love you too," Aki added, leaning

down to pat the girl's back. "Family is complicated. Sometimes the people we love are the ones we hurt most, but luckily for us, they're also the ones most likely to forgive us for our fuckups."

I couldn't help but glance at Connor, though he kept his eyes on Elisa and Isabeau, so I couldn't tell if Aki's words had impacted him at all.

As I debated what I could possibly say to him, a shimmer formed in the air next to us and a gateway opened, revealing Nemain and Mikhail. They stepped through, and it closed behind them.

"We're gone for a couple of hours and come back to you two mated"—she waved a hand between me and Connor before gesturing towards Isabeau detangling herself from Elisa's hug—"and whatever the hell this is?"

"Just going for a walk on the beach," Elisa said smoothly as she rose, slipping her hand into Isabeau's. "Ashling was kind enough to keep us company."

"Right," Nemain drawled, clearly not believing there wasn't more to this story but apparently willing to let it drop for now. Her green eyes glanced between Connor and me. "So the mate thing isn't going well, I take it?"

"Drop it." Connor gave Nemain a warning look.

"Extra grumpy Connor," Nemain replied with a sigh. "Great."

"Is this going to be a problem?" Mikhail eyed Connor like he was the wounded animal in a herd. "Because I can think of a solution."

"Still can't kill him." Nemain bumped her shoulder against Mikhail's. "Kaysea would be sad."

"Zareen could distract her."

"Did you learn anything useful?" I asked to steer the conversation away from Connor's untimely demise.

"Good news, bad news." Nemain frowned. "And worse news."

I rubbed my forehead. "Give me the good news first. I need something positive right now."

"I really pissed off Lughán." She grinned, clearly proud of herself. I waited for more information, but she didn't say anything else.

"How exactly is that good news?" I ground out.

"Because I'm positive I'll be able to lure him away tonight and Aoife will no doubt follow him. So that's two out of the five who will be easy targets." Then her grin slipped a little. "The bad news is that all the courts will be in the meadows behind the palace tonight. There is a meteor shower taking place, so the party is being held there."

"Which means everything is out in the open. Very little in ways of cover," Mikhail said. "Aside from a few random trees and boulders, everything is visible for miles."

"Is that the bad news or the worse news?" I asked, even though I wasn't sure what could be worse than that.

"The queens have publicly announced your banishment from their realms." Nemain at least had the grace to wince a little at that. "If anyone sees you, you'll be immediately detained."

"Or killed," Mikhail added helpfully.

Connor growled, and everyone but me eyed him curiously. On one hand, the fact that the idea of my death angered him gave me a little hope about us, but I knew that feeling would be immediately crushed if I looked at him only to find anger and betrayal still in his eyes.

I mulled over our limited options. If we waited until tomorrow and tried to attack in the morning or midday, we risked not getting any viable opportunities, leaving us only with the ceremony. It would be even harder to take them out there because Maeve would no doubt choose to stand close to the queens. Even if we somehow managed to lure her away, the queens would notice her absence at such an event, given that I'd told them about her plot.

There was also the fact that my magic was strongly pushing me towards tonight. "Did you see the dofheicthe anywhere?" I asked.

"No." Nemain shook her head. "But I felt him. If he's there tonight, I'll at least be able to sense his presence."

"If you can get Aoife and Lughán to follow you," I said slowly, "I can probably get Maeve to come after me. Just seeing me might be enough. If it isn't, my magic can give me pointers to separate her from the queens and the rest of the court. Coireall and Rowan have been sticking close to her side all week. If I can get Maeve, I'll get them."

"Still leaves us with the problem of being in the middle of a wide-open field," Connor grunted. "Maeve and the others won't go down easily, even with the four of us working together."

"We need a way to hide in plain sight." My gaze fell upon Isabeau, who was sitting on the gazebo steps with Aki and Elisa, the three of them listening to our plotting with rapt attention. Magic zipped through me, making it quite clear that I was on the right path. I glanced at Nemain. "What exactly are your feelings about child endangerment?"

Chapter Sixteen

"THEY'RE ARRIVING," I murmured as several groups of Tuatha walked through the gate that led to the palace and out into the meadow. Nemain had opened a gateway directly behind a large tree that she had scoped out earlier, so between the broad trunk and how far we were from where the fae were currently gathering, we had little risk of being spotted.

Isabeau had confessed that she had used her magic to hide Finn before, much to Elisa's annoyance, so we knew she was capable of extending the illusion to cover us. Though, after some practice, we discovered it was taxing on the young vampire girl, which meant we needed to conserve Isabeau's magic. She struggled a little more concealing sound and couldn't do anything about scent or physical touch. The fact that she could do anything at all was still truly shocking.

Nemain was confident she could lure Lughán and Aoife over to us. Hopefully we could take them out quickly and quietly before figuring out how to get the other three and dealing with the dofheicthe if and when he showed up. All while making sure the queens had no idea we were here.

Oddly, I didn't feel nervous despite how many ways this

could go wrong. I'd been waiting my entire life for this moment, and now that it was here . . . I felt exhilarated. We would pull this off, damn it, and then I'd have an entire life to live without this fucking vision hanging over my head.

An entire lifetime to fix things with Connor, because Aki was right. Nobody could hurt us like the people we loved, but they could also heal us. He still loved me—I felt it in my soul. I would figure out a way to win him back.

I breathed in the crisp night air and let myself sink a little further into my magic. Not quite as much as I had the night when I'd fully embraced it while I'd snuck my way through the crowded palace halls, but enough that I was in tune with any hints or nudges it sent my way. I had a feeling I would need them tonight.

"Pretty," Isabeau whispered from where she was standing on her tippy-toes to look at the meadow. The willow tree towered far into the night sky, long tendrils of deep purple and blue leaves extending down from its branches, stopping only a few feet above our heads, and the tree's roots rose above the ground and stretched outward quite a ways. We were behind one of the tallest roots, which was about four feet tall, so while Isabeau could barely see over it, we had to crouch.

"Here." Mikhail picked the girl up by the waist and raised her over his bent knee. Her feet landed on his thigh as she peered out over the root at the gorgeous landscape before us. The meadow had a wild and chaotic beauty to it. In the places where the fae were beginning to congregate, short yet thick grass of deep green grew, and tables had been set up here and there with food and drink for the partygoers. Large patches of wildflowers grew in random patterns, giving the sprites and other small fae dancing amongst the orange and red blossoms a faint glow.

The large black wolf behind us shuffled uneasily. Elisa hadn't been thrilled about bringing Isabeau in on this plan, and I couldn't say I blamed her, but Isabeau's illusion magic significantly increased our chances of pulling this off. To ease some of Elisa's concerns, I'd taken a blood oath before coming here that I would place Isabeau's life above everything else. If I had to make a choice between saving the girl and killing Maeve, I'd choose the girl.

This had mollified Elisa somewhat, but she'd still insisted on coming. Nemain had agreed but told her to shift to her wolf form because, much to the feline shifter's annoyance, Elisa had taken more interest in studying politics under Pele's tutelage than sparring in the ring. She was stronger than most vampires and incredibly fast, but she possessed no other magic and wasn't great at wielding a blade, so her wolf form was deadlier than her vampire one.

"Still no sign of the queens or Maeve and her asshole friends." Nemain's sharp eyes looked over the growing crowd of sidhe. "The meteor shower starts in ten minutes though, so it shouldn't be much longer."

"The queens will likely arrive just as it starts," Connor said. "They like a dramatic entrance."

Nemain snorted. "I'm aware."

"We'll give it a few more minutes, then Nemain and I should go mingle so we're ready to intercept Lughán and Aoife when they arrive." Mikhail lifted Isabeau off his leg and set her down, looking into her eyes. "You and Elisa should get settled. Queen Ashling will tell you when we need the illusion to start." He pointed a warning finger at the girl. "Remember, you are to stay put and give us a warning if holding the illusion becomes too much. Do not hurt yourself."

Isabeau rolled her eyes, not the least bit impressed by the big bad vampire assassin. "Yes, Dad."

Nemain and I snickered as Mikhail paled. Even Connor brushed a hand over his mouth like he was hiding a smile.

Of course, Nemain had to ruin the moment by opening

her big mouth and cocking her head at Connor. "So are you really going to deny the whole mate thing just because she didn't tell you right away? I mean, I didn't tell Mikhail and he wasn't all pissy about it."

"I was a little pissed," Mikhail mumbled, still perturbed by Isabeau's comment.

"Not your business." Connor gave Nemain a sharp look. "And definitely not the time."

"Disagree." Nemain grinned, and I resisted the urge to strangle her. Connor was right—this was not the time or place for this conversation, and I had no doubt that anything she said would hinder me further. All she'd likely do was enrage Connor more.

Nemain, Elisa pushed out in her raspy, telepathic voice. *Don't meddle.*

"Oh please." Nemain glanced over her shoulder at the wolf. "You're nosier than I am. Don't act like you're not curious about their relationship drama."

Elisa swished her tail back and forth but didn't disagree.

"We're about to face off against five incredibly lethal sidhe and probably a devourer fae if the dofheicthe shows up," Nemain continued. "I'm just saying, you might want to have your affairs in order before then."

"That is actually a good point," Mikhail said lightly.

"Thank you, vampire." Nemain grinned at him.

"You're welcome, shifter." He smiled back at her.

"Really wish you two had killed each other instead of whatever this is," Connor grumbled.

"They're here," I interrupted, pointing at where Maeve and her inner circle strode out into the meadow like they owned it. Nemain and Mikhail instantly zeroed in on them, all teasing forgotten.

"Showtime." Nemain hopped over the root, Mikhail following after her, then they walked a few feet away before she stopped and wrapped her arms around his neck and grinned wickedly. "Ready to piss off some snobby fae assholes?"

"Always." He kissed her deeply, and I felt a pang at how easy their love was. I knew enough from Kaysea's gossiping that it had taken them a while to get here, but they'd made it. Connor shifted uneasily next to me, and when I looked at him, I found his gaze on me—frustration seemingly warring with desire in his eyes. I felt a faint pull of the mate bond, as if it was struggling to come back, then a soft moan caused us both to jerk our heads back to Nemain and Mikhail.

Another sound of pleasure slipped from Nemain as Mikhail fed from her neck. I'd never been bitten by a vampire, but apparently, it felt really good.

"Damn," I muttered. "Maybe I've been missing out on the whole vampire thing."

"Don't even think about it," Connor said tightly.

I slid a glance at him. "Oh? Don't like the idea of some hot vampire sucking on my neck?"

"Can we just focus on the task at hand?" His jaw hardened, but he kept his eyes trained ahead.

I turned my attention back to Nemain and Mikhail. "They seem to be focusing real hard," I noted and was rewarded with a low laugh from Connor.

The two lovers broke apart, blood trickling down Nemain's neck, which she didn't bother to wipe away. Mikhail tossed an arm around her shoulders, and the two of them tottered off towards where Lughán and Aoife had split from the others to get some drinks, putting a little unsteadiness into their move-ments as if they'd gotten the party started early and were already a little inebriated.

Keeping my head low, I crept over the roots to the back of the tree. Isabeau was tucked into the base of it between two thick roots with Elisa crouched protectively in front of her. I frowned as my magic sent me a little nudge.

"Move over there." I pointed to the left. The roots in that spot didn't provide quite as much protection, but I was getting a bad feeling about where the vampire girl and her guardian wolf currently were.

Without arguing, Elisa rose and moved out of the way so Isabeau could slide past her, and the two of them rearranged themselves in the spot I'd directed them to. Once they were settled again, I concentrated on my magic, but it didn't give me any other pointers. "Get ready," I said, "and remember to let us know if you feel your grasp on the illusion fading."

The little girl nodded, fierce determination on her face. *Such an unusual family Nemain has pieced together*, I thought as I moved back to where Connor was still watching the party.

"How's it going?" I asked quietly, kneeling beside him. Nemain and Mikhail stood opposite Lughán and Aoife at the drink table closest to us. Our two targets had their backs to us so I couldn't make out their expressions, and it was hard to hear exactly what they were saying from this distance over the chatter of everyone else talking. But based on the way Lughán clenched his hands at his sides and the angry magic swirling around them . . . Nemain was doing an excellent job of pissing them off.

I'd never had any doubts about that part of the plan though. The question was, could she get them to follow her?

"I could be wrong," Connor said in an amused tone, "but I'm pretty sure Nemain just called Lughán a pussy."

"Ohhh . . ." I leaned forward a little more as Mikhail seemed to flick off some lint or something from Aoife's dress, who slapped his hand away. Nemain and Mikhail leaned their heads together as if they were whispering, but clearly whatever they'd said had been loud enough for the other two to hear, because Lughán had to grab Aoife when she flung herself at Mikhail.

Lughán was still holding her back as Nemain and Mikhail

laughed and started to walk away, but just as Nemain moved past Aoife, she tilted her wine glass all over the sidhe's pearl white dress. Nemain held her hands up in mock apology as Mikhail tugged her away, the two of them swaying with each step as they stumbled back our way.

"Wow." I shook my head. "Who knew Nemain could pull off such mean girl vibes?"

We watched as Lughán and Aoife angrily spoke to each other. "Come on," I muttered. "Take the bait."

For a second, I thought it wouldn't work. That they'd have enough common sense not to pick a fight with the Unseelie Knight the evening before they planned to steal the magic from the fae queens. But then Nemain spun around, continuing backwards—albeit with Mikhail's help as the two of them stumbled a bit—and flicked her fingers.

Blue flames popped into existence directly in front of Lughán and slapped him on the balls before winking out of existence. Aoife gripped him when he stumbled back, hands over his bits as he bent over from the pain.

"She's such a bitch." Connor laughed, and I knew, for once, he didn't really mean it as an insult.

The two sidhe had clearly had enough as they stalked across the meadow away from the rest of the sidhe to where Nemain and Mikhail laughed obnoxiously, still making steady progress towards the tree despite their ambling steps.

I looked around for Maeve and spotted her with Coireall and Rowan on the other side of the meadow. The queens hadn't turned up yet, and the three of them were likely waiting on their arrival. So far, they hadn't noticed the other two going after Nemain.

Unfortunately, Olwen had. The Seelie Knight stood a short distance away from Maeve and frowned in the direction of Lughán and Aoife. *Shit, shit, shit.* She took a step forward, only to be halted by Kalen and Badb, who both threw an arm around her shoulders and directed her focus in the opposite direction. Olwen glanced over her shoulder one more time before allowing herself to be pulled away.

I had no idea what they had told her to get her attention, but I was thankful for it.

Now, Isabeau! I thought as loudly as I could.

Done.

Even knowing I should be invisible to everyone who wasn't part of our group, I still remained crouched as Lughán and Aoife closed the distance between themselves and Mikhail and Nemain and the four of them made it to the other side of the tree. Then, a second version of Lughán and Aoife walked back out, heading towards the rest of the party. Knowing these two were illusions, my mind rejected the sight of them.

Stop, Isabeau said. *You're making it harder.*

Right. The more someone doubted an illusion, the harder Isabeau had to work to make them believe it was real. We were already asking a lot of her and I sure as hell didn't want to make this even more difficult. I looked away from the illusion versions of Lughán and Aoife, who were stalking off towards a different tree closer to the palace, where Isabeau would drop the illusion once they were out of sight again. At least people would see them walking away from our location.

Not foolproof, but hopefully good enough to buy us the time we needed and keep Olwen or anyone else from nosing around where we were. I had faith in Isabeau's illusions, but I really didn't want to find out how they held up against the fae queens. Connor crept over the roots towards where Nemain and Mikhail faced off against our first two targets, and I followed after him while scanning for the dofheicthe. No sign of him yet—maybe luck would be in our favor for once and he wouldn't crash our party.

"I've had enough of you walking around like you belong here." Lughán stalked towards Nemain, his magic flaring around him in a shimmering array of blues. He heavily leaned towards air magic in a fight but was no slouch with earth magic either.

"Devourer trash!" Aoife snarled, and the willow tree groaned slightly at her rage. She almost exclusively used earth magic. I eyed the tree and all the roots snaking out from it. Roots that would be great for someone with earth magic to use on us.

"Is she talking to me or you?" Nemain frowned and looked at Mikhail.

"You, I think," Mikhail mused. "Despite the devourer blood in my veins, everyone just kind of dismisses vampires."

"Poor little vampire." Nemain patted his arm.

A root snapped up from the ground and slammed into Nemain's side, flinging her backwards. Yep. Definitely a problem. Mikhail was barely fast enough to avoid the second one and backed up quickly to get out of its range as Nemain staggered to her feet where she'd hit the ground twenty feet away.

"Still pissed about the dress?" She laughed and pulled her short swords free.

"Swords?" Aoife sneered. "Really?"

"As much as I'd love to burn you both to ash right now and devour all that yummy magic of yours"—Nemain stalked closer, radiating menace—"that might bring some unwanted attention. My flames are a bit flashy, and the fae queens get a little pissy if I use my devourer magic at their shindigs."

Some of the confidence leaked out of Aoife's stance as she finally realized the situation she'd willingly walked into, then she shot Lughán a look, but he didn't seem as concerned about how everything was turning out. If anything, he looked eager.

I tapped Connor's shoulder and pointed to Aoife. He nodded and moved towards her while I slowly made my way towards Lughán. Isabeau was making sure the two of them couldn't see any of us while also preventing partygoers from seeing or hearing the fight.

The kid had mad skills. It was a little terrifying considering she was only going to get more powerful as she grew up.

"Enough of this." Lughán stretched his arms out in front of him, palms facing up, and his magic flared. Nemain and Mikhail both staggered to a stop as the air was sucked from their lungs. "Little hard to mouth off when you can't breathe, isn't it?"

Aoife laughed in delight and sent one of the roots crashing against Mikhail, who wasn't fast enough to dodge it this time. I lunged towards Lughán, needing to distract him enough for his magic to waver. Manipulating air around someone's body like that was just as difficult as controlling blood. I just needed to break his concentration for a moment; otherwise, Nemain would have to summon her devourer flames, and that would almost certainly draw Olwen's attention.

Just as I slid my dagger free and was about to jam it into Lughán's side, someone slammed into me and sent me sprawling across the ground. Nemain sucked in a gulp of air and stumbled back as Lughán frowned at the general area I'd fallen. He couldn't see me, but he'd either heard something or just sensed something was off. Just then, two silver blades sunk into his chest, only missing his heart because he'd moved at the last second.

"Eyes on me, prick," Nemain snarled and dashed towards him.

I saw a wall of earth spring up between them and two roots spiral towards Mikhail before I focused on my own problems. Throwing myself to the side, I rolled away from the dagger that would have pierced my chest if I hadn't moved.

On shaky legs, I rose to my feet.

"This feels oddly familiar." The dofheicthe chuckled. He hadn't dropped his invisibility, but thanks to Hecate's spelled flower, I could see a vague outline of his form. "Tell me, Merfolk Queen, are you the one responsible for that missing gap in memories?"

I couldn't let him know I could see him—or at least the general shape of him. That would give away my advantage.

Fighting fair was for suckers and soon-to-be corpses.

"Can't say we've had the pleasure of meeting before." He took another step towards me, and I forced myself to stay still, letting my head swing back and forth like I was trying to figure out where he was. Out of the corner of my eye, I saw Connor doing the same, only, he wasn't faking it. "Also, this is kind of a private party."

"I think you're lying." He let out a raspy laugh as he closed the distance between us, and I barely managed to hold in my flinch when his clawed hand shot out to wrap around my throat. "And I think you'll taste delicious."

"Again—" I choked and gripped his wrist with both hands. "You're a creepy fuck!"

"So you do remember me." Aoife's head rolled on the ground next to us, and the dofheicthe glanced down at it. "Shit. Syndra's not going to be happy about that."

"Don't worry." I gripped his wrist harder. "You won't have to tell her."

The dofheicthe let out a gurgled scream as Connor took a guess on where he was and lucked out, his dagger slamming into the devourer's neck. The three of us crashed to the ground before rolling around in a tangle of limbs. Pain flared as the dofheicthe did his best to finish what he'd started and rip out my throat. Our tumble stopped with me on the bottom and the devourer asshole on top of me after managing to knock Connor aside. I gripped his clawed fingers with both hands, trying to pull them off my neck, which meant I could do nothing as he yanked the knife out of his own damn neck and stabbed me in the side with it.

"You fucker!" I screamed.

He laughed and ripped the knife out. In desperation, I tried to freeze the blood in his veins and almost blacked out as my magic was pulled from me. Another snarl of pain tore from my lungs when he sank the dagger back into my side.

"Thanks for the snack," he purred as the wound on his neck healed more rapidly. "Your magic is delicious."

Gods, I hate devourers, I screamed internally.

"Ash!" Connor screamed at the same second I got a very strong feeling that I should move my head to the left.

I jerked my head as far left as possible, a half-strangled scream erupting from my throat as the devourer's claws tore more flesh, but the sword that slammed through his head pierced the ground an inch from mine instead of going through it. Small victories.

"Oh shit!" Connor swore as he yanked the dofheicthe's twitching but now visible body off me, then he knelt next to me and clamped his hands around my neck to stanch the bleeding. "Fuck!" He growled in frustration when nothing happened. My head felt a little woozy thanks to the blood loss, but I focused on healing my neck and then the stab wounds on my side.

I still felt like shit, but I staggered to my feet with Connor's help. Then I planted a foot on the dofheicthe's back and yanked the sword out of his head—and then brought it down on his neck.

"Creepy asshole," I muttered as his head rolled to the side, then I turned to hand Connor back his sword. "What the fuck, Connor?" I dropped the weapon and lunged forward to grab him as he stumbled, but he was way too heavy for me, so we both fell to the ground.

"Bi–bi–bit me," he ground out.

"Fuck, fuck, fuck," I chanted and carefully started searching him for the wound. We were both covered not only in our own blood but also the dark green blood of the dofheic-the. "Where the fuck is—oh, fucking hell!" A huge chunk of Connor's bicep had been torn out, and dark black veins spread out from the wound, creeping up his arm . . . and back down towards his heart.

No. A cold fear seized me, and I clamped my hands over Connor's bicep, ignoring his hisses of pain and pushing as much healing magic into it as I could.

"Ash." A hand closed over mine. "Ash."

I realized that at some point, I'd closed my eyes, and slowly, I opened them to find Connor's light green gaze locked on me. Tired, but more clear than before.

"You're okay?" I asked weakly.

He sat up and pulled me into his arms. "Yeah. Magic is tapped out but otherwise fine."

"It's really not the time for cuddling." Nemain sauntered over to us, covered in blood and looking quite happy about it. "We have to get ready for round two."

"Wonderful," I said evenly and glanced around us. The dofheicthe's decapitated body lay next to us, and Aoife's head wasn't far.

Guys, Elisa said, *Isabeau is struggling.*

I'm fine, the girl pushed the defiant thought out, and I sucked in a breath as I looked behind Elisa's large wolf form to where Isabeau crouched between the roots. Her pale complexion suggested that Elisa was right and Isabeau was close to being tapped out, but that wasn't what got my attention. Her eyes, which were usually a beautiful brown with green flecks, were now solid black with jagged white lines running through them like marble.

What in the ever-loving fuck was she?

Amazing, Isabeau replied. *Amazing is what I am.*

"You're spending too much time around Eddie." Nemain huffed.

"I told you that." Mikhail gave Nemain a pointed look before reaching down and grabbing a very broken Lughán by the ankle. "She just needs a bit of a top-up and she'll be good as new for part two." He dragged the bloodied-up sidhe towards the tree. Surprise flickered through me when I saw he was still alive, and I arched an eyebrow at Nemain in question.

She shrugged. "When you spend a lot of time with vampires, you kind of get used to keeping powerful juice boxes around. Waste not, want not, and all that."

"Here you go, kid!" Mikhail dropped the barely conscious sidhe in front of Elisa, who moved to the side enough to let Isabeau step past her. "Eat your vegetables."

Chapter Seventeen

Lughán's body thumped as it hit the ground, and Isabeau wiped the back of her mouth with her hand, which only smeared the blood around more. A tiny frown spread across her face as she peered at her now bloody hand. With a dainty movement, she stepped over the sidhe's corpse, walked towards Mikhail, and proceeded to wipe her face and hands on the back of his shirt.

Frankly, I was impressed she'd found a section of his clothes that wasn't covered in blood, but he did seem cleaner than Nemain, whose tunic was literally dripping blood.

Mikhail glared at Nemain. "This is your fault."

She just laughed and blew him a kiss. Once Isabeau was satisfied she was clean, she stepped back and folded her hands behind her back—it was a very Magos-like move. Kid was picking up all sorts of habits.

"So, just to be clear"—Connor cleared his throat—"we care about swearing in front of the little ones, but we're fine with them killing people?"

"Bad people," Nemain defended. "Plus, she's a vampire—it's not like being a vegetarian is an option."

"Actually, Elisa has been a vegetarian the last few months," Mikhail commented.

"That's not my point, and you know it!"

An amused glint shone in Connor's eyes as he looked at Nemain. "Interesting parental strategy the two of you have."

I barked a laugh as Nemain gaped at him like he'd just dumped a cold bucket of water on her. "We're not parents!"

"Oh?" Connor arched an eyebrow. "Last I checked, Finn lives with you, as does Isabeau. You took both of them in and care for their well-being. Is that not what parents do?"

I pressed my lips together hard as I tried to contain my laughter. Mikhail and Nemain both looked like they'd swallowed something rancid and were trying not to hurl it back up.

"Elisa is clearly the parental figure in this situation!" Nemain pointed at the wolf, who had her tongue hanging out and mouth parted in what had to be the equivalent of a wolf smile.

No, I'm very well established in the older sister role.

"Do you want me to call you 'Mom?'" Isabeau asked sweetly.

Nemain's face paled further, and Connor held a fist over his mouth as he tried to cover up his laughter, but it did nothing to hide the way his shoulders shook.

"That's it!" Nemain growled and stalked over to me. "Let's go. Isabeau, work your magic."

"Yes, Mom."

Connor lost it and gave up trying to hide his laughs. Mikhail just had this weird look on his face like he didn't know how to react to this turn of events. Who knew that a nine-year-old vampire kid would have been the one to cut the vampire assassin and mouthy feline shifter down to size?

"I'm telling Kaysea no more cookies for you." Nemain pointed a finger at Isabeau, who just rolled her eyes at the ludicrous statement. The kid's reaction to the threat was correct—

Kaysea would absolutely sneak her cookies behind Nemain's back. The feline shifter clearly knew this too, because she glared at the devious child one more time before looking at me and waving a hand at her face. "How do I look?"

"Gods, this is weird." I shook off my laughter as I scrutinized Nemain's appearance, or rather the appearance of the fae in front of me. Isabeau had managed to pluck the image of Syndra from my mind and had overlaid the fae's looks onto Nemain. The shifter's golden-brown skin was a few shades lighter, and her ash-blonde hair was now a dark gold. Isabeau had kept Nemain's clothes and weapons the same but hidden the blood, and instead of piercing green eyes set in a pretty face with bold features, sharp blue ones from a breathtakingly gorgeous face peered out at me.

The likeness probably wasn't perfect, I'd only seen Syndra the one time, but from a distance, it was good enough to fool people.

"Maeve will buy it," I finally said. "We just need to get the timing right."

"That's your job." Nemain glanced at Isabeau. "Hide us from sight until Ash gives you the go-ahead, and do not move from that spot. That first fight was the easy one."

Isabeau nodded and settled back into her well-covered spot between the tree roots, Elisa hunkering down in front of her. I looked at Connor, chewing my bottom lip. I'd healed his physical injuries, and the black veins were thankfully gone, but he had no magic. Lughán and Aoife had been difficult enough, but Maeve, Rowan, and Coireall were stronger than they had been. Nemain was a lethal fighter, but she was at a disadvantage in this fight since she couldn't use her devourer flames this close to the queens without drawing attention.

It wasn't that I didn't have faith in Connor's fighting abilities, but he'd already been injured once. Maybe I could convince him to leave . . .

"No," he said flatly.

"What?" I flinched as my magic practically screamed that it agreed with Connor on this.

"You were thinking about asking Nemain to open a gateway to get me out of here." He crossed his arms. "I'm not going anywhere."

"But you don't have any magic left," I argued. "Once they figure that out, they'll zero in on you as the weak link."

He scoffed. "I'm hardly helpless. Nemain can't use her magic and you're not asking her to leave. The vampire doesn't have any magic to begin with."

Not exactly true. Mikhail could vanish into mist, and he was a scary bastard who was faster than Nemain with his sword.

"What is your magic telling you?" Connor pushed, and my mouth flattened into a hard line because my magic was still adamant that he needed to stay. He laughed, but there was no humor in it. "That's what I thought."

"Don't worry," Mikhail drawled. "I'll make sure the delicate little princeling stays alive."

The delicate little princeling yanked a dagger from his thigh and hurled it at Mikhail's face, but the vampire's hand shot out and caught the blade without even looking and tucked it into a spare sheath on his side.

Something bright flashed in the sky above us, and we all looked up. "The meteor shower is starting," I murmured.

Technically, it would last for a few hours, but everyone would be the most distracted in the next few minutes. This was our perfect window of opportunity.

Nemain followed after me as we skirted our way around the tree until we were in sight of those gathered. Hundreds of sidhe were scattered around the meadow, all eyes directed up at the wondrous sky as stars of brilliant white fled across it, leaving glittering trails in their wake. Magic filled the air to an almost intoxicating degree, but I kept my attention focused.

The queens were seated on a slight rise in the meadow, overlooking everyone else. Kalen, Badb, and Olwen were with them. I scanned the crowd until I found the three we were looking for. Maeve had either found another upraised portion of the meadow or, more likely, she had made one. It wasn't quite as high as the one the queens were sitting on, even she wouldn't go that far, but it was a statement all the same. Coireall and Rowan stood slightly behind her, all three of them watching the stars like everyone else.

I stepped forward a little when my magic nudged me to the right.

Now, Isabeau, I thought loudly.

A bead of sweat formed at my hairline because Nemain and I were in plain sight to anyone who looked over now. If Olwen or the queens dropped their gazes from the sky and spotted us, we were fucked.

Another push from my magic to take a step forward. I did, Nemain moving with me, and we faced each other as if we were conspiring. The hair on the back of my neck crept up, and I turned my head just enough to see Maeve staring at me from across the meadow.

"She's looking," I said quietly.

Wordlessly, Nemain pulled one of her daggers free and passed it to me, holding on to it for a few seconds, as if she were warning me about something. Then she spun on her heel and headed back to the tree, and I followed obediently. Even without looking, I could feel Maeve's gaze drilling a hole into the back of my head.

They're coming, Isabeau said. *I can feel their minds drawing closer.*

Something in her tone was off.

Are you okay?

I'm hiding all five of you from sight again, and I made illusions of the three of them that stayed behind where they were standing. Strain coated her words. *But someone is suspicious. I can feel them poking at it.*

Probably Olwen, I grumbled. *Do you need to drop it?*

No, she ground out. *I can hold it a bit longer.*

"I take Maeve," I told Nemain as we made our way back around the tree. "The three of you need to overwhelm the other two. Hopefully the odds will help compensate for the fact that none of you lot can use magic right now."

"If it comes to it, I'll use my flames," Nemain said tightly.

I shook my head. "The Unseelie Queen tolerates a lot from you, Nemain, but there are going to be questions when these five disappear tonight, and if you make a big show of your magic, those questions are going to be directed at you."

"I'll deal with it."

We were almost to the back of the tree when I grabbed Nemain's arm and pulled her to a stop. "You're already helping me out of an impossible situation, I won't let you throw your life away."

"Please," she scoffed. "You're hardly the first friend to put me in a nasty position. It's practically a right of passage to becoming one of my besties."

I blinked before slowly saying, "Maybe you need some different friends."

"But then I wouldn't get offers to come to the fae realm to kill a bunch of assholes." Nemain grinned wickedly before jogging over to where Mikhail and Connor waited. I walked to a spot about twenty feet out from the tree and away from the others. A tingle ran up my spine, and I glanced around until I found it. The dirt was damp where an underground spring was slowly bubbling up towards the surface.

Perfect. I called the water towards me, letting it spread further across the forest floor so it would be available when I needed it.

Maeve stepped around the tree's roots, Coireall and Rowan flanking her, and the three of them continued towards the back of the tree, where Nemain and the others waited for them. They walked past me, and Maeve paused, letting the other two continue on. Then her golden eyes scrutinized the area, and I knew the second she felt the unusual amount of water pooling up.

I barely had a second to pull the water towards me before heat erupted across the ground, causing steam to rise from whatever water I hadn't been able to grab. Nemain and Connor launched themselves at Coireall, swords flashing as the sidhe male drew his own with one hand while calling flames into his other. Mikhail popped into existence behind Rowan and drove his sword through her back. The sidhe screamed as she fell to her knees and tried to wrestle the water from my grasp to launch at Mikhail.

Her magic reached into the large ball of water behind me and pulled out a stream that she sent straight towards the vampire, elongating it into a spear. I let it get a few feet away from him before I changed its course, and shock flashed across Rowan's face right before the spear pierced her throat, sending a spray of blood across the grass.

A bellow of rage tore from Coireall as he hurled fire at Mikhail. The vampire vanished into mist and reappeared behind Nemain, where he knelt on the ground, the scent of burned flesh filling the air.

"Brought some friends, I see," Maeve said lightly, as if she wasn't the least bit concerned about Rowan bleeding out. Her flames flittered across the clearing, forcing me to step further back, away from the others, who still fought Coireall. "Good play with Syndra. I thought it odd that she would ally with you —she's not a fan of the merfolk for some reason—but I didn't think you'd be capable of such trickery." She glanced around the clearing, her eyes hovering over several spaces between the roots.

"Turns out it wasn't hard to find people willing to kill you and your buddies." I took a few steps to the left so I was facing the tree. As much as I wanted to put myself between Maeve and Isabeau, Maeve was already clearly suspicious that someone else was here. Isabeau was currently keeping herself and Elisa invisible as well as hiding all of us from the partygoers. I suspected that if her magic started to drain, the girl would choose to keep the rest of us hidden over continuing to hide herself. Maeve turned her body with my movements so her back was to the tree and all her attention focused on me.

"Stronger people than you have tried to kill me over the years." She shrugged.

I let my eyes slide momentarily to where Rowan lay unmoving in her own blood. "By my count, you're down three." A pained, pissed-off snarl sounded from Coireall, followed by another wave of fire. I saw it out of the corner of my eye before I felt the heat of it against my skin. Their fight had moved almost behind me, but I wasn't willing to turn around to make sure my friends were okay.

"You think there aren't more people frothing at the bit to rise up against the queens?" She laughed. "Lughán and Aoife were outliving their usefulness, and Rowan has been plotting to stab me in the back for years. You did me a favor."

"I think you want all the power of being a queen with none of the responsibility," I said honestly. "A queen is supposed to serve her people."

She snorted. "I see why the prince fell in love with you. His parents believe the same. That loyalty must be earned and rewarded." A wolfish smile stretched across her lips. "Tell me, Merfolk Queen, how much will you sacrifice to protect those who have chosen to follow you?"

The water from the ground snapped up, creating a twenty-foot wall between us and everyone else. Maeve's flames crashed into it a second later before shooting towards the tree. Only the push of my magic let me react fast enough to send some water to cut it off.

Fire met water, sending a column of steam into the air. If Elisa and Isabeau had stayed where they'd originally settled down, that would have put them directly behind Maeve. Even with my magic warning me, I wouldn't have been able to react fast enough, and they would have been incinerated.

So much of my water had burned off in blocking Maeve's attack. I pulled more from the earth, and it wound its way up my body like two twin snakes ready to strike.

"Who is it you're protecting, Ashling?" Maeve mocked, sending more flames towards the roots of the tree like whips. I met each one with a shield of water. "Someone gifted with illusions, I take it?"

For once, I didn't have a good response. Instead, I sent tendrils of water slithering through the grass to wrap around Maeve's ankles and then poured magic into them the second they made contact, turning the water into ice, which pierced her flesh.

"Fuck!" She hissed and burned away my watery snakes. The second her attention was diverted, I hurled a dagger at her face. A root snapped up, and the blade sunk into it. With a wave of her hand, the root retreated, and Maeve plucked the dagger free as it left. She held it up to her face and smelled it, wrinkling her nose. "Really? Working with daemons, now? You are a disgrace to all the fae."

"They make good shit." I flicked my hand, and the dagger leapt out of Maeve's hand and back to mine. The poison on it was particularly toxic and I couldn't risk stabbing myself, so I slid it back into my sheath.

"When I'm queen of all the fae realms, I want you to know that I'm going to boil the merfolk out of their beloved oceans."

Bright orange flames flickered around her hands as she held them up. "It's part of my deal with Syndra. Like I said, she really doesn't like you."

"Yeah?" I drew more water from the underground spring. "Got to say, the feeling is mutual."

Nemain cried out a warning, and my heart stopped beating when Connor let out a pained grunt before being flung backwards. He crashed to the ground between Maeve and me, burns marking his right leg and two daggers buried in his ribs.

"Connor!" I screamed.

A ball of flames hurled towards my face, and I barely ducked back out of the way. Coireall grinned at me from across the clearing. The right half of his face was coated in blood, and based on how he stood with one arm cradling his ribs, he wasn't doing too well. He was almost as skilled at manipulating fire as Maeve, and based on the burns both Nemain and Mikhail sported, he was holding his own against them.

My attention was drawn away from Coireall as Connor struggled to rise to his feet. There was no way I could get to him before Maeve, and when my gaze darted to her, I saw the same realization in her eyes as they lit up with delight. She glanced over her shoulder at the roots, where Isabeau and Elisa were still likely hiding. I couldn't see them—Isabeau had hidden them from everyone because it was easier for her that way—so it was possible they'd moved, but that would mean they'd deviated from the plan of remaining fixed to that spot. From what I knew about Elisa, she didn't seem like the type to change from the agreed-upon course, for better or worse.

"I'm curious, Merfolk Queen, who will you choose to save?" Maeve flung her hands out to the sides, and flames poured out of her. The earth around me erupted as I pulled all the water up at once, sending walls of it to guard Isabeau and Elisa, Connor, and myself.

Maeve's flames beat at my walls, and I had to pour more of my magic into them. Sweat dripped into my eyes as I fiercely tried to blink it away. I couldn't hold this forever—it was taking every ounce of my concentration to keep Maeve at bay.

Then Coireall joined the party, letting out a deep, rumbling laugh as he hurled his own flames at me as well as at Nemain and Mikhail. Out of instinct, I pulled a wall of water up in front of us, but I wouldn't be able to hold it much longer—I was already stretched too thin.

Fuck it. "Now would be a great time for your freaky devourer magic!" I screamed at Nemain. It would complicate matters with the fae queens, but at least we'd be alive to deal with that complication.

"Sure would!" she yelled back. "Except this asshole stabbed me with one of those nullifying daggers!"

"Same," Mikhail ground out. Guess that explained why he hadn't vanished into mist.

Godsdamn it all. That meant I was the only one with any sort of magic to combat Maeve and Coireall. We outnumbered them, but they outmagicked us. Fan-fucking-tastic.

"Let's make a deal," Maeve said evenly. Either she was an excellent actor, or she wasn't the least bit strained after using so much magic and I had severely underestimated just how much power she had. "Illusion magic of this scale is rare. I would have use for such a person. Given that you've taken away several of my loyal followers, I find myself in need of replacements."

I ground my teeth as I pulled more water from the earth. The underground stream was running out, and even with as much magic as I poured into the watery shields around every-one, it wasn't enough. Maeve's flames were eating their way through.

"Do you hear me?" Maeve's heavy gaze fell on the tree roots. "Reveal yourself. Save the life of your friends."

Don't! I shoved more magic against Maeve's. *Don't you fucking dare.*

I won't watch you all die, Isabeau replied, and Maeve's smile widened.

"No!" Nemain darted out from behind the wall of water keeping her safe and flung a knife at Maeve.

A whip of fire knocked it out of the air, and a second whip lashed the shifter across the chest. An agonized scream tore out of Nemain, and Mikhail was suddenly there, pulling her back behind my watery shield.

The world around me narrowed as my vision wavered. I was pouring everything I had into keeping us all alive for a few more minutes.

"Honestly, I thought you'd be stronger than this." Maeve made a disappointed sound before laughing. "You're young, aren't you? What are you? Two centuries?"

"One, actually," I bit out.

"Ha!" The fire burned hotter, and I dropped to my knees. "You got a boost from the merfolk throne and thought it would be enough. Darling, I've seen a thousand years come and go. You are nothing."

A half-strangled scream slipped from me as I tried and failed to push the flames that flicked through the water and licked my hand.

"Ash," Connor called out from where he was barely standing. Less than ten feet separated us, but I wasn't capable of moving, and if anyone stepped out from behind the water, Maeve or Coireall would burn them to a crisp.

"I'm sorry," I said softly and met his gaze. "I wish we had more time."

The look in his eyes was pure agony.

"Enough," a soft but firm voice called out.

Maeve cut off the flames she'd been wielding against all of us, and Coireall did the same. I let my water shields drop as well, and the water pooled to the earth. I could snap it back up if I needed to, but I would take any reprieve I could get. Black spots clouded my vision, and I shook my head, trying in vain to clear them away.

The movement made it worse, and I would have collapsed if Connor hadn't lunged forward to grab me. He wrapped an arm around my waist and held me upright as we both looked to the tree.

Isabeau blinked into existence. For a second, I thought my vision was failing me because I didn't see Elisa with her. Was she still hiding the wolf from sight? The vampire girl looked even paler than she had earlier, and blood was trickling from her nose and ears. She was damn near tapped out and hadn't said anything.

It had been my idea to bring her here. Even if I hadn't made that blood oath, I would have done anything in my power to keep her safe. Letting Maeve take her wasn't an option.

Unfortunately, I didn't really have any plan beyond that. Then I felt it. Through the pain of the burns on my hands and forearms, between the fuzzy spots of my mind while I struggled to stay conscious as my magic waned, that little tug to the north. To where the tree cast a shadow on the ground, which was further obscured by a particularly tangled web of roots.

To where Elisa crept towards Coireall, her black coat blending into the darkness.

I quickly averted my gaze so I wouldn't give away her position. We would have one chance to seize the opportunity Elisa was about to create for us.

"A vampire?" Maeve's lip curled as she stared at Isabeau. "All that power wrapped up in a mongrel of a child."

"Syndra will know how to leash her to us," Coireall grunted.

"That's what they're for." Maeve waved at all of us.

"No." Coirreall pointed angrily at Nemain and Mikhail. "They killed Rowan. Their deaths are mine to claim."

"It's hardly our fault that you and your lover chose to follow her." Nemain pointed her sword at Maeve.

Mikhail frowned in the direction of Rowan's corpse. "She was pretty easy to kill. If anything, I think you owe us. I was really hoping for more of a fight."

"I've fought humans who were tougher to take down," Nemain agreed.

Elisa crept closer.

"Quiet!" Maeve snapped and sent a cool look towards Coireall. "We take them all alive for now. If the girl steps out of line, I'll allow you to kill one of them in front of her."

"I'll behave." Isabeau sniffed and stepped forward. I suspected the timidness in her voice was fake, but I was pretty sure the fear leaking from her eyes wasn't. My fingers curled into fists at my sides, but I forced myself to remain still. "Promise you won't hurt them?"

Maeve smiled at the girl. "You're in no position to demand things, mongrel, but if you do exactly as you're told, you'll increase the chances of their survival."

Roots snapped behind Isabeau and shoved her forward enough that Maeve could grab her. The young vampire cried out as Maeve twisted her arm, and the only reason I didn't launch myself at the sidhe was because Connor still had an iron grip around my waist. Despite the exhaustion I could feel coming off him, he held me firmly in place.

Maeve saw the fury on my face and laughed. "I'll give you this, Ashling, you've made it rather far in life considering how young you are and the fact that you're just a mermaid. Pity you didn't come to me sooner. I could have used you and taught you many things."

"Such as?" Out of the corner of my eye, I saw Elisa adjust

her stance like she was getting ready to lunge forward, and Mikhail and Nemain had both gone predatorily still.

Maeve's grip on Isabeau's arm tightened, causing the girl to exhale sharply. "Friends make you weak."

I bared my teeth. "Bitch, you don't know my friends."

Then Elisa launched herself at Coireall, her large wolf form slamming into the sidhe's back, and sank her teeth into his shoulder. He screamed as he crashed to the ground, and I summoned water up from where it had been pooling around Maeve's feet and spun it until it was a thin spike of whirling liquid that sliced through her wrist. Isabeau stumbled away from the sidhe and started to run, only to be blocked by a wall of fire.

Another wave of fire forced Nemain and Mikhail to abort their attack on Coireall, which meant they could do nothing as he swung a blade behind himself and stabbed Elisa.

"Elisa!" Isabeau screamed.

The wolf didn't release the sidhe though, just started shaking him like a rag doll, even as blood poured from the wound on her neck.

"Get the fuck off me!" Coireall screamed, and fire erupted from him. Elisa yelped as it crashed into her and sent her flying until she hit the ground a few feet away. She struggled to rise before collapsing with a pained whimper, large patches of her fur burned away.

Isabeau ran towards her, but was snatched up by Coireall. I froze where I'd been poised to send another spike of water through Maeve. Her golden eyes were alight with rage as she looked at me and then Isabeau, her gaze finally falling on Elisa's crumpled form. "Kill the wolf."

"With pleasure." Coireall smiled as Isabeau fought to break free of his hold. A circle of flames erupted around Elisa, creeping inward to slowly burn her alive.

Maeve's wall of flames still blocked Nemain and Mikhail,

who were pacing behind it. They could take Coireall down—I just needed to give them the chance. If I could piss her off enough, Maeve would direct all her magic at me.

Of course, given how weak I felt, I didn't know if I'd be able to hold her off, but I couldn't let Elisa die. It would destroy Isabeau. Plus, she'd come here to help me. My goal had always been killing Maeve. Me surviving came second.

I rallied the last of my strength and focused on the blood running through her veins while also sending what remained of the water through the grass to circle around her feet.

Maeve sent me an annoyed look. "Really? Even if you weren't on the verge of passing out, you could never overwhelm my magic enough to control my blood. I expected something better from you."

"Nemain's right." My words were slurred as the world spun around me. "Gotta love fae arrogance."

The water rushed up from the ground to coat Maeve's skin, and before she could burn it off, I shoved every last ounce of magic I had into it. The water solidified into thousands of needles that shot straight into her flesh.

Maeve screamed, and the wall of fire separating Nemain and Mikhail from Coireall shifted towards me. Connor pushed me to the side and I crashed to the ground, then he threw himself back the opposite direction, away from Maeve's chaotic flames.

Realizing he no longer had Maeve protecting him, Coireall tried to jerk the flames from Elisa towards Nemain and Mikhail but screamed as Isabeau twisted in his grip enough to sink her fangs into his arm.

"Keep your hands off my fucking kid!" Nemain shoved a clawed hand straight through the sidhe's neck just as Mikhail gripped his hair and yanked, tearing his head clean off.

I let out a relieved breath that ended in a bloody cough as pain shot through my chest.

"You may have won the battle." Maeve twisted the knife she'd shoved into my heart. "But your friends will lose the war. Pity you won't be there to see it."

A sword shoved through her chest, stopping an inch short of piercing me as well, and then her body was hurled away. Connor's face filled my vision, and he said something, my name I thought, but the darkness that had been calling me for the previous few minutes grew stronger as my body went languid against the ground and I stared up at the night sky.

"No-no-no-no," Connor chanted as he pulled me into his arms, the knife still embedded in my chest. "You need to direct the healing to your heart so I can pull the blade out. Fucking heal yourself, Ash!"

"Can't," I mumbled. "Tapped. Out."

Coldness started to replace the pain, and I knew that wasn't a good sign. Nemain and the others crashed to my other side. Everyone was screaming, but none of them had healing magic except Connor, and he couldn't access his magic thanks to the bite from that prick devourer. There were a thousand fae on the other side of the meadow, but none of them would heal me without the queens' blessings, which I knew they wouldn't give.

"Do something!" Isabeau sobbed.

"It's . . . okay. We won." I raised a hand to cup Connor's cheek. "One last night"—my eyelids fluttered as I struggled to keep them open—"under the stars . . . with you."

"I don't accept that!" Connor screamed, sounding so far away as my heartbeat slowed and the world faded.

Fire erupted inside my chest, and I sucked in a gasp of air as my back arched off the ground. It hurt. Everything fucking hurt. Suddenly, I was very aware of the gaping hole in my chest and every injury I'd sustained during the fight against Maeve as my body rapidly knit itself back together.

Between the agonizing breaths, confusion filtered in. This

magic coursing through my body and soul right now . . . wasn't mine.

I felt it then—that link between Connor and me—the one that had broken on that rooftop. The mate bond thrummed between us like a living thing. He wasn't healing me, I realized, but the bond linked us—body, soul . . . and magic. I was using his magic—that he still couldn't access—to heal myself.

"Is it working?" Isabeau asked frantically. Elisa sat behind her, still in her wolf form, not looking great, but at least she was alive.

"Yeah, kid," Nemain assured her. "It's working."

"Come on." Mikhail held his hand out to Isabeau, and she slid hers into his. "Let's give them some space."

My body sank into the earth as the pain gradually lessened. Connor stared at the wound left by the dagger, the discarded weapon lying on the grass next to us.

"You accepted the mate bond," I said a little uncertainly. On one hand, I was thrilled, but at the same time, I was terrified. It wasn't like he had voluntarily done it. This had clearly been a last-ditch effort to save my life. What if he regretted it? Mate bonds could be undone, but just the idea of having this with him only for him to reject it later sent another spear of pain through my heart.

I wasn't sure if I would survive that.

"You're mine." His light green eyes flashed. "I'm still really fucking pissed off at you, and now even more so since you tried to die on me instead of spending the next century making up for all the bullshit you've been spinning."

"What?" I sputtered. "I saved your life, you asshole!"

"You tell him, Ash!" Nemain yelled from somewhere behind us.

Connor raised his eyes to glare at her for a moment before dropping them back down to me, something in them softening as he leaned down to kiss me. "Let's go home, my love."

Chapter Eighteen

"Apologies, Galather," Kaysea said in a polite but firm tone. "But the queen has an appointment that cannot be missed."

I fixed my features into a very apologetic expression and faced the merfolk I'd been dodging all week. If he'd had any legitimate concerns, I would have heard him out, but I knew he just wanted to complain about the deal I'd negotiated with him and his rival last week. He was almost eight hundred years old. It was time for him to start acting like a damn adult.

"So sorry, Galather." I held a hand over my heart. "But I'm afraid Kaysea is right and I don't have a moment to spare currently, but I have complete faith in your abilities to make good on the agreement with Elmon. There is no one better qualified than yourself."

I was pretty sure a rock with a face drawn on it was better qualified, but I hid that thought behind an earnest smile. Galather puffed up his chest. "Of course, My Queen. I will handle things personally."

He strode off with a determined step, and I let out a relieved breath as soon as he turned the corner.

Kaysea let out an amused chuckle. "You're really getting the hang of this whole queen thing."

She wasn't wrong. In the weeks since we'd successfully stopped Maeve and prevented Balor's return, I'd been able to just . . . be queen. No more being half present while plotting how to prevent my vision from coming true. No more sneaking off for days at a time to eliminate a threat or collect information. Now, I got to spend all my time with my people, listening to their problems—both big and small—and doing everything I could to make them right.

The threat of Balor was still ever present, but I had faith in Nemain. After all, who better to take on an egomaniac fae king than an unhinged, borderline psychopathic shifter and her equally deranged vampire.

Check. Fucking. Mate.

At least that was what I was going to believe for the next few months. I needed a fucking break from apocalypses. Maybe I could convince Connor to have a pj party and we could watch some trashy tv shows while he rolled his eyes and pretended not to be invested in the drama.

"Where are you going?" Kaysea asked when I started down the hallway in the opposite direction of the throne room. While I still preferred my more casual meeting place, I'd been spending more time in Naewynn and the grand palace here. Things between me and the fae queens were still tenuous, and I needed to consolidate my own power base, but it was easier to do that from our capital city.

I paused and looked at Kaysea. "It's late. I was going to grab something to eat and review some correspondence in my suite." I would have preferred to go to my home in the hidden realm, but my schedule was packed with meetings the following day, and it made no sense to travel back and forth. Next week, I'd be taking a couple of days off and spending most of it there . . . with Connor.

My fated mate.

It still hadn't fully sunk in yet that he was mine. The mate bond hummed happily in my soul. In a perfect world, we would have been able to spend the previous few weeks together, enjoying our new mate status. Unfortunately, I'd had to deal with the political fallout from everything that had gone down between me and the fae queens.

They had lifted my official banishment from their realms but made it quite clear that I wasn't welcome to drop by for a visit. Many of the Tuatha families had taken this as permission to start fucking with the merfolk and testing my power. Tensions were running high between Tír fo Thuinn and the rest of the fae realms. Kaysea was doing an amazing job of smoothing things over where she could, and when she couldn't . . . Connor would step in.

Because, apparently, sometimes violence really was the answer.

Between the two of them, they handled most of the problems. I suspected Nemain was also keeping an eye on things since I appeared to be on the short list of people she genuinely liked.

Aside from threatening arrogant sidhe into behaving, Connor had also taken a trip to one of the death realms with Nemain to visit his sister, Myrna. He'd invited me to come, but I'd suggested he go on his own for the first time. He'd been quiet when he'd returned—whatever they'd discussed had taken an emotional toll on him—but in some ways, he seemed lighter, like he was finally able to move on from her death and stop blaming himself.

He'd even volunteered to spar with Nemain once a week to

improve his skills with a sword. The first couple of sessions hadn't gone particularly well and they'd both walked away bloody and pissed off, but I had hope that they could figure their shit out.

"You have one more meeting to attend to." Kaysea gave me her best *quit your bitching* look, which, I had to admit, was pretty good.

"Fine," I grumbled, "but you better bring me some of Zareen's cupcakes tomorrow. I want the red velvet ones with sprinkles."

"Yes, My Queen." She bowed dramatically. "I shall brave the dangerous lair of the daemon and offer my body as sacrifice so that I might bring you sweets."

I rolled my eyes. "You mean you're going to walk into the kitchen wearing nothing but your 'Kiss the Cook' apron and bat your pretty eyelashes."

"Oh, I won't have to bat my eyelashes." She winked at me and then pointed down the hallway in the opposite direction of where I'd been going. "Now go. You can thank me later."

"Thank you later?" I snorted as I wandered down the empty hallway. "Unlikely." At this late hour, I no longer took visitors unless they had an invitation, which nobody did, except whoever Kaysea had let through.

I had very much been looking forward to curling up on my oversized chair with its fluffy cushions and a bottle of wine while I read through a mountain's worth of paperwork. Connor had been away these last few days, helping with some aqueduct construction in the dragon realm. I missed him terribly, but we'd have some time just for ourselves soon.

The large, silver throne room doors were cracked open, and none of the guards were in sight, which made sense because I'd dismissed them when I'd gone to what I'd thought had been my last meeting. Naewynn was not only our capital city, it was also our largest. The palace sat above the surface, but the rest of it stretched out far beneath. We actually planned on expanding an entire section, and I'd been discussing the timeline with our architects.

I paused for a moment before entering the room, checking in with my magic to see if it had any warnings to give me, but it seemed . . . excited. Weird. If Kaysea thought whoever I was meeting would pose a problem, she would have made sure there were guards stationed here and probably would have come with me.

Pushing the doors open the rest of the way, I strode into the room and stopped when I saw the person sitting on my throne. A sinful smile curled along my mouth as I closed the doors behind me.

"And what grievances do you have to air this evening?" I drawled and started walking towards him. "I will do my best to rectify them."

"There are so many." Connor cocked his head as he watched me approach, heat flaring in his eyes. "To start, I've been having the same dream the last three nights, and I just can't get it out of my head."

"Oh?" I reached behind my neck and untied the top of my dress. It fell down and pooled at my waist, my breasts only covered by my wild curls. "Pray tell, what type of dream has been troubling you?"

"Well, you see . . ." His voice was a little rough as he spoke, and gods, did I love it. "My mate—an absolutely stunning creature—is queen."

"Is she?" I slowly tugged the dress over my hips and let it slip all the way off, never once breaking my stride. "She must be all kinds of cunning and wicked to not only gain a crown but to have such a princely mate."

"She is that and more," he agreed. "Her jokes aren't always funny, but nobody is perfect."

"Hmmm." I climbed up the steps of the dais until I stood

before him. He widened his legs further so I could stand between them, his hands still on the arms of the throne—but based on how hard he gripped them, I knew he was struggling not to touch me. I flicked my hair back over my shoulders so I was completely bared to him. "And what does your absolutely perfect mate have to do with the dream?"

"In this dream, we do something we haven't done yet." His smile was so carnal, it had me clenching my thighs together as wetness pooled between them. "You see, she has this throne"— he tapped his fingers several times on the dark wood that was inlaid with silver—"and we have yet to properly coronate it."

"How tragic." I inhaled with mock horror before sliding onto his lap. "So, just to make sure this is addressed correctly, how about you tell me exactly what happened in this dream?" I unbuttoned the top of his pants. "I'm a bit of a details person." I loosened another button. "And I like to get all my facts right."

He groaned as I pulled his cock free and ran my fingers up and down his thick length. "You are wicked."

"It's one of the many things you love about me." I laughed huskily.

Connor's lips crashed against mine, and there was so much need in the kiss that I instantly forgot about our game. His fingers dug into my ass, pulling me closer, and I let out a feeble protest because I had to release his cock.

He chuckled as he nipped my bottom lip. "I missed you."

"It's been three days." I smiled, tracing a finger across his jawline.

"Too long." He kissed me again and swallowed my moan when his fingers slipped between my thighs and swirled in the slick heat they found waiting for them. "I think you missed me too."

"Nope," I said playfully, earning me another nip on the lip, this time, hard enough to draw blood.

"Perhaps I should stay away longer next time," he mused while still teasing his fingers through my wet flesh but deliberately avoiding that throbbing bundle of nerves. I raised my hips, chasing his movements, but he just moved his fingers away until I let out a growl of frustration.

"Connor . . ." I glared up at him.

"Yes, My Queen?" Light danced in those pale green eyes.

"I might have missed you," I said smoothly, and he grinned at the lie he could see written all over my face. There was no might about it. The only thing that had gotten me through the previous few days was the knowledge we'd have time away together the following week, and even then, if he hadn't surprised me by showing up tonight, I probably would have come up with an excuse to go to the dragon realm tomorrow.

"Hmm." He plunged two fingers inside me while his thumb brushed over my clit. A litany of curse words poured from my lips as my hips bucked up. His smile turned wicked as he plunged his fingers in and out while putting more pressure on my clit with each brush of his thumb. Within seconds, my pussy clenched around his fingers, and I threw back my head and screamed as the orgasm ripped through me.

"Okay." I breathed roughly. "I missed you. Now do that again."

"So demanding." He clicked his tongue as he lazily swirled his fingers around my still trembling clit. "But as I was saying earlier, I've been having a dream about you and this throne that I'm going to need you to reenact for me right now."

"What—" My words were cut off as Connor gripped me by the waist, picked me up, and proceeded to impale me on his cock. "FUCK!" I cried out as my body adjusted to having him buried deep inside me.

Connor didn't give me time to recover, his fingers digging into my waist as he raised me up and down on his hard length.

"All I've been able to think about is watching you fall apart while riding my cock on this throne. This should have been the first fucking thing we did."

"Agreed," I panted. "Real fucking oversight on our part."

I started to match each of Connor's thrusts, and he released his hold on my waist, one hand gripping my ass while the other entangled itself in my hair. His head dipped forward, and I arched my back as he latched on to my breast and sucked hard on my rigid nipple. My thighs clamped down over his as I kept up the relentless pace. Then he switched to my other breast, the hand wrapped in my hair falling to squeeze and fondle the other one.

Pressure built in my core, and I could feel myself teetering on the edge once more. When his fingers pinched my nipple, that was all it took to send me over, and I let out a strangled moan as the climax hit.

"You're so godsdamn beautiful." Connor pulled back to watch me unravel as I trembled over him, struggling to keep up any pace while my mind devolved into nothing but bliss. His heated gaze slid from my face and down past my breasts to where we were joined together. "I still can't believe you're mine."

"I am yours," I gasped through panted breaths. "And you are mine."

My words were his undoing, and for the second time, I found myself being easily maneuvered by his strong arms. This time, Connor lifted us both and spun me around until I knelt on the throne, facing the back. He gripped my right leg and moved it until it rested on the arm of the throne, and I instinctively grabbed the back to stabilize myself.

His fingers bit into the curve of my hips a second later before he slammed into me. We both groaned as he set a punishing pace. The smooth wood splintered where I was holding on, but I didn't let go. Instead, I arched my back, allowing Connor to thrust even deeper. He growled, one hand digging further into my flesh while the other slid down my front to swirl two fingers around my clit.

"Come for me, My Queen," he ordered, and I whimpered as those clever fingers pushed down the swollen and sensitive flesh in time with each of his thrusts. "My mate."

I saw stars for a second as the pleasure ripped through me for a third time and Connor groaned his own release. My legs shook as he continued stroking my clit until he'd emptied himself inside me.

My thoughts floated in a pleasant haze as he slid out of me, then he gathered me in his arms and repositioned us until he sat on the throne with me in his lap once more. I leaned my head against his shoulder, enjoying the way his scent wrapped around me. Part of me wanted to just stay like this forever. Spend the rest of my days letting Connor short-circuit my brain so I could stop stressing about every little thing.

One problem: we were sitting on my throne, which represented a long list of all those things I stressed about.

"Stop." Connor glared down at me.

I blinked and looked up at him. "What?"

"Stop thinking about all the problems outside this room and just be here with me."

"Is that an order?" I gave him a cheeky grin

He gave me an exasperated look. "Ash . . ."

"Fine, fine." I nestled further into his embrace. "You might have to do something in a bit to distract me again though."

"Oh, I will," he purred. "I have many, many plans for this evening. Like I said, I missed you."

I laughed. "Good."

"Let's return to your chambers for round two." Connor leaned down and kissed me before nudging me off his lap. "I already requested food and wine to be left for us, so we won't have to leave for at least twelve hours. He walked over to where I'd dropped my dress, swept it off the floor, and tossed it to me.

I arched an eyebrow at him. "For someone who complained about being a prince, you sure do take advantage of all the perks."

"I'm not a prince anymore." He smirked as he blatantly took in my naked body. "I've been upgraded to consort."

"Hmm." I tugged the dress back on and took his hand, letting him pull me to the door. "Imagine all the benefits that would come with being king. I could dig out the extra throne . . ."

"You promised me I could just be a pretty figurehead." He slid me a side-eyed glance. "All the benefits, none of the work. It's perfect."

I huffed a laugh. "But think about it?" We reached the door, and I halted, standing on my tippy-toes as I leaned against Connor's broad chest. "If you get a throne, then we'd have to have another proper coronation for it."

His grin gained a sly edge again. "Oh?"

I nodded. "Might even get down on my knees for my king."

"Fuck," he muttered and rubbed his face. "Can't we just do that on your throne?"

"Nope!" I said cheerfully before swinging the door open and stepping into the hallway, only to squeal when Connor grabbed me and threw me over his shoulder.

"We'll talk about this further in bed. I'm pretty confident I can change your mind."

He absolutely could, but I wasn't going to tell him that. Instead, I just giggled as he raced us through the hallways to get back to my—our quarters. Tomorrow, I'd once again worry about all the problems I faced as queen and the issues we faced as a whole with our growing list of enemies.

Connor set me down just outside the door to my—our—

royal suite. "You're going to pay for that sass." His eyes had a wicked glint to them that gave me all sorts of ideas.

It still didn't seem real. My fated mate. The one I had fought so hard for, even knowing I would likely lose him.

I held up my index finger. "Pointy promise?"

"Mo chroí." He looped his finger around mine before leaning in to whisper across my lips. "It's a promise."

Epilogue

A LONG-WEARY SIGH slipped from his lips when he reached the third bar and caught her scent. Leave it to his sister to find the shadiest bar in the shadiest part of town. It'd been the same two hours west of here in Warsaw . . . and in Prague . . . and in Milan before that.

Nothing he could say would convince his sister to give up this fight—this war they had inherited—and he would never abandon her, even if this was not the life he would have chosen.

C'est la vie. He snorted. *Such is life. Thanks, Nemain.* Of course a feline would have had such a fatalistic outlook.

Two people burst out through the front door of the bar and hurried down the street, leaving behind a pungent, bitter smell. Fear mixed with tension. He'd gotten better at parsing scents over the years. At carving the emotional imprint from them.

He crossed the street and entered the bar, nobody stopping him or asking for an ID. This wasn't that type of place. Not only because of how seedy it was, but because it didn't cater to humans. Before he'd left Emerald Bay, the lookaway ward around it would have sent him on his merry way, but he'd learned a lot since then. The blinders had been ripped off, and now the ward did little more than cause an itch in the back of his mind.

A few pool tables that had seen better days took up one corner of the bar to his right. On his left was a long counter with a dozen stools. The bartender, a middle-aged-looking man with dark hair, was serving some locals, none of them paying any mind to the fight brewing towards the back.

Everyone appeared human, but that didn't mean much. They could have been humans who were keyed into magic and all the creatures that shared their realm, or they could have been some other supernatural wearing human skin for the evening. He didn't smell any other werewolves besides himself and his sister.

None of the patrons mattered as long as they didn't interfere.

He slapped three hundred in the local currency onto the bar as he walked past. "For the damage."

The bartender nodded without missing a beat and pocketed the money.

"My friend asked you a question," a broad-shouldered man said to someone the wolf couldn't see . . . but his nose told him exactly who it was. Although he could have guessed without having to rely on his werewolf senses. Different town. Same story. He was getting tired of this.

"And I told your friend," a cold, feminine voice responded, "to fuck off. What part of that wasn't clear?"

"I think it's time we taught the dog a lesson," another man chimed in, and several others jeered.

The werewolf fought back another sigh. Why couldn't these idiots just leave it alone? He could have been enjoying a nice meal right now.

Might as well get it over with. He strode around the group of men, revealing the woman they were talking to—or he supposed "threatening" was more accurate. At 5'7" with a curvy build and stunning hazel eyes, she didn't exactly radiate menace.

"You don't want to do this," he said evenly.

Six pairs of eyes swung to him. The woman glared, but the five warlocks just laughed.

"Pretty sure we do." The big one who'd been speaking when he'd approached snorted.

"I wasn't talking to you." The wolf in human skin flashed him a smile that was all teeth before focusing on his sister. "Let's go."

"No." She crossed her arms.

"Damn it, Stela." A bit of growl leaked into his voice as his frustration with his sister's antics finally broke. "Couldn't you just go one night without picking a fight? They're not even vampires. Just warlock assholes."

"Hey! Who the fuck you calling asshol—"

The werewolf waved his hand sharply through the air, cutting off the warlock who'd taken offense. "You promised you'd behave when you left earlier."

"And you said you'd stop being such a wet blanket." She arched a perfectly sculpted eyebrow. "Guess we both lied, bro."

The big warlock looked back and forth between the two werewolves, likely noting all the similarities in their facial features, eye colors, and expressions. "You're . . . siblings." He frowned. "Vamps have been going on about a couple of were-wolves—brother and sister—who have been making a nuisance of themselves this past year."

"Nuisance," Stela scoffed. "We've killed at least twenty of those fuckers and a handful of you dickwads too. Pretty sure that qualifies as more than a nuisance."

"Really, sis?"

She gave him an innocent look.

"What the fuck did you just say?" The warlock who'd been

doing most of the talking took a menacing step forward, any lingering amusement gone from the faces of the other warlocks now. Three of them had drawn daggers with markings carved into them, and he could feel the magic in the room rising like a static charge.

"You really should have walked away." The werewolf's voice deepened as the wolf rose, another thing he'd gotten better at—although control was still an issue.

"And *you* really should learn how to count." A faint purple glow flared over the ring on the big warlock's index finger. "Five against two, asshole, and the vamps pay for any were-wolves—dead or alive."

The warlock opened his mouth again, likely to speak whatever words would activate the spell in that ring, but he never got the chance. Warm blood splattered across the werewolf's face. He wrinkled his nose. Some of it had gotten into his mouth, and the taste was terrible.

More blood flew as the warlock coughed and dumbly stared down at the fist shoved through his chest. The look of surprise was fairly amusing.

"You really should have listened," the werewolf said mildly before he ripped out his heart, blood dripping from his clawed hand, and dropped it onto the floor. "Four against two now."

Chaos erupted.

Spells slammed into him, and one of the warlocks used something that burned through his flesh until he could see flashes of bone. It barely slowed the wolf down though. One thing he'd learned since leaving Emerald Bay was that once a fight started, you didn't stop moving until your enemies were dead. Plus, as a werewolf, he could heal from just about anything.

A warlock barked out a harsh word before ropes appeared from out of nowhere, wrapping around Stela's legs and upper body. He'd missed her arms though, and she grabbed a nearby chair, broke off a leg, and threw it hard enough that it went through the warlock's eye and poked out the back of his head. The ropes fell away, and she pounced on the other warlock just as the werewolf tore the head off another.

He looked around, barely winded. Warlocks dead. Locals entertained. Not the worst of nights.

The bartender surveyed the damage, frowned at the dead bodies he'd have to deal with, and grunted before going back to pouring drinks. That was one benefit to shit like this going down in shady bars, they really didn't give a flying fuck about anything.

Of course, the bartender would have had the same response if it'd been Stela and him bleeding out on the floor.

His sister stepped around the dead bodies to stand in front of him. "*Now* we can go."

The wolf rolled his eyes. "Let's grab our stuff and get out of town. Word of this is going to spread." He sank a hint of chastisement into his tone. It wasn't that he cared about killing warlocks—while he may not have been as bloodthirsty as his sister, the warlocks were more than happy to target the wolves and had been doing exactly that for the past year—but they'd just gotten into town a week ago, and he'd been hoping to stay for at least a few more. Being on the move constantly was getting exhausting.

"Quite a mess you two made."

The two wolves spun around to face the woman who had snuck up on them. A hard thing to do around werewolves. Not just a woman—a witch. The spicy aroma of herbs clung to her skin, and he recognized the magic in it.

But just because she was a witch and not a warlock didn't mean she was a friend to them. Both he and Stela had learned that lesson the hard way—her even more so.

"What do you want?" he asked, wanting to get to the point so they could get the fuck out of there.

"The vampires and warlocks have teamed up and are stamping out the wolves . . . and the witches who oppose them."

"Oh, do the witches actually give a fuck now?" Stela sneered.

Dark eyes looked at his sister, revealing nothing. "You are young, and there is much you don't understand."

"We understand death just fine," he cut in before his sister did her best to kill the witch. There was something about this woman that said she wouldn't go down easy, and he had learned to trust his instincts. "We've been hunting warlocks and vampires all over this continent—never encountered a witch standing up against them."

A faint smile played across her lips. "We're not really the bloody barroom brawl type. Our methods are a little more . . . underhanded."

"More like nonexistent," Stela muttered.

"How's this for being straightforward?" The witch stepped closer to the wolves, causing both of them to tense, and said quietly enough that only their ears could hear, "Soon, the vampires will get what they've been after all along—more power and magic, enough to wipe out the wolves once and for all. And in exchange for this, they will help the warlocks do the same to the witches."

"Who are you?" he asked sharply. "And how do you know this?"

"I am Lestari," the witch replied. "You'll have to wait to find out how I know this until we reach our destination. There are others who need to hear this."

"What destination?" He narrowed his eyes.

"It's time for you to return to Emerald Bay, Andrei." The witch smiled.

Greymalkin Press Shop

The Lost Legacies series is also available directly on the author's shop - Greymalkin Press - and you'll find bundle deals for the ebooks and audiobooks!

Signed paperbacks with character artwork, exclusive paperback omnibuses, and special edition hardcovers are also available!

Author's Note

Thank you so much for reading A Shift in Tides!

I had a lot of fun with this one, lol. When Connor made an appearance in A Shift in Shadows, I knew I eventually wanted him to be somebody's love interest. But I honestly had no idea who... until Ashling stepped into the light.

Connor appears to be an asshole to everyone (which, TBH, he kind of is) and Ashling comes across as shady (which she totally is).

I loved the idea of two people who have come across as one way in the series and exploring the reasons why. It was also fun to write about two people who had been in a relationship that ended badly and them getting a second chance.

And Ashling's inner monologuing was incredibly amusing to write.

I know that it's a bit unconventional to write a series that alternates between a main character book and then a side character one; but I truly love getting to show Nemain from a different point-of-view. Especially as we enter the last half of the series when things start to get more intense.

Huge thank you to my editing and beta team. They

continue to keep me sane and chuckling as I read their comments complaining about the emotional damage I inflict upon them. Heh.

As always, it would be incredibly appreciated if you could leave an honest review on Goodreads or whichever platform you prefer. Reviews are super important for authors and we really appreciate it when y'all take the time to leave one! Plus, it helps other readers find us :)

LOST LEGACIES GUIDE

<u>CHARACTERS:</u>

Ashling - the new Merfolk Queen who replaced Kaysea's parents. Comes across as a bit shady because she somehow always seems to know things that she shouldn't.

Bryn - newbie valkyrie; her soul is bonded with Finn's and she is his guardian

Cerridwn - dragon, sweetheart of Eddie; daughter of the dragon who rules their realm

Cian - feline shifter with necromantic magic; twin brother of Nemain; has a strained relationship with her but still loves her fiercely

Connor - Kaysea's older brother; former prince to the merfolk throne. Has a tense relationship with Nemain because he holds her responsible for the death of his other sister, Myrna.

Damon - teenage vampire on the run from the Vampire Council

Dante - necromancer, incredibly powerful and in a long-term relationship with Nemain's brother Cian

Eddie - a dragon who owns and runs a shop of magical oddities and supplies
Elisa - oldest of the teenage vampire runaways
Emir - leader of the Warlock Circle
Finn - fae child of the exiled fae king Balor; a prophecy about him says he will bring about the end of the realms
Isabeau - child vampire that the teenage vampires take care of and treat as a younger sister
Jinx - a fae cat known as a grimalkin, him and Nemain have been together since she was born; he's grumpy and has the ability to inflict bad luck on others
Kaysea - mermaid princess and bestie of Nemain; Myrna was her twin sister; older brother Connor is very protective of her
Lir - fae devourer hybrid, serves as the right-hand of the exiled fae king, Balor
Luna - another grimalkin (because the only thing better than one cat is two cats); unlike Jinx she is sweet and cuddly
Magos - old vampire warrior, his past is a bit of a mystery but he's loyal to Nemain and their relationship is similar to that of a an uncle/niece despite not being related
Mikhail - former vampire assassin of the Vampire Council; nephew of Magos
Misha - part of the teenage vampire group, looks very similar to Elisa but they don't know for sure if they're actually related, either way they consider each other brother & sister
Nemain - feline shifter and fae hybrid with devourer magic; all around freak of nature; raised by Macha and Nevin who she only learned recently were actually her aunt and uncle; biological parents are Badb and Kalen
Niall - fae devourer hybrid who is in a relationship with Sigrun. He used to serve in Balor's army.
Pele - daemon who runs the local tavern, The Inferno; close friends with Nemain who she has been in an ongoing casual poly relationship with for centuries

Sigrun - valkyrie, exiled from her people after the events of Ragnarok; has a wolf companion named Gunnar and a magical cat named Viggo

<u>REALMS:</u>

*Note, this is not an extensive list of all the realms because there are many. Only those relevant to the story are mentioned.

Human Realm - the modern world that humans are familiar with; most humans are completely unaware that their realm is one of many or that magical beings walk amongst them
Meenri - the main realm controlled by the daemons after they fled their original home realm

Fae Realms

Mag Ildathach - belongs to the Seelie Court; name means multi-colored plains
Mag Mell - belongs to neither the Seelie or the Unseelie; like all death realms it is difficult to fully comprehend or travel in without necromantic magic; currently where Dante & Cian call home
Tír fo Thuinn - despite being referred to as a realm, this is actually a territory that stretches across all the fae realms, it is the dominion of the sea fae, all the oceans and seas belong to them
Tír na mBeo - only realm shared by the Unseelie & Seelie Queens

Fallen Realms

Kanima - former realm of the feline shifters; this is where Nemain's parents were born; it fell to devourers and the survivors fled to the human realm

Cerulle - former realm of Magos and Mikhail; also fell to devourers; survivors fled to the human realm and were later killed during the vampire and werewolf war

250

Cerulle - former realm of Magos and Mikhail; also fell to devourers; survivors fled to the human realm and were later killed during the vampire and werewolf war

About the Author

Maddox Grey is a queer nonbinary elder millennial who still remembers vividly what it was like to be emotionally damaged by the season two finale of Buffy the Vampire Slayer.

They write morally grey characters who fall for equally unhinged morally grey love interests. And the banter flows as fast as the action in the stories they craft.

When they're not putting their characters through hell, Maddox is playing video games, reading smut, burying their nose in comic books, or hiding behind a pillow while they watch horror movies.

To get regular email updates about new releases and other announcements, be sure to sign up for the newsletter on maddoxgreyauthor.com

facebook.com/maddoxgrey.author

instagram.com/maddoxgrey.author

tiktok.com/@greymalkinpress